ROBIN LANE-DOUGLAS

The Fighting Men From Buxton

This book is a fictionalized account based on the lives of real men and women from Buxton, Maine.

First edition

Cover art by Dina Sutin Productions

This book was professionally typeset on Reedsy.
Find out more at reedsy.com

DEDICATION

This book is dedicated to George and Shirley Lane, my parents, not only for their love of their family but, who started me on the genealogical journey at the age of 18.

Acknowledgement

To my husband, Desmond Douglas, Jr., my brother, Richard (Richy) Lane and nephew, Jesse Lane; my love to you always. Thank you for so much more than I can express here. I have been blessed to have each of you with your support and participation in everything I do and being there for me at all times.

I am so very grateful to my teacher, Cindy Simon and classmate Linda Hafford for their support and helpful critique during our Creative Writing Course. The hours we spent together, sharing our lives and work (with a dash of humor), resulted in friends for life.

1

1754

THE FRENCH AND INDIAN WAR

At first glance Fort Halifax didn't look like much. A rather small unfinished garrison. It contained two block houses and two long buildings. It didn't look like it could hold all the men in its buildings and yards. Around the fort, people had built their homes to live under the protection of the fort. Traveling with my father, Captain John, my brothers John and Daniel and I, Jabez, and the rest of our company arrived under the command of Sir William Pepperell's 51st regiment. Our orders were to complete the fort and deter the Indians from the burning of homes that have been on the rise. It was spring and the march was long and hot.

I heard my father, John, who was Captain of our company remark that it was a good location overlooking the Sebasticook and Kennebec rivers in Winslow, Maine. It was the main waterway for which furs and goods along with men would travel down. John, my oldest brother asked my father "Who is this fort being named for?". My father replied, "the 2nd Earl of Halifax, son. His name is George Montagu-Dunk and he is the British colonial secretary." This to me, an eleven-year old boy, meant nothing. Just a lot of names for one man. There were men, old and young all around me. Daniel, my other brother, is most definitely more sociable of the three of us. He was off to catch up with the other boys his age he had met on the march. John and Dad were deep in conversation with the other men from camp as to organizing the plan for building up the fort. I was quickly gathered by a bunch of other boys to learn the drum calls. The different calls were explained to me as signals for the men, to march but, most importantly were used when in battle to direct the men such as; move left, right, forward, retreat.

By the end of the day, I would have rather been working with the men than working with drums. I became friendly with Ezekial, another drummer boy, who really had the hang of it and worked with me after the others had gone to find food. Ezekial understood my frustration. "Jabez, having command of these drums is probably the most important work we could do for the company. This could save lives." While I thought that through, he went on to explain. "Of course, you are right by the Colonel or the commanding officer's side in battle to communicate with the men". "It's very important you listen carefully to them and send out the proper signals". He instructed me through the first drill slowly and gradually as I caught on, he sped it up to the proper pace. When he was somewhat satisfied with my progress, we ran as fast as we could to find our food.

I managed to get a plate and found my father and two brothers sitting on the ground together and with a quick good bye to Ezekial, hurried over to see what news they had. Father was tired and so John filled me in on the details of the work done that day.

Father was at the Siege of Louisburg that was located on Cape Breton Island many miles north in Canada, nine years prior in 1745 and had received a musket wound in the side. Some of the men here were at the Siege with him. His wound never fully healed and it bothered him more often than not. He never let it show as he always managed to keep ahead of the men, guiding them, watching out for them and making sure everyone pulled their own. By the agility of his movements and the loudness of his bellow, you would not know of the trouble this wound gave him. His men respected him as I had learned on the march. Everyone seemed to have a subtle watch over him. It was remarkable that he never lost his love for adventure.

John told me it was imperative that the fort be finished as quickly as possible as the Indians were now being influenced by the French and as a result were becoming more and more more hostile. I listened as he relayed what the scouts had learned.

Daniel, with an aggressive slap to my back said, "So Jabez, my little brother, how did learning the drums go today?" "Not very well.", I muttered. I would rather be working with the ground and help with construction. My father responded, "Jabez, it's important you learn. Many lives will depend on the correct signals". To which Daniel added, "be sure to stand behind the officers because drummer boys are the targets. By bringing you down, the enemy knows they can halt communication." "Daniel!" my father railed at him. "Stop trying to frighten your brother!" Suddenly I wasn't as hungry. My father, a rough man, said "Son, your smart. Keep your wits about you and pay attention. Now eat your food. There is going to be a lot of work to do around here. Keep your eyes and ears open. Learn what you can. Be aware of the men around you. These are good men, most of them are farmers like us. You have to earn trust just as they will have to learn to trust you." I was confused at his calling himself a farmer, because he was never home and most men described him as a celebrated Indian fighter. I was too tired at the moment to question him, so I went directly to bed.

As the days wore on, I finally mastered the different signals I had to learn and the men continued their construction of the fort. It was to have three living quarters and a blockhouse. During the construction of the fort, scouts came and went. One day, the scouts returned and reported activity from the north. The Acadians were originally British settlers as far back as the early 1600s. The French wanted to claim the Acadian territory and as much of the area as their own for their fur trades. The British settlers would not swear loyalty to the French. The French in response, put those men and their families on ships. Some ships were sent to England and some sent southward towards Louisiana. Others fled to the outer islands of Nova Scotia. We were to work with the British building forts to repel this idea.

Summer was soon turning into fall, John and Daniel had an excellent command of their rifles and father made sure they worked with me on how to use one. John called me aside when rumors began to spread that we would be moving on. "Father wants you to learn as much as you can, as do I. I know your young but your smart. "I listen to the officers as much as I can when they speak with each other.", I told John. "Good" he replied. "But always remember to take stock of each officer. Some have a good sense of strategy and tactics while others can be foolhardy". You must obey orders, but heed what is going on around you". "I don't like these English officers" I admitted to him. They treat their dogs better than they treat me. He took a deep breath. "I understand, Jabez, but they are career soldiers. You can learn from them, but use the lessons carefully. They don't take well to taking cover behind a tree to fight. The Indians fight using cover and ambush and we colonists learned to adapt to this." With a nudge and a grin, he suggested, "Perhaps you should stand behind the fool that stands in the open to fight." Looking up at the brother who I respected so much, his face became serious again. "When things get serious, use whatever method you deem necessary at that time."

John and Daniel spent as much time as they could with me. I enjoyed this time with my brothers, even knowing the seriousness of why I was being taught. They were determined that I knew all I could. Even teaching me how to make my own musket balls. The lead arrived in small blocks. The idea was to melt the lead and pour it into two, half circle molds that were pressed together as they cooled to form a ball. Once that process was complete, the rough edges would be trimmed to make the ball smoother so as not to ruin the barrel of our muskets and to provide better aim. I had watched them perform this ritual many times at home but, now they were having me do it myself. I felt more like one of the men learning this, than I did playing an instrument I absolutely hated.

My father on the other hand, was caught up with taking care of his command and making sure his men were prepared with what would be needed.

Father was quite serious when he informed us, "Boys, the fort construction is almost complete. We have gotten word that raids are happening nearby. One poor fellow was killed and scalped and a few other men were taken as captives." John said to Father, "Is it true that there are survivors on their way here?" "Aye.", responded Father. "Some believed that they would not be bothered." Daniel jumped in to the conversation, "Why do they believe that?". Father patiently explained, "Some believe if they don't take a stand for the British or the French, they are not in danger. In fact, some of these murders are because the settlers refuse to align with the French." I asked, "Why don't they just leave?" Father looked at me calmly and said, "Son, these people settled here. They have worked very hard to build their homes and raise their families. They make their living here. This is their way of life. Now the French sends in their soldiers and have recruited Indians to pressure them how they will live and take away everything they have built. Hopefully, when you have your own family and home, you will not have to suffer an invasion of a government informing you how to live or else have everything taken away from you."

I glanced over at John who was nodding at Father's words. I didn't fully understand but, I had seen a few of the people who managed their way to the fort. They were depressed and most only had the clothes on their backs.

Daniel jumped up in a temper, "Then why are we inside a fort. We should be chasing them back North where they came from!". John grabbed Daniel by the sleeve of his arm and pulled him back down to sit. Father took a deep breath, "Daniel, we don't have enough men here yet. Governor Shirley has been informed and has agreed to send more men. All we can do at the moment is keep an eye on them with scouts and try to help as many people as we can. Understood?". Daniel sullenly answered, "Yes, Father". John asked Father, "What have we heard from the surrounding forts?" Father went on, "You might as well know. The other forts in the area report that plantations were being attacked and burned to the ground and the settlers were fleeing to those forts for safety. So, you see, the situation is quite dangerous. I want you boys to stay within sight of the fort. No wandering off." All three of us agreed to our father's wish.

In the following weeks, more survivors appeared and most were escorted south to a safer area. I wondered at what their fate would be. Father continued to keep a watchful eye on us if were outside the fort to gather wood. Fearing for our safety and the other men, no one was allowed beyond the walls alone. Father would select men to go out with a scouting party and I could not breathe until his return.

With the spring of 1755, many men had arrived at the fort to take over. We returned home to care for our farms. We arrived home, at Narraganset Township, No. 1 in April. On May 8, John married Elizabeth Hancock. He had spent a lot of time visiting her and her family before we left for the fort.

The morning of the wedding, Mother had carefully cleaned his clothes and made a fuss over his appearance. Father sat in a corner of the room watching her with a smile. "John, stand still!", she begged.

John turned to Father, "Please tell her I look fine!". My father who could command men so easily, seemed to always back down from Mother when she made her wishes clear. He urged, "You will let your mother do what she needs to. Until then, I suggest you stand still or you will be late to your wedding." With that he had himself a good laugh. He let mother go on for a little bit more and then took some pity on John. He stood up and walked behind her as she worked on John's hair. His tone was always soft when he spoke with her as it was at this moment. Resting his hands on her shoulders he turned her toward him, "My love, he looks well enough. Let's get our nervous groom to the ceremony." I didn't understand the tears in her eyes and I watched as my father put his arms around her, holding her for a long while. Finally, she composed herself, looked up at Father and they gazed at each other for a moment before she said, "You're right, we should head out." Father smiled that smile he always shared with her, patted her gently on the back and guided her toward the door. The four of us followed them out.

It was a grand affair. Elizabeth was quite pretty, beautiful in fact. All the town folk came out to celebrate that day. The weeks before the wedding, these same people came together to help build a home for the couple. I spent many days that summer helping him clear the land for planting. I got to know Elizabeth quite well. She was a very kind and sweet person. If John was anywhere near her, she could not take her eyes off of him.

During the winter, Isaac Hancock, Elizabeth's brother, seemed to spending a lot of time around my sister, Joanna, stopping by our home with the silliest of excuses. Once he brought a turkey he had shot. After he left, I asked father if Isaac thought us terrible hunters. My question sent my father in such a fit of laughter, he lost his breath. Joanna was always quite friendly toward all the men that seemed to want her attention but it was Isaac she seemed to like spending time with most.

Father and I were working in the barn and I asked him, "Father, is there something wrong with Isaac?". Surprised, Father looked at me, "Why do you ask?" Disgusted that he had not noticed Isaac's behavior I spelled it out, "Well for starters, he stutters and turns red when he talks to Joanna. When he sees her, he is in such a hurry to get to her, he trips over his own feet. There must be something very wrong". This to my agitation made my father laugh. Seeing that I didn't find it funny at all, he tried to regain his composure and said, "Jabez, he's sweet on her. He is nervous that he may offend her in some way. I think he hopes to marry her someday."

We stood at the barn door watching them walk toward the house and I asked, "Did John act like that with Elizabeth?". "Aye", he responded. I looked up at him and said, "Were you like that with Mother?" "Hell, no!", he bellowed. At my silence, he said, "Well maybe just a little." Having gotten under his skin about the subject, he wagged his finger at me with a warning, "You just wait until it's your time!". He was humored at the thought and I walked away with a retort, "Not likely!" Walking away I could hear his laughter and I honestly thought the whole idea quite absurd.

In the early spring of 1756 Father brought us together for supper at our home. He had just returned from a visit with Sir William Pepperell. Father had been under his command at the Siege of Louisburg and knew him quite well. William Pepperell was a prosperous merchant who lived in Kittery. "Lads, Pepperell has informed me the British are making preparations for an Expedition to Crown Point in New York come spring. He has asked us to join his regiment. Unfortunately, Pepperell's health is not well so he will not be going with us. This will be a long hard trip. The roads are hard and there are mountains to climb. I will be out to muster men in the next couple of weeks. John, see to Elizabeth. Daniel and Jabez, you will help your mother and

Joanna with preparing stores for the house before we leave." Daniel spoke out, "I think the house has everything it needs." Father aimed his temper at Daniel, "Check again! Check every part of the house, make sure the barn, the animals and the equipment are in perfect order. When your done with that, hunt for some meat to store and gather berries." "Gather berries!", Daniel thought himself above woman's work. Father's glare didn't stop him there. "I should be out with you recruiting." Looking at my father's reaction, I dreaded what he was going to say to Daniel. Thinking I might calm him I offered, "I think I can handle it." Father, through his temper, didn't hear me as he rose from his chair still glaring at Daniel. "Boy, I would like to see how well you recruit when I tan your back side so badly you won't be able to leave with us!" Daniel's bravado ended. He thought himself the best fighter in town. The thought of staying behind with the women would be more than he could handle. He gulped, worried that this would be his fate and gave in. "I'm sorry Father. I will do as you ask." Still glaring at Daniel, he said in a steely tone, "Get to it, now!". With that he walked out of the house.

John sat there with a disgusted look on his face toward Daniel. He glanced over at me and I nodded my head toward Daniel and simply said, "Dummy". We spent the next week going over everything. It was still too early for berries to pick but, we did manage to hunt down a deer and some rabbits and prepared them for storage. Father seemed pleased with the work that was done. We were ready to leave.

On an April morning we formed and started our march. Our father's company now belonged to Pepperell's 51st regiment under Colonel Joseph Dwight, headed to Crown Point. Father was not doing well on the march. He became quite ill. John steadfastly remained at father's side. As Father had promised, the march was brutal. There were no clear roads in many places and more mountains to get over or around than I cared to count. We were almost to Crown Point when Father could go no farther. The company halted to give him a rest.

After sitting with my father for a little while, I joined John and Daniel for something to eat. There were a few men gathered. John as Lieutenant, and John Mirick as Corporal, were discussing whether to move on or stay a day or so. The decision was made to stay for a few days and then decide. On the second evening, Father looked worse, his face seemed to have a gray pallor and his breathing was much worse. The three of us John, Daniel and I sat by him. John shook his head from side to side slowly towards Daniel. Daniel's shoulders drooped and I felt the heaviness develop in the pit of my stomach when I realized, this would be the last time we would all sit with our father.

Father was feverish and in much pain. He looked at us all, one by one and said, "My boys, you've become good men and good soldiers. I'm so very proud of all of you. I've done my best for you. Don't forget your training and what you are fighting for, mainly the right to your homes and families, which you will all have one day. Watch out for each other." To Daniel he said "You are a brave lad. Learn to use a little caution in what you say and do." His eyes came to rest on me. "Jabez, my good lad, I see your intelligence. You are as brave as your brothers." Fighting back the tears that were filling my eyes, I was at a loss and all I could do was crouch down with him and hold his hand. "Promise me all, you will take care of your mother and sister." We all assured him we would.

After a few moments of silence his breathing became more labored. He asked Daniel to take me off as he wanted a few moments with John. He loved our mother and his last words to John were for her but John never told us what they were. Such a heavy message for a son to bring home to his mother. It was about an hour later that John walked over to us and his look told us that Father's suffering was over. We sat together in silence deep in our own thoughts. One of the men came and spoke to John. They had dug a grave for Father and when we were ready, they would help us. We went to our Father's lifeless body, John saw to it that he was properly dressed. He was wrapped in his blanket. John took Father's musket and gave it to me with words to care for it. We carried him to where he would be buried and carefully placed him. John took the shovel from one of the men and began to cover him. The man tried to take the shovel back but the unwavering glare on John's face made the man back up a few steps. I looked at all the men standing there to help. I never saw grown men with tears in their eyes. Through my own tears, I looked at the other men that had known him; lived and fought with him, who did not try to hide their grief. The pain in my chest was unbearable. I had idolized my father but they knew him better than me for they had spent more time with him and I at only 13, had not. Then they bowed their heads in prayer. We stood there for a long while. When they were done, Daniel quietly took me by the shoulder and we went back to camp. I went to my bedroll and laid down. I heard the men talking. It was decided that Father's command would be passed to my brother, John. He instructed everyone to get a good night's sleep as we would be heading out with the first light. Everyone settled in for the night. The usual nightly banter was replaced with the deafening silence.

The next morning, everyone roused and we pushed silently ahead. No time for grieving. Looking back clutching Father's musket, I'm glad of the time I had with him. At times I thought him hard on us but, he wanted us prepared. Now I would look toward my brothers and that was a comfort for me. I would find in the days ahead how men in war looked after each other.

We made it the Fort at Crown Point that day. The stench was awful to my nose. There was filth everywhere. Evidence of slaughtered animals and sickness was all around. It was overcrowded with twenty-five hundred men, more than at Fort Halifax. John saw to it that our company had a place in the fort and called us all together. He had met with the Colonel and relayed the news with us. John informed the company, "We are to stay put here for now. The fort is so overcrowded and dirty that men were getting sick. They bury from five to eight men daily." There will be hunting parties for food and we should stay together in our own company. Because of the overcrowding he warned that tempers were already becoming short. He urged us to stay close and not get caught in the bickering. John in a very steely tone informed us all he was not going to tolerate that behavior from any of us. But then, John never did tolerate that kind of thing. He also shared with us that Generals Shirley and Johnson, are in charge of the campaign. This was not good news because the gossip in camp was that they were disagreeable to one another.

Colonel Joseph Dwight seemed a sensible god-fearing man and had known our father. He took time to see my brothers and I to express his sympathies. He also shared a few stories of being with him. He told us a story about Father having been the first man wounded at the Siege of Louisburg back in 1745. "The men including your father were dropped from the ship in boats to make the landing. Well, no one had judged how fast the current was and the boats were caught in it and drifted past where the landing was to take place. They made land in a terrible spot. It was steep terrain for them to get up and the French were just firing down on them. They still made it up there. Your father was wounded getting up to the top. That didn't stop him, he kept crawling up and the men kept up with him. No one knew how badly he was hurt until the battle was over." John said to the Colonel, "We were never told the story of how he had been wounded." Colonel Dwight nodded, "That sounds like your father. He was fearless. In battle, I was always proud to know he was under my command. Nothing stopped him", he said in a wistful voice. I looked down at my father's musket, wondering at how many adventures it had been through with my father.

Colonel Dwight changed the subject saying, "I'm disappointed with the lack of men, supplies and ammo that showed up." John replied, "We brought everything we were given. Didn't any other supplies get here?" The Colonel shook his head in the negative. John asked the Colonel, "Is the British attitude changing toward the colonials at all?" The Colonel responded, "I'm afraid not son. Even I'm the target of their ridicule." He went on to share with us, "Shirley was replaced by Lord Loudoun a British officer and is being sent back to England. Loudoun has a poor opinion of the Colonists." Daniel who up until this time had been quiet, aimed his anger at the Colonel, "The British officers AND soldiers have been less than kind to us colonials. How many wars are we fighting here? Then this Lord Loudoun wants to integrate us? You are never going to get colonial cooperation with his attitude. We had heard on arriving at the fort that the Brits were planning on separating us." The Colonel placated Daniel by saying, "Please don't worry, Daniel, the British soldiers don't want to sleep with us either. The other colonial officers find him inept. Hopefully not at the cost of men." With that he stood to leave and parted saying, "My best to you boys, call on me if you need anything. I'll do the best I can for you." With that he was gone and we were left with our thoughts.

In June we were sent to Fort William Henry. John kept his company together and we spent as much time as we could outside of the fort, away from the sickness that was rapidly spreading. Getting away from the stench, even for a few hours, was a mercy. We were sent out on a few scouting parties and once or twice encountered a few Indians. The Seneca and Mohawk were a fierce and handsome looking Indian. The Mohawk fought beside us. On one patrol, I had been coming out from the woods after answering an urgent call of nature and stopped still hearing a noise close to me. I waited a few moments before I spotted a lone Seneca coming up behind one of the men, hatchet raised. I don't know how I moved so quick but, I slammed that drum so hard on his head, he dropped with a thud. There was a look of disbelief on Daniel's face as everyone turned toward the noise I had just made. All John said was "right then". I picked up my rifle and looked down at the drum, now damaged beyond repair. Daniel said, "Where are you going to get another drum?". I shouldered my rifle and snapped back at him, "I don't give a damn about another drum. I hate the damn thing!" John only stared at me, not ever having heard me curse. A few men had the Indian tied up in no time. Daniel looked at the captive and with a huge grin announced, "Well, will you look at this. Jabez has caught his first Indian. With a drum, no less!" All of the men found it humorous. Finally, we walked on and drums were never mentioned to me again. Other than that, the scouting parties were usually uneventful.

On the night of August 11, the French advanced on Fort Ontario. Mercer was in command and gave the order to abandon the fort. From there the French went on to Oswego. The word received was gruesome. The walls crumbled from the onslaught of fire. As soon as the Indians and French took over the fort, they got into the rum and proceeded to get drunk. A few British tried to escape, but were tomahawked. Then, they beat the colonel calling him a coward. The prisoners were brought to Montreal. Some of our regiment was with them. Only one man was able to escape.

Lord Loudoun, in disgust decided to halt the Expedition. Daniel and I now looked to John for what to do.

"I think it's time to return home. Mother and Joanna will not spend another winter without us." So, we will muster out at least for the winter and see what comes of everything in the spring. There was no argument and at the next muster call, we did not sign.

Upon reaching town, we reached John's house first. Elizabeth was holding their newborn baby girl, Sarah in her arms. John was in awe. Elizabeth put the babe right into John's arms saying, "Meet your Father, Sarah". The little girl opened her eyes and looked straight at him. The hard months we had just endured melted away from his face as he looked down at his daughter. Daniel and I wandered around the farm a bit so they could have a few moments to themselves. We got the horses hooked up to the carriage to take Elizabeth with us to Mother's house. We would all break the news to Mother together this day. As we got close to home, Daniel and I were in front on our horses and Joanna was the first one we saw. She was beautiful than we left. She cried, she laughed and didn't know who to run to first.

Seeing Mother, all I wanted to do was run into her arms. Instead, I stood frozen in shock. She was much thinner and looked so tired. She yanked each one of us to her crying and looking into our faces to see what changes had occurred. There were plenty of tears as we talked about the loss of Father. "I am glad you were with him" she said. I couldn't bear the thought of his dying alone with no comfort in his last moments". She found some peace in knowing he was properly buried. Finally, Joanna and Elizabeth started supper. Mother informed John and Elizabeth they would stay the night. A babe should not be out in the cold night air. There was no argument. As the women cooked, the three of us went out to tend to the animals and bring in wood for the fire. We took note of what needed fixing.

The women cooked all the food they could fit on the stove. I saw on Mother's face that she had it hard while we were gone. As did the other women left behind. They became a sisterhood of their own. They took care of each, helped each other with the children and the farm work. She gave us all the news that happened while we were gone; who got married, who had babies and the antics of the townspeople. When supper was over, she looked at us with a far-off look in her eyes. She said, "My babies left me almost two years ago and men have returned". With that her motherly instincts took over and she sent us off to bed.

John stayed with her a few minutes longer and I know he relayed Father's last words. I heard her sobs late in the night. Leaning over to the side of my bed, I gave Father's rifle a pat. John and Elizabeth left after breakfast. It felt good to be home.

We weren't home more than a month when Mother passed away. At thirteen years of age, I had Daniel and Joanna to take care of me.

2

LIFE AT HOME

I now had other things to get busy on, such as the farm. I often thought of mother when sitting quietly at night inside this home. I think life was hard for her. While father spent so much time protecting his family and neighbors most of his life, she was spent most of it alone raising her children, keeping the farm going. When my brothers and I grew strong enough we were taking on more and more chores to help with the family.

Coming back from the war, we found the farm needed so much work. Some of the fields were overgrown, the house needed some desperate repair and winter was on us. Once that was done, Isaac Hancock, who was Lieutenant in our company, married Joanna. Isaac was also the brother of John's wife, Elizabeth.

After Joanna married, Daniel returned to the War and was a participant in the Battle of Quebec. He was present when General Wolfe expired from his wounds in battle with Montgomery and Daniel helped gather balm to cover the General's body. He aided in erecting fortifications at Halifax, N.S. His stories were many and he often fancied himself as Peter the Great.

Since Mother's death, Joanna took on a motherly role toward me and on Daniel's return she attempted to do the same with Daniel but she failed miserably. Daniel would get impatient with her and send her home to Isaac. Daniel and I lived as bachelors in the house my parents built.

Joanna and Isaac's first child, John, was born in 1757. Then came Mary in 1758 followed by William. They were handsome children and I had spent much time with them. Daniel and I grew quite attached to her children and spent many hours playing with them. Daniel, for all his manliness could be found making dolls for his nieces (Joanna's and John's children) out of corn husks. He had used dried apples for their heads which were clever looking.

Daniel and I arrived one morning at Joanna's home to a tearful Mary. Daniel jumped down from his horse and swooped her up. This war hardened man could never stand to see a woman or child cry. "There girl, what is wrong?" he asked. She was so tiny, she almost disappeared into his arms. She was sobbing hard but managed to get the words out. "I was holding my doll while Father was feeding the horses and one of them snatched the doll." With that she showed it to him and sure enough the horse had taken the "apple head" right off of it. It was so amusing I practically fell off my horse getting down. Daniel glared at me for laughing, put her down and took her by the hand saying "Let's see what we can do about it". "I'll take you to the mare and you can give her a sound beating", she ordered. My laughter grew more intense. He snarled toward me saying, "We won't beat the mare but I know your uncle over there is about to receive one."

I escaped Daniel's idle threat to the house in search of Joanna. I knew she was in the house as I could smell the food. Her cooking was the best around. Entering the house, I was greeted with her cheerful smile and a huge hug. She was still beautiful after having three children. "It's so good of you and Daniel to come help Isaac today" she said. "It will be nice to have plenty of good food for the next winter. It's been hard to work caring for the children and Mother". On our return, we learned that the women were reduced to picking berries and were quite thin. "I know" I replied. "Isaac is a good man. And he is going to spend a day helping us tend to the fields at our place. We should all be able to plant well this year."

I liked spending time with Joanna. She was always cheerful and so much like Mother. I reminded her of it during our conversation. Joanna had a wistful smile on her face and said, "Mother once said to me, 'I've spent most of our marriage waiting for your father to come home from one of his adventures'. Joanna said, "She always kept a candle in the front window for him to come home."

I said to her, "I wonder if Daniel will stay close to home when he marries." She stopped what she was doing and said, "I knew he had taken a fancy to Molly." I replied, "He still fancies himself as Peter the Great. Poor Molly. He calls her Moll Peter." Joanna, I thought would faint. "Dear God", she said. "Doesn't he understand that Moll Peter was Peter the Great's mistress, Catherine? It doesn't come across as very nice." I found it rather hilarious. "Relax Joanna, it's all in fun and she finds the humor in it." Joanna seemed to calm down. She said, "I still don't like it and you should not encourage him."

With that, the door burst open and Daniel entered with the children in tow and Isaac behind them all. Mary holding her now repaired doll. Daniel went right over to the food and was immediately slapped when he reached for food. A firm look from Joanna and her words "When the food and everyone else is at the table." I gave him a sideways glance to the children. Joanna was raising her children with manners and he was breaking one of her rules. She told the children to wash their hands and as soon as their backs were turned, she handed him a biscuit. I rolled my eyes in exasperation. She was a softy when it came to Daniel. As soon as the children reappeared, we all sat for our lunch. We were enjoying Joanna's wonderful cooking when, with a twinkle in her eye, she said to Daniel, "So when do you plan to marry Mary?" The fork stopped halfway to his mouth. "I haven't asked her yet!", he said. Joanna with a huge grin retorted, "Well, if you truly love the girl, you best get asking. I notice a lot of the young men are vying for her attention." "I know!", he exploded. I couldn't resist teasing him myself and said to Joanna, "He's had to use more than words to chase a few off." Daniel glared at me and Joanna gasped, "Daniel!" I only added to her shock saying, "Yep. He'll take on any man in town but is afraid one beautiful woman and her father." Isaac who had been silent, couldn't hold the laughter back any longer. Daniel gave all three of us a withering glare, slammed his fork on the table with a "Bah!" and left the house. We finished our lunch in high humor.

Daniel was gone for a few hours and returned. Joanna was on the porch and Isaac and I were standing in front of the barn. His head was high, walking with a swagger and an idiot's grin. He walked toward Isaac and myself but Joanna clearly heard it as well from where she stood. "October!" he roared and went right on by us and into the barn. The three of us watch him disappear into the barn. Once he was lost inside, we all burst out laughing. Daniel apparently didn't appreciate our humor, because a horse's harness went flying by our heads. This only made us roar even more with laughter.

On a beautiful day in October of 1762, the wedding day was beautiful. The hardest part was keeping Daniel away from the rum before the ceremony. Daniel and Molly were a handsome couple. They did clearly adore each other. During the feast everyone remarked on how they were the most beautiful couple ever married in the meeting house. There was plenty of food and plenty of rum. I was very surprised to see that Daniel drank sparingly after the ceremony and could not wait to get his bride home. He was the happiest and proudest I had ever seen him and was even quite amiable to all the teasing he received. It was clearly one of the happiest days I shared with my brothers and sister in many years.

During the celebration, a young girl who turned out to be Molly's cousin, seemed to be everywhere I went. She was around eight or nine years of age and I obliged the child with a dance after which, she found every excuse to be at my side. She was really a sweet little girl. Finally, her mother came over and took the child by the hand and said, "Sarah, come away and stop pestering Mr. Lane." The child to my shock, very seriously said to her mother but loud enough for everyone to hear. "Mother, I will marry him one day." To cover the mother's embarrassment, I leaned down and responded, "I can't wait for the day. It will be beautiful, my dear." The child beamed with pleasure and with that her mother whisked her away. Her father, Joshua, stayed behind and talked with me a while. He said, "I've never seen her behave like that. Thank you for being so kind to her." Before I could respond, Ephraim Sands, who could always be counted on for a jest said, "Let's celebrate! There is at last one lady in town who wants to marry the man". The jest put Joshua at ease and we all raised our mugs to Ephraim's toast. The wedding continued on for a long while with dancing and teasing and we finally all staggered back to our homes.

With Daniel married and in his own home, I continued building up the farm. By now, I had gotten used to living alone. I did miss the dinner table banter and John encouraged me to engage more in Town business. There were a few disagreements to solve but mostly the decisions were on how to make the town prosper more. John served as Moderator for the Town and I mostly was engaged with the drawing up of Lots and their sale. In the next few years, the prosperity grew and we were mostly engaged in lumber.

One day in 1764, while working on my farm, Joshua Woodman came flying toward me on his horse. "Jabez, you must come quick. A tree has fallen on Isaac Hancock, Joanna needs you." I asked if our brother John had been warned. "I'm on my way over there now." I was already running for my horse before he could finish speaking. I had no idea as to Isaac's health until I arrived at Joanna's. There was already a crowd around her home. As soon as I arrived, the crowd parted and I strode right to the door. I found Joanna inside. She ran to me, tears streaming down her cheeks. "Oh, Jabez! He's dead!" Stunned, I could only hold her as she wept. Soon, John was there and he embraced her. She finally calmed. John informed her that the children were taken to Joseph Woodman's home. The men arrived carrying Isaac's broken body. A few women went into the house to sit with Joanna and keep her inside while John and I went outside. Isaac's brother, John, was part of the group, clearly distressed himself.

While John uncovered the body, I asked, "How did this happen?" John Hancock spoke, "A group of us had been together and after working, had some ale. There was a discussion as to who was the best lumberman and Isaac got involved in a bet. The next thing, wagers were made and he picked up his axe and started chopping. The tree came down and he didn't get out of the way in time." Their father, William Hancock, who had just arrived, caught the end of the conversation. My brother moved aside so William could be near his son's body. When Isaac's brother, John, started to speak, William turned toward him without a word. It silenced his son who stood rooted to the spot at his father's expression.

John, my brother, went into action. The Woodman's were to attend to making the coffin. John and I brought Isaac in to be cleaned and attended to by the ladies. William sat quietly with Joanna. I went outside and spoke with Reverend Coffin. He was well respected in his short time here in the town. "Jabez", he said. "I would like to sit with your sister." I walked with him to the door. I spoke with him a few minutes. Reverend Coffin said, "Poor Joanna with three small children. Such a tragedy." I replied, "Obviously, I will look after her and the children. John and Daniel of course, will do what they can."

As he entered the doorway to the house, Daniel and Molly arrived. Molly had baskets of food. Daniel and I helped bring the baskets in. Some of it was already prepared. She placed this food on the table and went straight to the fire and began cooking more. She wasted no time in getting Daniel and I to assist her with her work. Finally. Isaac's coffin arrived and the women went out while the men gently placed Isaac inside. Joanna tearfully bent over Isaac and placed one last kiss and a few parting whispers before the coffin was covered. Molly took Joanna aside while we took Isaac out. Everyone followed us to where Isaac was to be buried. Molly held on to Joanna the whole time. The Reverend spoke a few words. When he was done, Molly guided Joanna home. Both women in tears. I stayed to help finish the work to be done with John, Daniel and the Hancock men. We headed back to Joanna's home. Many more people had arrived with food and to comfort Joanna.

John, Daniel and I stood together while people milled around. Isaac's father, spoke very little. He and his wife sat silently grieving. The Woodman's brought back Joanna's children. William held onto them tightly and finally the tears let loose on his cheeks. This reduced his wife to openly crying. We brought the children into the house for Joanna. She quietly spoke with her children about their father. Watching her, I realized how much strength my sister possessed. She swept aside her own tears and calmly talked to the little ones. I spoke to John saying, "Joanna and the children can come live with me. I have plenty of room." John replied, "I don't think she will have any of it. Regardless, let's give her a few days with the children and talk to her then." "That's fine", said Daniel. He went on, "I have already been informed by Molly that she is spending the night here with Joanna. So, I will come back for her tomorrow and look in on things." John said, "I will come back the day after if Jabez can come on day three." I nodded my agreement. Once that was decided, John said "Let's all be here in four days to have this discussion with Joanna."

On that day, the Hancock's accompanied us to see Joanna and the children. It became quite clear on that visit, that three brothers and two in-laws were no match for Joanna. Once we were all seated, John spoke first. "We have all talked and think it would be wise for you and the children to stay with Jabez for a while." Daniel offered, "Of course you are welcome to stay with Molly and I." She calmly sat there looking at each of us. She spoke softly when she said, "I thank you all for the offer but the children and I will stay here. John Garland has offered to buy baked goods from me for his tavern. That should help me in feeding the children. I would only possibly need help with the farm once in a while." Daniel stupidly said, "You can't stay here by yourself." For the first time, I saw Joanna's temper and I squirmed sensing that John was feeling the same way. "You didn't mind one bit leaving Mother and I here alone while you went off to fight your war!". Good point, I thought.

To calm her, I said, "Joanna, we just want to help. I want you to know, you are always welcome to come stay with me. Please don't be upset with us." She softened her tone and said, "I really need to try this. I need to be busy and this seems like a good solution right now and the children must stay in their home." John said, "There really isn't much more to be said, without upsetting you more. It sounds like a good start for you. We will help you in any way we can." "Thank you", she said rising to her feet. She ushered us all to the door and I believe she might have been still a bit angry as she firmly slammed the door behind us. John was glaring at Daniel who looked back at the rest of us saying, "What did I do?". I gave him a dead pan look saying, "Dummy" as I headed toward home. I heard William Hancock let out a giggle as I walked away.

In the next year, Joanna did quite well with her baking. I would head to the tavern to enjoy the ale and hear the latest gossip. The Town held its meetings there and by the conclusion of these meetings, everything she had cooked was eaten and enjoyed. Joanna would often come and help serve the food. After leaving the tavern with John and Daniel one night, I said, "I believe Mr. Garland is quite taken with Joanna." Daniel quite filled with liquor said, "How did I not notice this?" John and I watched him stagger in front of us and we exchanged a quick grin. John said to me, "Don't say it". I said to Daniel's stumbling back, "Dummy".

Within weeks, our suspicions were confirmed. John and Joanna decided to marry. They said their vows to each other in December of 1765. A year after Isaac's death. They were a good match and he clearly adored her. She soon became well known for not only her cooking and beauty, but she was greatly admired for her hospitality and intelligence. She soon became known as Ma'am Garland. In the years ahead, travelers would come from all around to visit the Garland Tavern.

The town needed roads in and out to accommodate carriages. The roads being so rough, carriages got through with a great deal of difficulty. John was soon involved with the committee in handling this task. He was quite capable of leading men to get things accomplished and quite soon, our road greatly improved. This aided us in getting our goods to Saco and Biddeford.

With prosperity taking shape with the farms and the Saco River so close by, the imagination of many to build mills began to take shape. In 1769, I, along with Captain John Elden, Deacon John Nason and Isaiah Brooks were approved by the Proprietors to build a Gristmill at Salmon Falls. The farmers no longer needed to carry their corn to Saco to be ground. Once the gristmill was finished, a sawmill soon followed. Our town was taking shape and more people began to move in and settle.

There was a comradery among the people and on special occasions and Sundays when church sermons would break for lunch, during warmer weather, the townspeople would enjoy banquets outside. The women would bring a feast of food, musicians brought their instruments and of course the men brought plenty of liquor. Adults and children would enjoy the dancing and games.

The little girl Sarah would always manage to find me and drag me out for a dance or two. She was growing into a beautiful young woman. Her brothers, Benjamin, Samuel and Joshua kept a close watch over her and I liked them all very much. They worked with me at the mill. Many times, Sarah would appear with baked goods. I was absolutely charmed by this young woman. By the time she had turned 17, the brothers started dropping hints. Finally, after suffering a year of their harassment, Benjamin led the charge.

She was walking away from us at the mill and I had stopped to watch her slender form walking away. Benjamin stood beside me and said, "You understand she is eligible to marry? You're so busy working every day, you don't realize she adores you." I looked at him and said, "Aye, I realize that. It just struck me she is no longer a child. Not sure how I feel about that." With that, Benjamin chuckled, slapped me on the shoulder and said, "That's why you have lived until now. We've never worried about her with you. But if you have any feelings for her, it's okay by us to court her." I looked at the three grinning brothers and felt foolish. "You've got this all planned?" Samuel couldn't wipe the grin off his face saying, "She still says she is marrying you, been saying that for years. Are you going to do something about it? Father is becoming quite busy with eligible suitors coming to the house to see her." When I started to stammer, they were uncontrollably laughing. With that, I stormed over and mounted my horse and galloped toward her retreating figure.

I caught up to her quickly and she seemed surprised at my approach.

I jumped down and took a long hard look at her. She gazed back at me perfectly calm. I was at a loss. I knew then, at that moment, this was the woman I wanted to spend the rest of my life with. All I could manage to say was, "I don't want any other man courting you. Understood?" Before she could respond, I reached out, brought her to me and gave her a long, well-meaning kiss that I'm sure I bruised her lips. When I released her, the power of my feelings over her had me rooted to the spot. She still stood there quietly with absolute happiness her in her eyes gazing back at me.

Finally, I said to her, "Let me walk you home." With my horse's reins in one hand and her hand in the other, we slowly headed that way. She had always been easy to talk to and so she started the conversation. "Did my brothers finally get to you?", she started. I sheepishly admitted, "They caught me watching you walk away and took me to task for it." "Oh?" she said. I leaned over and said to her, "I've been watching you walk away for quite a while now. Actually, I look forward to watching you arrive with your basket in your hand." She looked back at me with that smile and I saw the blush take over her face. I hadn't meant to embarrass her so I added, "I look forward to your company each day. It makes me very happy to see you." We were now approaching her home and there her mother stood. She took in the sight of us walking toward her, hand in hand and her mouth formed a perfect "O". We calmly got to the door and I gave Sarah an impulsive kiss on the cheek, "May we go for a walk this evening?" Sarah nodded with a huge happy smile. I could only smile back. I nodded toward her mother and bid her a happy day, mounted my horse and headed back toward the mill. All the while, her mother stood there not moving a muscle.

On my return, I never said a word about it to the brothers but they looked uncomfortable thinking they may have gone too far with me. I felt they should squirm a bit. We finished work and I hurried home. I took care in washing to make sure I was absolutely clean and my hair combed out. I put on my best clothes and headed to the Woodman house.

Outside to greet me were her three brothers and her father, Joshua. Joshua said, "I believe you're here for Sarah?". "Yes, sir", I cheerfully answered. "With your permission, I would like to walk with her a while." Samuel said, "We'll all walk with you and Sarah a bit". I was still irritated at being the butt end of their joking today and I managed a growl towards them saying, "You may walk in another direction!". That wiped the silly grins off of their faces. Joshua said, "You may walk with Sarah", and then he raised his voice toward his sons adding "While they walk the other way!" He turned back to me and winked, "You take care of my daughter." At twenty-nine years of age, I felt like a young school boy. I tried not to run to the door to knock. Out came Sarah. If it was at all possible, she was even more beautiful to me at that moment than she was this afternoon.

For two weeks we walked each evening. Some nights her mother had me come for dinner. At the end of two weeks, I asked Joshua if we could have a few minutes. We went outside away from the house. I asked him for his daughter's hand in marriage. In a serious tone he said, "If she'll have you." My smile dropped at the unexpected comment before I realized he was teasing me. He went on in a more serious note, "I want her to have a happy life and you must promise me to do your best at my one request." I answered him solemnly, "I promise you that." I offered him a handshake and he uncharacteristically gave me a quick hug. He offered to send her out and I thanked him. We went for our walk and I took her to where she always remarked was one of her favorite places and I asked her to sit with me there.

I didn't know how to start and suddenly felt nervous. The darned woman sat beside me and softly said, "Yes, Jabez". Surprised I said, "But I haven't even asked you! You're as bad as your blasted brothers!" She smiled knowingly. So, I went ahead with my planned speech. "I have come to love you with all my heart. I wish to share my life with you." With a deep breath I asked, "Will you marry me"? She was quickly in my arms and said, "Yes. I've been waiting on you for ten years. I want to marry you as soon as possible."

A month later, on August 27, 1772, with my brothers standing beside me, we married. Every member of both families attended as well as most of the town. Elizabeth (John's wife), Molly (Daniel's wife) and Alice, Sarah's mother, made her a beautiful dress. Her hair was brought up and adorned with wild flowers. Her eyes were a crystal blue. Her father escorted her toward me and my heart hammered in my chest. She was beautiful and her face shone with her happiness. I could not take my eyes off of this woman as she gazed back at me. The ceremony was blessedly over quickly and I could take my bride in my arms. I wasn't interested in the feast, I wanted to take her home. So many people had come to witness the marriage and celebrate, we had no choice but to stay. The women were trying to whisk her away but I had my hand firmly clamped around her waist.

Ephraim Sands came to us with mugs of ale in each hand. Behind him were the Woodman men and my two brothers. He said, "Come Jabez. We must celebrate with a toast." When I reached for the ale, the women got their way. "It's only for a few minutes, Jabez.", they teased as Sarah was hustled away. Ephraim laughed and joked, "Don't worry my friend, they will bring her back."

The fiddles were already beginning to play and people were beginning to dance. The food was brought out and the men were handing me one ale after another. Daniel was beginning to feel the effects of the liquor. "Congratulations, little brother. You look handsome together and here's to a happy life." With that he threw back his head to drink to his toast and the liquor poured down either side of his face. The men were in hysterics at this. Daniel could only laugh at himself. Her brothers were standing with John enjoying his conversation. I thanked them for their help with all the preparations. Benjamin toasted, "To my new brother in law. May you always keep Sarah as happy as she is today." Samuel added with a serious expression, "The three of us have decided to come and live with you both to make sure." I froze with my mug half way to my mouth. John to my frustration said, "Aye, best idea I've heard all day." I looked at him in complete shock. For a few seconds we all stood there looking at each other. Daniel broke the tension when he doubled over laughing, spilling his ale yet again.

I stood with them a few minutes more and after enduring a few more minutes of their harassment, wandered off to find Sarah. I took her by the hand and we walked toward the dancers. She looked toward our brothers and said, "They are having themselves a good time." I looked over at the fools, still enjoying their joke and said, "It seems my brothers have joined your brothers in tormenting me." With that, she smiled even more and squeezed my arm. We joined in with the dancing. All five of the brothers each took a turn dancing with Sarah. I found Joanna to dance with her as well as Molly, Elizabeth and Sarah's mother.

Much sooner than I expected the afternoon faded and the cool night air moved in. Sarah leaned over and whispered, "Let's go home." I nodded and hand in hand, we said thank you and farewell to everyone. Our home was very close and we walked quietly. I was so proud of my new wife and told her so. We entered home and saw that the ladies had somehow gotten in. They had completely cleaned the house and I found there was new bedding. They had even left some prepared food on the table for us. It was very sweet and Sarah was touched. But I didn't care about the house or the food. All I cared about in that very moment was this woman in front of me.

I found I enjoyed my married life with Sarah more than I had expected. I couldn't wait to get home for supper each evening and she would still bring her basket filled with lunch to the mill. She was a good cook and kept our home neat and tidy. She not only had become my wife but, my best friend. Each night, we shared what we had done, seen or heard that day. We were very content in our marriage.

One morning, after only a few months of marriage, she looked a little pale and was quiet while we had breakfast. After a few bites, she jumped up and ran outside. Baffled, I ran out to her and the poor thing was violently losing her breakfast. I took my jacket off and placed it over her shoulders to protect her from the cold. I stayed with her until I felt sure she was finished. She was very weak on her legs when I brought her back into the house so I guided her to bed with orders to stay put today. She didn't argue. I cleaned up the kitchen, checked on her and stood there not knowing what to do. She decided for me. "Jabez, you are not going to stand there all day staring at me." I reluctantly left the house. Still quite worried about Sarah's incident, I went to her parent's home, I knocked on the door and after explaining what happened, asked Alice to check in on Sarah. She reassured me she would.

I left the mill early that day and found Alice had been there all afternoon. "Is she all right?" I asked. "She is just fine." she responded. I took her hand and said, "Thank you for coming today. I have never seen her so sick." Alice smiled and walked past me saying, "She's not sick you dolt." "What do you mean?", I asked her. She just smiled and said, "She's waiting for you." Confused, I strode into the house and there she sat, calmly. "How are you feeling?" I questioned her. "Fine, my love" she answered with a smile. "Your mother says you're not sick. Did you not tell her about this morning?" She nodded. In my frustration and with my voice raised for the first time toward her, I said, "Then, what is the meaning of this?" She sat in front of me with a proud smile and said, "It's a common in women when they become pregnant." I was dumbstruck. "A baby?" was all I could manage. She was still stood there calmly. I swept her into my arms. "A baby! This is wonderful!"

And so, the following months I hovered over her and she in turn enjoyed her state. We were excited and could not wait to meet our first child. She didn't seem to mind her clumsiness in the later stages of pregnancy but I did all I could to help keep her comfortable. She refused to take it easy and kept herself quite busy. She spent her free time making clothes and I spent mine with her brother Samuel, making furniture for the soon-to-be addition to our family. Samuel and Sarah had always been very close and I enjoyed his company. He was a hard worker and a good man.

Finally, one day, Sarah said, "Go and fetch my mother." I didn't bother to saddle the horse and sped over to find Alice. I ran toward the house yelling, "Alice!" The door swung open and out she ran. She continued to run right on by me, without a word, toward Samuel who hoisted her onto the wagon he had just arrived on, demanding he take her to my house. I went to mount my horse to follow but Joshua had me by the arm. "It's women's business, son. You don't want to go near that." He tried to give me some ale but I wasn't interested. I was impatient, wanting to go home and be near her. I could only pace back and forth until Daniel's wife Molly arrived and said, "Jabez, you can go home now. Sarah is fine." Molly assured me that both the baby and Sarah were just fine.

I sped home to see that Joanna, Elizabeth, Alice and a few other ladies were hovering over Sarah and the baby. When I stepped in, they had quietly gone outside. There was Sarah, very tired, proudly holding our son. I drew the blanket aside and checked this new being from head to toe. He was perfect. I sat with her a while and she soon fell asleep. Alice came in and put the baby in the cradle and rocked him to sleep. "Alice, thank you for all you have done." I said. "My first grandchild." Was all she could say staring down at the baby.

Once the baby was asleep, she took me outside and we found that her husband Joshua, my brothers, as well as Sarah's brothers had arrived. I went back in and picked up the sleeping baby and brought him out to his aunts, uncles and grandparents. Alice was very stern about keeping the baby covered and urged me to put him back in his cradle. I reluctantly did so and went back out again to join the others. Everyone was anxious to know what we were going to name the child and although I would have liked to announced it with Sarah by my side, I couldn't resist. We have decided if it is a boy to name it Samuel. I looked pointedly at her brother. He absolutely beamed with pleasure at this. Daniel walked over to Samuel saying, "Well, Uncle Samuel, I believe the baby needs changing!" At his look of shear fright, we all burst out laughing.

In just a few days, Sarah was up and running her house again. Our lives were centered around our son. I marveled at the happiness that had come into my home and how changed my life was in this one year. Joshua and Alice spent every free moment with us doting on their grandchild. His uncles and aunts came by frequently. Joanna's girls made cloth toys for the baby and absolutely doted on their cousin.

The girls would come and visit with Sarah while I attended meetings at the tavern. There was word that things were becoming strained in Boston with the British. John was very involved in the events that were unfolding and had even made a few trips to Boston to see for himself and attend meetings with a group that called themselves 'The Sons of Liberty'. The news he brought home were becoming more unsettling as time went on. I could only hope his warnings would not prove true.

3

1773 - 1774

In 1772, Narraganset Township, No. 1 was duly approved as the Town of Buxton. Buxton was incorporated as the seventh town in Massachusetts. On May 24, 1773 we formed and attended our first Proprietors Meeting of Buxton. John and I became even more active in town affairs. Businesses and farms continued to grow. It may have been a time of peace through the country but, growing towns did come with their own set of disputes and difficult decisions. We held Proprietors meetings to dissolve our own disputes, record selling lands and make decisions for the good of the townspeople. We did our best to resolve issues amicably. John had a very diplomatic mind. His interest went beyond the town borders and he liked to keep up with the news around the Colonies. He maintained his friendships he had made with men from the previous war who lived as far away as Boston. Through these friendships, he was able to keep abreast of what was going on throughout the colonies.

For many years, the English arrogance was suppressing the colonists. The British found after the French and Indian War their monies depleted and so to raise money, Parliament passed two Acts in March of 1765. The first one, The Quartering Act which would require the colonists to house British soldiers in their homes as well as feed them. Many parents slept in fear for their children, especially the young girls who suffered the advances of some of these men. That same day, they passed the Stamp Act. This required colonists to buy stamps for such things as legal documents, newspapers and so on. The colonists were refusing to comply.

The taxes they were imposing brought us nothing in return. News from Boston sent a message of an unwanted wind of trouble. The English still looked down their noses at the colonists and tension was transforming into resistance. John and Captain Elden warned us that these events were going to lead toward a rebellion.

The Tea Act May 10, 1773 (just a few weeks after Samuel was born) was passed to help the East India Company who was in a financial crisis. Five ports (one being Boston) were selected to receive the tea. Each town, including our own, were to buy this tea whether they wanted it or not. The citizens thought this totally unacceptable.

In December John Mason asked John to travel with him to Boston. I saw him at church on Sunday after their return. When the church broke for lunch, John came toward me, "Have you a minute, Jabez?" I could tell by his tone he was excited about something and said, "Yes". Daniel strode over to say hello and when he heard us telling our wives we would be right along, he turned to Molly and urged her to go with them.

Once, they were on their way I asked John, "Is this about your trip to Boston?" "Aye." John replied. He looked around to make sure we weren't being heard. "You have heard of the Sons of Liberty?" Both Daniel and I said we did. John began his story, "Well we heard they were having a meeting at a tavern called the Green Dragon and got invited to attend which we did. Once we got there, we were vouched for by the man who invited us. The place was crowded. While we waited in the tavern, I learned that the upstairs is a Masonic Lodge." Daniel interrupted, "Did you go up to see it?" John wasn't annoyed by the question and answered, "No, unless you are a member, you are not allowed." John continued on, "We had an ale and I enjoyed some conversation with other men that were there. Finally, some of us were taken downstairs into the basement. The man who spoke to us was Paul Revere."

He paused and I had to ask, "The man we have heard so much about?" John's smile was wide, "Aye, Jabez." He became animated at that point with his story, "It all happened so fast, I went with the men to the Old South Church to join the protest. There were thousands of citizens outside the church. Our group went into the church and had our faces painted to look like Mohawks, given tomahawks and clubs and were told to wait." Daniel boomed, "Good Lord, why do that?" Again, John answered him, "So we would not be recognized on the streets going to and coming back." "You went with them?", I had to ask. "Yes, of course. "How many of you dressed as Indians?" asked Daniel. "A couple hundred" replied John.

The protesters outside headed down to the wharfs while we were told to remain. We were divided into three groups before the signal was given. I followed with my group through the crowds, onto the wharf to the ship we were assigned to board. The Captain on board didn't give any trouble. His only request was to not damage the ship. We spent most of the night breaking up the barrels and dumping them into the harbor." I stared at him in disbelief but on he went. "When we were leaving the wharfs, I looked at the harbor. It was strewn with barrels and tea floating everywhere." "Did the crowd stay all night?" asked Daniel. "Yes", answered John. "Where did you go from there?", I asked him. John replied, "We all followed the plan. We cleaned up and left the city immediately." "I fear there will repercussions from that bit of fun you had" I chuckled. Daniel elbowed me in the side and retorted, "We missed ourselves some fun, little brother." I couldn't help but roll my eyes derisively.

We did not have to wait long to find out what they would be. On June 20, 1774, we all gathered at the Garland Tavern for a Proprietor's meeting to hear the word from Boston. My brother John was chosen Moderator. Captain Elden read the news. The British proclaimed three more Acts on Massachusetts. The Massachusetts Government Act was put into place putting the government of Massachusetts almost entirely under direct British control. The Boston Port Act in 1774 was the King's retaliation to the colonies which closed the harbor of Boston until the cost of the tea that was dumped was repaid. The Massachusetts Government Act was passed by the Parliament of Great Britain and approved by the King in May of 1774. This would take away the rule of the Massachusetts Charter passed in 1691 and would give the English appointed governor control of Massachusetts.

When Captain Elden was done reading, there were a few moments of silence. He then explained, "The situation is further complicated. There is wind that the British are fearing that they are losing hold over the colonies. Boston is overrun with soldiers there and more are coming. Word is to disarm the local militias." Tristram Jordan interrupted, "They have been trying to do that since '69". John spoke up informing Tristram, "I have been to Boston, citizens are being harassed without provocation. I've seen some of it and heard stories while I was there." This silenced the crowd.

Captain Elden went on with his speech, "Boston has asked each Town to draw up resolutions regarding this. I nominate John Lane, myself, Samuel Merrill, Samuel Hovey and John Mason be appointed as a committee to draw up resolutions on behalf of the Town in concurrence with the Committee of Correspondence in Boston." After the nomination was made and seconded, there was a short discussion and being that there was no argument about the proposed Committee, we went on with the business of the Town.

The Committee spent every night for two weeks drawing up their response. On June 24, we met again at the Meeting House to hear the Response on behalf of Buxton. Captain Elden after opening the meeting went directly into reading the Resolves. John as Moderator read the words that had been written:

Resolve 1st that Self Preservation is the first Law of nature and that taxation without Representation is subversive of our Liberties.

2. Whereas an act of the British Parliament hath been passed for closing up the harbor of Boston, we think this is unconstitutional and under these grievous and unheard of impositions we are to remain until an unreasonable Demand is Complied with and we consider this attack upon us as utterly subversive of American Liberty for the same Power may at Pleasure Destroy the trade and Shut up the Ports of Every other Colony in its turn so that will be a total end of all Liberty and Privilege.

3. that this town approve of the Constitutional Exertions and struggles made by opulent Colonies through the Continent for Preventing so fatal a Catastrophe as is Implied in taxation without Representation, and that we are and always will be Ready in Every Constitutional way to give all assistance in our Power to Prevent so Dire a Calamity.

4. That a Dread of being enslaved ourselves and of transmitting the chains to our Posterity is the Principle inducement to these measures.

5. that this town Do Return their Sincere and hearty thanks to all the cities, towns and persons in America and to Boston in particular who have at all times nobly exerted themselves in the cause of Liberty.

Voted that the town Clerk transmit a true copy of these Resolves to the Committee of Correspondence in Boston. Voted that these Resolves be Recorded in the town Book. a true Entry attest JOHN NASON, Town Clerk.

All present were in agreement with these Resolves. They were promptly sent along with Resolves from towns all over to Boston. With the widespread support from the Towns, The First Continental Congress met on September 5, 1774 in Philadelphia. There were delegates from the thirteen colonies except for Georgia. There were important delegates in attendance. Among them were John Adams of Massachusetts and George Washington of Virginia.

Governor Thomas Gage's response was almost immediate. He rejected the petition. His response was three-fold. First, that the inhabitants of this province are to be disarmed. Second, the province is to be governed by Martial Law and third, that a number of gentlemen who have exerted themselves in the cause of their country are to be seized and sent to Great Britain.

In late September, the Governor's response was read at Garland's Tavern where a group of us had gone (as we often did in the evenings). The conversation got downright ugly. John and Captain Elden were disgusted. Peter Emery joined into the conversation, "Do you honestly think they would come this far to take our guns? The trouble is actually in the bigger cities and towns." Captain Elden responded to him, "Yes, I do believe it will happen to us. If it starts in one place, where do you suggest it will stop." Peter argued, "But we are in the wilderness, how would we protect ourselves and our homes? Besides, this is in retaliation for the dumping of the tea." John bellowed, "Do you honestly believe it would not affect us? Think man. We are forced to pay every tax Great Britain that levels on the colonies and none of the taxes collected benefit the colonies." Old man, Ebenezer Redlon chimed in, "The Governor himself is acting on Britain's behalf, did you not hear his response to our Resolves? He has the backing of the King's army."

Now everyone was yelling, John and Captain Elden stood and waved their arms to quiet down the volume of noise. John Garland who was filling the men's mugs interjected, "Think on this. England taxes their colonies to fund their causes. The tax money we pay, benefits people and government in other countries. They are not going to let go of the American money pot peacefully. I think the best way IS to disarm the population and bring more troops in. Without the right to defend ourselves and our homes, we are no better than slaves to a tyrant. That leaves us with no rights at all." Peter Emery had a shocked expression on his face and said, "I had not thought about it in that way. What you say makes sense and I am with you all in whatever you decide to do." Daniel slammed his mug down on the table in front of him saying, "Well said, Mr. Garland." With that, Daniel let out a belch that could drown out any conversation. Daniel went on to say, "Without our guns, we won't be able to hunt for food, let alone defend homes or our livestock from the wolves that come in at night." John now stood and gazed about the room and added, "If and when troops arrive, will you be happy to have them exercise their rights to take quarter in your homes? Would you stand still watching them take advantage of your wives and daughters? Wipe out the food you toiled for all summer so you and your family can starve all winter? Garland is correct in his opinion. There is no better way to take over a colony or a country for that matter, than to disarm the people. This my friends, is what will happen." The conversation we just listened to, hung over us all. No other words were spoken until Captain Elden decided to end it by saying, "Go home and talk with your families. One thing is for certain, we must wait to see what comes of this."

I stayed after the meeting to finish my ale. John and Daniel sat down with me. John let out a huge sigh and said, "That was a difficult meeting." Daniel still agitated from all he heard responded, "England is not going to let this go peacefully. Some of these people are living in denial." "Aye", agreed John. I voiced my concern, "I worry that if we have to leave to fight, the women will be left alone." We all pondered that thought a few minutes before John spoke, "Our women are resourceful. We must prepare them for what may come." Daniel added, "They would have the advantage. We should encourage them if the red coats should arrive here, they should hide in the woods." John was encouraged by the thought saying, "I don't think the red coats would remain in a deserted town more than a few days. They might do some damage but, the women and children would be safer." I warned my brothers, "They should definitely not run to the fort. The red coats will want to take it for themselves for cover." John agreed and went further, "The men that cannot fight, I'm sure will get the women to safety. We need to speak to our wives." "Agreed.", bellowed Daniel and I nodded. John went on to say, "I would feel better if we have some plan for the women. After that, all that remains now is to wait and see what England's next move will be."

My brothers and I chose to bring our wives together and invited Joanna and her husband for an evening dinner. Joanna's husband, John, had been listening to our conversation and offered, "Why don't you bring your families here for dinner tomorrow? We will not have any guests staying. Joanna and I would love to see everyone together." "That is a great idea, thanks John.", I replied. Daniel said, "My thanks as well, if big brother here agrees, we will take you up on the offer." John looked at his brother-in-law and John nodded saying, "I'm sure Elizabeth would enjoy seeing Joanna. She doesn't get to see Joanna very much."

We all arrived the next evening and enjoyed our dinner. Joanna served a feast and our wives brought food to add to the table. Once dinner was finished, the cousins were anxious to play games and the wives were intent on helping Joanna clear the table. The sound of the children's giggles while they played in another room and hearing the women banter back and forth brought forth a feeling of contentment.

John's wife Elizabeth dropped their infant son in his lap and who promptly fell asleep in his arms. Sarah handed Samuel over to me but he wasn't interested in sleeping. In Daniel's lap sat Charlotte, almost a year old, who just laid content in her father's lap watching Samuel squirm to be put down. Poor Molly was well into pregnancy with yet another child. If she was uncomfortable with her pregnancy, she showed no sign of it. John Garland held his daughter Patty. There the four of us sat with our infants waiting for the women to join us.

Finally, Daniel began to lose his patience and demanded they come join us. Once they settled into their chairs with us, Daniel tried to hand Charlotte over to Molly but a sharp look from her negated that idea.

John started the conversation, "Ladies, we have been discussing what may happen in the future and thought it best if we had some thoughts in case we have to leave for a war." Elizabeth's face paled visibly at her husband's words. Elizabeth looked so fragile and I was concerned for her health. In a frightened voice she said, "Surely you don't think it will happen?". John leaned over to pat his wife's hand and nodded. Molly spoke up in utter rage, "That's right, if there is to be a fight or a brawl, count on the Lane's to lead the pack!". I was stunned at her outburst. Daniel's jaw dropped, the usually temperate Molly was in a full-blown fury and it was quite obvious Daniel had not expected this reaction from her. John Garland thinking he was helping said, "Molly, I would not be left behind either." That only made the situation worse. Molly turned her temper towards Garland railing at him, "Why not! Don't worry about any of the women you men will be leaving behind!".

I looked at Sarah and Joanna who sat motionless. This was going badly and I had to say something to calm the woman, "This is why we are all together this evening. We want to make preparations for all of you while we are gone." Molly spat back at me, "And what would that be?". To my shock, Sarah spoke gently to Molly, "I believe it just may well come to war. What kind of men would we have if they did not fight for better lives for our families? I have been listening to what is being said in town. We are unfortunately being forced to stand up for ourselves. Do I want my husband to leave? Absolutely not!" I had been avoiding such conversations with her but she had wisely kept her own counsel until now. Sarah smiled sweetly at us all saying, "Please, tell us your ideas".

Daniel started speaking with a nervous glance at his usually gentle wife, "Our hope is that Red Coats never get to our town but, if they do, it's important that you get somewhere safe." Elizabeth said, "Going to the fort would be best, I should think." John said, "No, my dear. The soldiers would want to make it their quarters." Joanna finally spoke, "I propose at the first word of their coming this way, bring your children here to the tavern. We have all the guest rooms so, that would make staying together much easier. If they do enter the town, we can flee into the woods to hide or try to get to another town for help." I liked the idea very much and Daniel spoke to Joanna, "That is very good." To Molly he said, "I would feel better knowing you would do that." Molly with pursed lips nodded and Sarah added, "I will plan to bring supplies from our house to help us." Elizabeth joined in, "My children are older and will help out with the younger children as well as any work that we might need done." Joanna looked about the table and said, "That's settled. We ladies will have each other if needed. You men will do what you must and come back to us safely."

The conversation was decidedly over and we talked about each other's children. When Sarah let out a yawn, I rose and thanked Joanna and John for the evening dinner. That caused everyone to stand and ready themselves to go home.

With Samuel bundled up in my arms, Sarah and I headed home. Sarah said in a choked voice, "I don't want you to leave." "I don't want to leave you, my love", I whispered back. At her silence I added, "I have never been so happy as I am with you and our son." In response she wrapped her arms around my arm and moved in closer to me while we walked. "I love you, too." We walked quietly home, each of us deep in our own thoughts.

While these events were happening, the town continued on with its business. At home, I watched Samuel grow. He was now a healthy toddler and walking. When I came into the house at night, he would toddle toward me as fast as he could with his arms up knowing I would scoop him up into the air. The sound of my child's laughter, made the tiredness disappear from my body. He chattered away in my lap while Sarah would put the food on the table each night. Most nights I ate dinner with him in my lap while Sarah and I talked. It was usually about the mischief Samuel had gotten into that day while I was off working. She would find the humor in it when telling me and we couldn't help but laugh. Each night, while she cleared and cleaned the dishes, I would get Samuel ready for bed. It was a fatherly ritual I never tired of. Once he was asleep, Sarah and I would sit outside his open window on a warm summer night or cozied up close to the fire in the winter.

A few nights before Christmas, the men were called upon to gather at Garland's Tavern. Nathaniel Hill had come with the New Hampshire Gazette and we were anxious to hear news. Nathaniel read the news aloud to us. The Gazette told of Paul Revere's warning that British ships were on their way to Fort William and Mary, nearby in New Hampshire to seize the weapons and ammo there. The New Hampshire militia responded by raiding the Fort and seize the weapons and ammo before the Brits arrived. The newspaper further declared the capture prudent and proper with a reminder, 'the ancient Carthaginians had consented to "deliver up all their Arms to the Romans" and were decimated by the Romans soon after.' As predicted, the British were in fact getting closer to our little town.

Captain Elden spoke to us saying, "We have received England's response to our affairs. All eyes turned to Captain Elden and he went on, "England has ordered the Governor to disarm the colonists. It is decreed that town meetings would be allowed only once a year." Moses Atkinson said, "How do they plan to do this without killing most of the citizenry?" John responded, "Governor Gage is well aware, if shots are fired on the citizenry, it would be calling for war." Captain Elden interjected, "The Governor's idea to seize the gunpowder was intelligent on his part. Our guns will be useless without it. His troops have been successful at raiding the powder houses in the neighboring towns of Boston and taking away our ammo and weapons that are stored in them. Charleston powder house has just been taken. I am enlisting a company to come with me to join other militias to help deter the red coats." "And so, it begins.", said Peter Emery. To that, Ephraim Sands cautioned, "We should be careful to whom we speak. There are some in this town that are loyal to England." Some men nodded and a few looked around the tavern assuring ourselves that we could speak freely. We all were aware of those who opposed our resistance.

Reverend Coffin walked in while we were discussing the news. He had long argued that we should not engage the Red Coats. The Reverend was well liked by the townspeople and as a man of the cloth, we understood his wanting a peaceful solution. Ebenezer Redlon, however, had no compulsion about taking on the Reverend Coffin. "Are you a Royalist?" he demanded. The reverend answered, "Aye. Their troops helped to protect us from the French and Indians. Better to be under their Government than another." Immediate grumbling followed this comment. Ebenezer shot back at him, "There aren't any red coats here Reverend. There were many colonists fighting with the British against the French and Indians. The Red Coats didn't win that one by themselves. Your protection, food and housing does not come from Britain, Reverend. Best you remember that."

The Reverend stood stock still. Captain Elden jumped to his feet. "Ebenezer, stop!This is a godly man.", he commanded. Ebenezer picked up his mug and shot back, "Then let him preach God's laws. Does he think holding his bible up in the air will stop a cannonball from landing on this town?" The Reverend spoke up, "No, I don't Ebenezer. The British are not trying to take away our rights to self-defense." Ebenezer actually laughed at that last comment and spoke to the Reverend as if he were speaking a child saying, "Okay, Reverend. Think of it this way, the Red Coats confiscate our guns, now Reverend; wolves, Indians or a military force tries to harm us. What do you suggest we defend ourselves with? The Reverend supplied no answer but kept his eyes on Ebenezer and implored, "Maybe you would start attending Church on Sundays?". Ebenezer rolled his eyes in a derisive manner saying, "Not with the foolishness you utter." The Reverend gave up on Ebenezer and after speaking to a few men, left the Tavern. Shortly after, most of us headed home.

I couldn't wait to get home. I told Sarah of what happened that evening. A look of fright appeared for a second on her face but she quickly recovered herself. She calmly said, "I hope it doesn't come to violence between the townspeople." I answered, "Let's hope not. We won't know until things worsen." She asked me, "What do you think will happen?". I told her, "In all honesty, I am unsure but, we can only hope for the best." She said, "I can't help but worry about it." In a bit of bravado my response was, "I would probably want to shoot them but instead, I would have them run out of town." I knew she had been worried about it since our conversation at the tavern. I felt better being able to come home and speak to her freely. I learned from confiding in her that she was not apt to do anything foolish. When she visited with other women in the town, she kept silent on her opinions and maintained her friendships.

I was done with the conversation for the evening and she could sense it. "Come", she said, "You need to get some rest." I stoked the fire and she put out the candles. I took one of the candles from her and went to check on our sleeping son before I joined her.

4

1775

The beginning of the year, the Red Coats were spreading out further inland from Boston to seize more of the gunpowder. On April 18, the Red Coats left Boston for Lexington and Concord to seize American arms there. It was there, the colonists made their stand and the dreaded shots were fired.

We received word within a couple of days and in response, on April 24 1775, I marched with my brothers to Biddeford on an express from Colonel Tristram Jordan. Captain Elden had already left town with a few good men. Some of the men that left with us were:

Andrews, William
   Atkinson, Moses
   Boynton, Daniel
   Boynton, Isaac
   Boynton, John
   Bradbury, Elijah
   Brooks, Robert

Brooks, Samuel
Clay, Benjamin
Clay, Richard
Cole, John
Rounds, Lemuel
Flood, Henry
Hancock, John
Hill, Prospect
Elwell, Benjamin
Redlon, Ebenezer, Jr.
Sands, Ephraim
Towle, Phineas
Whitney, Stephen
Woodman, James
Woodman, Joshua
Woodman, Benjamin
Woodsum, Abiatha
Peter Emery
Cole, John Sr.
Cole, John Jr
Cole, Samuel
Edgerly, John
Hancock, William
Redlon, David
Redlon, Ebenezer
Smith, John
Wilson, John
Woodman, John
Woodman, Nathan
Woodman, Nathan Jr.
Woodsum, John

Woodsum, Samuel.

The night before I left with Daniel and John, I spent alone with Sarah. Leaving her and Samuel behind was probably the hardest thing I had yet done in my life. These past few years, I had been as happy and content as any fortunate man would be. I knew that the women of the town would take care of each other. Sarah's worry was evident. I knew her thoughts were full of fear and I tried to ease them. "At least the planting is done. Molly will come by and help as much as she can. I hope to be back before the harvest", I told her. I could see tears forming in her eyes. "Jabez, I am so afraid something will happen to you!" I tried to summon a chuckle but it seemed to get stuck in my throat. "My love, I will be back. That I promise you. I will send news as much as I can." With that, I held her all night, my thoughts on her health and that of the babe she carried. I didn't share it with her but, my fear was for her and her health. Caring for a home, a farm and small children was hard for a woman alone. I saw that as a boy when Father marched off.

The next morning, I woke before Sarah. I laid next to her gazing at her sleeping face. I drank in every angle of her face and form. My heart weighed heavy realizing it would be a while before I would hold her to me again.

I forced back the morose thoughts and got up to check on Samuel. He was just waking. With a huge innocent smile, he threw his chubby arms up for me to lift him. He let out a little squeak when I clasped him to my chest a bit too tightly. I brought him out to the kitchen listening to him chatter away. By God, I didn't know how I could leave my family behind. Soon Sarah came out and began making breakfast as if it was a normal day. I was amazed at her cheerful calmness. I knew inside her emotions were in a turmoil. We both wanted these last moments together to be a pleasant memento for each other and our son.

Her mother and father had come early that morning to see me off. I found a few moments alone to speak with Joshua. He said, "Good luck, Jabez. Get yourself home soon." I shook his offered hand and said, "I would really appreciate your keeping an eye on Sarah and Samuel while I'm gone, Sir." He smiled and said, "You're not to worry about that. Alice is not going to let Sarah out of her sight very long until the baby is born and even then, poor Sarah won't get a moments peace." We both laughed at the thought. Alice was very close with her daughter and I knew she would move a mountain if it appeared to be in her daughter's way. He placed his hands on my shoulders and plead, "Promise me you will keep my sons as safe as you can." I looked him directly in the eye and said, "I promise. They are my family, too." His expression was one of acceptance but, I understand the man's fear for his sons. I started to turn away, hesitated and said one more time, "I promise."

With one more hug for Samuel and a lingering kiss and a long embrace from Sarah, I mounted up and joined the others. From behind I heard Samuel yell, "Papa!". My stomach twisted at his call. I turned and mustered up a smile and a wave and rode on.

We reported to Cape Ann in Gloucester. Once arriving, we had a vote on who would be Captain. After good-hearted arguing, John was voted in as Captain, Daniel as Lieutenant and I as Ensign. We were now a company of fifty men in the command of Colonel Foster's Regiment. We were to remain there as part of the defense on the seacoast. The days were spent building up defenses around Cape Ann. Whalers were being sent out to catch any ships that would supply the British.

Colonel Jordan had summoned John and when he returned, he called the company together. He informed us, "I will have to leave for a few weeks to head up to Boothbay. It has been requested that I deliver supplies and meet with the Penobscot to get their cooperation." "Why you?", asked Daniel. John returned, "All I know is that someone presented my name to Continental Congress."

Phineas Towle stepped forward and said, "Begging you pardon, Sir, but what news do you have from Boston?" John was happy to answer saying, "Boston is under siege. The colonists have the surrounding hills and is at an advantage. The British have very little access to the city at this point. Houses are being ransacked by the Brits for food and goods. Daily they are being harassed with a sniper's bullet."

"When do we leave?" asked Benjamin Woodman. "I am going alone.", responded John. He quickly added, "There is a company of men already up there that are to aid me. Daniel will be in charge while I am gone." Daniel puffed himself up saying, "Aye. I can manage that while you are gone."

The night before he left, Daniel and I managed to have supper with John. He read the letter Washington had sent for John to read to the Penobscot.

"Our liberty and your liberty are the same, we are brothers, and what is for ours for your good, and we, by standing together, shall make those wicked men afraid and overcome them and be all free men. Captain Goldthwaite has given up Fort Pownall to our enemies. We are angry at it and We hear you are angry with him and we don't wonder at it."

After he read it, I said, "So, it seems that you are to find out what is going on at the Fort AND calm some angry Indians." John sat quietly in thought. Daniel broke the ice when he said to him, "Don't worry about things here, John. We will keep ourselves out of trouble while you are gone." John responded, "I'm sure you and Jabez can manage things here. I'm not sure how well I will be received with the Penobscot."

We were quiet for a minute while we ate. Daniel was quite thoughtful when he spoke to him, "John, you are the perfect person to go. Your honesty and honor are the reason why you have been chosen. People respond to you better than any man I have ever met." John said, "Coming from you, that means a lot. Thanks, Daniel."

John's attitude seemed improved at Daniel's words. He turned to me and said, "What do you think, little brother, can you make sure Daniel keeps our company out of trouble?" I looked at both of them, "We'll have to hide the liquor." While Daniel looked like I had struck him, John's laughter filled the air. Daniel and I looked at each other and joined in with the laughter. It felt good. Because, in fact, we were worried about John. We just weren't about to let him know that. We finished our supper talking about the men and John's upcoming adventure. I gave John a quick brotherly embrace good bye and good luck and turned to leave as Daniel did the same. Behind me I heard Daniel's voice, "Keep that hair attached to your scalp and get back here." I stopped for a second, not looking back. All I could do was roll my eyes as I walked away. I'm sure John felt comforted by that parting remark. John left the next morning with the whole company to see him off.

During the second week of June I received a message from my sister, Joanna, of the birth of my second son on June 2. Sarah had named him Jabez. Sarah and the child are doing well. The family was doing fine and missed us. I was happy and relieved at the news. I hated this time away from Sarah. I wanted to get home to see for myself but could not. I'm sure every man here felt the same way.

I shared the news with Daniel and we had a pint of rum to celebrate. We talked about missing our wives and families and had a drink to that. I read the letter I received to Daniel, "Joanna says Jabez's features take after me where Samuel looks of more of his mother's side." I should have known Daniel would have fun with that. He spent an hour regaling me and the others who came in to have a celebratory pint with us, "The poor babe, Jabez, to go through life with his father's look. What is to become of the poor child". I endured everyone's teasing with good humor as well as the congratulations by all. It was a welcome reprieve from the work and the watchful waiting going on here.

The last week in June, while out working with the men I got word John had returned. It was a good day to stop our work early because the summer heat beating down us resulted in slow moving men. No one objected. I got back to town as quick as I could and found John. Apparently, there were a lot of men who wanted to hear about his trip.

When I arrived, he started talking. He began, "I had good success with the Penobscot. Fort Pownall is undermanned but Colonel Goldthwaite who is in charge there is continuing to do his best with what he has got. Unfortunately, he had to turn over his cannons to the British and is being condemned for it. He did not have the men to defend the fort. The Colonel introduced me to a man by the name of Andrew Gilman. The man speaks their language so I brought him as my interpreter. When I arrived at their village, I met with four chiefs and they agreed to send a chief and three young braves with me to Watertown." "Who is the chief?", asked a voice from the group. "Orono.", he replied. He went on, "He's also the Grand Chief of the Penobscot and he is white." "What!", Daniel voiced in belief. John just went on again, "They believe he was kidnapped as a child. He has blue eyes and is light skinned. I was told he had blond hair but it is white now. He is extremely intelligent. Anyway, we arrived in Watertown June 19th with Chief Orono, Joseph Pease, Poveris and one other, just two days after the Battle of Bunker Hill. Two days later, the 21st of June, this group was on the floor of Continental Congress. I presented them to a Committee from the Continental Congress and Orono spoke very well there."

John continued his story, "I was informed that a few days before we arrived in Watertown, George Washington from Virginia was made the Commander in Chief of the army. "So, what is this new Commander in Chief like?", asked Ephraim. John answered, "I don't know, he has not gotten there yet. All I know about him is that he owns a plantation in the South and fought in the French and Indian War." John Boynton said, "I don't recall that name." His son, Isaac, said, "Sounds like we will be hearing a lot more of it, if he is in charge of all the armies." "Aye.", said John.

Behind him, four Indians came up and stood still. John introduced them to his company. With a wave of his arm to the men behind him, John said, "These are our guests for a day or two. I'm confident you will be hospitable with them." Daniel was the first one to move and the others followed behind him. The Chiefs were greeted with handshakes and welcoming remarks. That evening the men shared their meal with the Penobscot. John, Daniel and I joined them. For the most part Orono himself did the talking and it was primarily with John. I observed a mutual respect between them. When the meal was finished, the Indians found a place to sleep fairly close to John's tent.

Daniel and I followed John to his tent and once inside I broke the silence, "How long are you here for?" John looked at me and said, "I didn't mention that." I answered, "It was what you weren't mentioning out there that caught my attention." John with a wave of his hand replied, "A few days." I have to bring supplies up to Falmouth." "Are we going with you?", asked Daniel. "No, I intend to get right back here. I have been ordered to return to my duties here and a ship will bring Orono and his men the rest of the way to Boothbay."

John left with Orono within a few days. It was true about Orono. He spoke well and was in fact quite intelligent. He carried himself tall and proud. The men that accompanied Orono were cautious but quite friendly toward us. When John left with them, the men all turned out to bid them good-bye and wish them well. I watched John at the rail with the Chief as the ship moved out toward sea. They looked quite comfortable and at ease with each other.

It took John two weeks to return and on his first night back over our evening meal, he did tell more of his story about his travels while we ate. He had returned to Falmouth with the Penobscot and remained until July 4 when they sent a letter back to Cambridge. He told us

about a letter that Orono sent back to Watertown which read:
"*Falmouth, July 4, 1775.*

"*Sir: We have been here five days and did expect to go home with the supplies for our tribe in a sloop. But we are told Captain John Lane must return to Watertown before supply can be sent, we have agreed to go home in our canoes, though we should rather go in said sloop. We be, leave to let you know it is our desire that Captain Lane be appointed truck-master, with full power to redress any insults we may receive from the white people when we come in to trade. You may depend on our friendship and assistance*

if required.

"*We are your humble servants.*
"*Olenah,*
"*Messhall,*
"*Joseph,*
"*Pooler.*
"*Andrew Gilman, Interpreter.*

July 8th, 1775, the Provincial Congress resolved to supply the Indians of the Penobscot with goods not to exceed in value, three hundred pounds and to take furs and skins in exchange. John was satisfied. He was quite impressed with the Penobscot people and Chief Orono. The company John raised in Falmouth consisted of people from the area and as well as Indians from the surrounding tribes. This new company was sent to Fort Pownall to help defend the area.

A few days after arriving at Cape Ann, John boarded the ship with supplies to be delivered. He was gone for another few weeks.

Meanwhile on August 8 a frantic call ran through the town. There was a British ship chasing an American schooner into the harbor! The alarm was rung and all the men turned out. We watched as the Captain of the American schooner "Hannah" grounded the ship. In all the faces around me, I could see the panic in the townspeople. It looked like we were to be attacked. Men sent their wives and children to safety away from the town. Most looked on in awe.

Our company came together and Daniel chose a spot for us to be ready. Daniel went to receive orders from Colonel Foster and I stayed with the men. There were two American schooners but one stayed with the British ship. It didn't take long to figure out the British had captured it.

Daniel came striding back and said, "Look Jabez, there are British onboard the schooner out there." I replied, "They are dropping some boats off the British ship. I can read the name it is the Falcon and I think they are going to take the grounded schooner too."

Daniel now spoke to all us, "Men, on my word, fire on the boats as they get close to the grounded schooner. We've got to help those men", he added. As soon as the boats started to row. Canon fire from the ship began. I yelled, "Take cover!" I could feel in my chest the repercussion of cannon fire and the sound of the ball whistling over and passed our heads into the town. The noise was deafening and disorienting. Without looking I could tell by the noise of splintering wood, that a couple cannon balls had hit a building behind us. Seeing the fear in the younger men's faces I got up and running in a crouched posture along the line I yelled, "Heads down, eyes forward, the enemy is in front of you!" The men responded and I took position at the other end of the line.

We watched as the dories loaded up and the men started rowing. "Now!" yelled Daniel. Our company along with the others on the shoreline started firing. Our bullets didn't reach until the boats came closer to the schooner. Daniel ordered us to keep firing on the boats heading toward the grounded ship. The British ship again fired their canons focusing on the Town. It was an attempt to distract us from the grounded schooner.

I rose, running to alert Daniel of another party of boats now coming toward the shore instead of the grounded schooner which was now boarded by its attackers. Daniel yelled at me pointing toward the landing party, "Go!". Without hesitation, I yelled for Phineas Towle, William Andrews, Moses Atkinson, Daniel and Isaac Boynton and Ephraim Sands. We ran toward the boats coming and a group of townspeople came up behind us. We had all gotten there as the men were getting out of the boats. With just a few shots fired, we captured these men. Still the canons boomed sending their destructive balls toward the town, but at least we had managed to stop this group of men from setting fire to the town.

In the meantime, one small boat managed to get away from the grounded ship with a few men back towards the Falcon. The rest of the British men were now trapped on the grounded vessel. The Captain, we later learned his name was Captain Linzie, realizing his defeat, sent the captured schooner in to rescue his men. The American prisoners on that ship mutinied against Linzie's men who held them, took them captive and reclaimed their ship.

The battle that had started at noontime, had lasted until seven that evening. To our surprise, there was very little damage to the town itself from the cannon fire.

Once the firing stopped, I went with the men to see what needed repairing. Daniel caught up with me and my small party. He asked me, "How did you find things?". I answered, "The damage is minimal." He nodded and uttered, "Thanks. I have to report to the Colonel right away." He took off in the Colonel's direction and I turned to the men. Every face expressed their tiredness. I took pity on them and said, "That's all we can do for the moment. The women and children are afraid to come home with the British ship still in the harbor. What we need to do now is find some food. I want you to all rest immediately after that. I'm sure some of us will be doing picket duty during the night." Phineas Towle stepped up and said, "I will see to food if someone can find us some wood to cook with." Ephraim Sands added, "I will help Phineas if we want the food to be edible." A few men chuckled at that. In the end, Daniel and Isaac Boynton along with Elijah Bradbury took off to find something to burn. James and Joshua Woodman went to help see what food was available. The rest went to cleaning the rifles and counting the rounds in readiness for another attack.

Within an hour, our supper was cooking and Daniel arrived. "Any news?", I asked him. "Aye, we are to be up and ready to picket at 4:00 in the morning." Moses said, "At least we will be able to get a few hours' sleep. The poor devils who have this shift have been fighting all day. Hope they don't drop off in sleep." The men were quiet while they ate. Once they were finished, it was a quick moment to clean and they all went immediately to their beds.

It felt like I had just fallen asleep when I was awakened by Moses Atkinson. "Jabez! Jabez! Come on son. It's time to head out." "Are the men ready?", I asked. "Aye, Daniel is already out there hollering." My muscles were sore and my body was rebelling at being up at this hour and this caused a little groan from me. Moses didn't offer any sympathy, "Show me one man out there who's feeling hale and hearty and I'll do your cooking for a week." I rushed out behind Moses and joined the company. Daniel smirked and said, "Nice of you to join us, little brother." With that we walked off into the darkness to relieve the other men.

As we sat out there, listening for any strange noise, the light of dawn appeared. Samuel Woodman sat beside me. He whispered, "Do you hear that?" I whispered back, "Aye, its coming from the ship." The sound of the voices of a ship waking up traveled over the water to our ears. "Should we alert the Colonel?" he again whispered to me. "Not yet and be quiet", I barked. I wanted to determine if I could hear any words spoken. After a few moments more, I could see the sails being hoisted on the ship. "Look Samuel", I pointed, "The sails are going up. They are leaving." I turned to him and ordered, "Go to Daniel, see that he sends word to the Colonel". "Aye", he answered and took off to find him. Blessedly the British captain and his ship were disappearing from view. Daniel appeared beside me as I watched and said, "I believe it's over". Without looking at him I spoke, "Maybe so but, we should keep watch in case this is a ruse." He nodded in agreement, "I will go to the Colonel and see if he agrees." The Colonel did in fact agree and for the next two days we stood guard along the beach.

In the days and weeks that followed, the Town became fearful that the British would come back in retaliation of their defeat. The Town immediately went to work repairing the damage and further securing its defenses. The Colonel sent word to General Washington and in response Washington sent ammunition and along with that came Major Robert Macgaw and his riflemen. A much welcome sight by us all. They helped in rebuilding the old fort and putting more breastwork up along the beaches. They were long hard days for us all. The townspeople set to work helping us with construction as well as supplying us with food and blankets. The women sent us their treasured silverware to be melted into more musket balls.

Gloucester seemed by now pretty well prepared in case of an assault from the British. Daniel received word about a week after the battle that John was on his way back from Fort Pownall and that the Chiefs of the Penobscot and the St. John Indians held a conference. The Chiefs resolved "to stand together' with our brethren of Massachusetts and oppose the people of Old England that are endeavoring to take our lands and liberties from us." I was cheered to hear of his success.

A few weeks brought John back to us. To our chagrin he was not to be staying with us long. He was barely off the ship when he informed us, "I'm headed to Cambridge. Congress wants a report." Daniel relayed our story of the attack to John who sat silently until Daniel finished the telling. The Colonel sent word while we sat together that the Colonel wanted to see John. When John returned, he informed us, "The Gloucester Committee of Safety assigned the prisoners captured from the "Falcon" to go with me to Cambridge to see General Washington." I spoke up, "John, I would like to make the trip with you." John thought for a minute and his answer was, "No. I really need you here to watch over the rest of the company." I was more than a little irritated remaining here. For the most part, things were quiet. I wanted to see for myself what was happening in Boston. I was quite bored with the monotony of daily drills and the quietness here. Instead he appointed a few privates to go with him.

A few weeks after John had left for Cambridge there was some excitement nearby in Gloucester. The "Hannah" was outfitted with cannon and made part of Washington's fleet. Its intention was to help defend the area. It was in and out of the harbor daily. There were a few British ships that chased him back into Cape Ann harbor but they quickly turned back. Finally, on September 5, Broughton escorted a ship called the "Unity" in. The alarm was raised and everyone ran to the beaches ready. The ship anchored peacefully. Captains Somes and Smith went alongside it in a boat and asked where they were from and where were they headed. They said they were from Quebec and were headed for St. Eustatia. They were wanting some water. The Captains were suspicious so, they invited them ashore and the Captains sent boats out to seize her. Sixty-eight sheep and forty-five oxen were taken and brought ashore to graze. After questioning the men on board, they found that the ship had been taken by the British and they were actually heading to Boston. The British on board were taken as prisoners. A few of my men were posted for guard duty over the prisoners until it is decided what to do with them.

Moses came to me after doing a few hours of guard duty. "Are you wanting me for patrol this evening?", he asked. "No.", I answered. I asked him, "How is it guarding the prisoners? Have they been quiet?". Moses shrugged his shoulders and said, "Not bad. I just wish something could be done about them." I was surprised at the comment and asked, "What makes you say that?". Moses said, "I don't trust them. We also have people around here that are still loyal to England and I fear they may try to free them. It worries me, we may have to fight our own people." I understood his worry and agreed with him saying, "I believe around here, Loyalists are few. I hope that is the case and no one is foolish enough to try." He wasn't placated by my words at all and said, "Nonetheless, will be happy to hear when something is decided." Moses left me and I thought hard on his words. I had not thought of people here that might sympathize with them. That night I went out to see the men at the campfire and cautioned them about Moses' words.

The next afternoon Daniel came to me and said, "I am to bring the British prisoners to General Washington in Cambridge." "I heard", I replied. I was wondering where he thought I was all day. The news of it was everywhere. "When do you leave?" I asked. He answered "In the morning". "I will be taking the Captain and ten of his men. When the Colonel's men searched the ship, they found letters on board written to officers in Boston. Apparently, it confirmed they were heading to Boston". "What did the letters say?" I asked him. "I don't know", he replied. "They are to be kept sealed and given to General Washington". I bid him to be careful and safe journey. I'm sure he will be coming back with a great story to tell.

I would most certainly miss him while he was gone. He was very proud to have the responsibility. I, along with the rest of the men left behind, spent the next few weeks patrolling the area and posting lookouts for English ships that might appear.

Moses Atkinson in our company, was a great help and worked just as hard, if not harder than the others. I learned to rely on all of the men, but him most of all. After one particularly long, hard day I invited him to have supper with me. He was quite pleased with the offer and once everything was settled, he showed up at my tent. I greeted him with a "Please, come right in.". Thank you, Jabez.", he said.

He looked unsure of himself and I opened up the conversation with, "It's so quiet in here without my brothers. I'm pleased to have some company to eat with." Moses responded, "The men were saying how quiet it is without Daniel for a few days. We are accustomed to hearing him bellow from somewhere in camp." I laughed at his comment and we sat down to eat. After a few bites he remarked, "This is quite good. I sure appreciate your kindness." "Think nothing of it.", I said. I went on with, "It's the least I could do for everything you've done to help me keep things in line." Moses chuckled and added, "You can't do it alone. I hope I'm not crossing any boundaries." I looked up from my food and repeated, "Like I said, I appreciate you taking on the responsibility with them. The men are receptive to you as well." Moses nodded his head and I tossed out a jest saying, "Until we have a mutiny on our hands, let's keep things as they are." His surprised look at the word 'mutiny' caused me to chuckle. My laughter brought forth a sigh of relief when he realized I jested. Within seconds Moses, himself, was laughing. He said, "Mutiny! At least it would give us something to talk about around here." Once we sobered and had finished our meal. He rose and said, "Again, thank you for the meal." I responded, "Your welcome. I was grateful for the company tonight."

He left and I finished cleaning the remnants of dinner. I went straight to bed. As I lay there, I realized I hadn't shared a laugh in a few weeks. I took my duties seriously and with everything left on me to take care of, I had not taken much time to socialize other than wandering around to check on the men in the company. Moses is a good man and he cared for everyone around him. My last thoughts that night, as every night, were of Sarah and the children.

Daniel, along with John, was back by mid-September with orders from General Washington for the Committee of Safety for the town of Gloucester. I was just finishing dinner when they strode in.

Both looked tired but excited about their journey. I asked Daniel if the prisoners gave him much trouble on the way. "No, we kept a good eye on them. On land, I think they were completely lost. Pretty much kept them moving so they were too tired to think of running from us."

As I was making them something to eat, I asked what the news from Boston was. Of course, Daniel had plenty. He related to me, "The Colonists have the British pretty much pinned down in Boston. They are not allowing them much movement. As a result, the Brits are confined in the city of Boston and pretty much remaining on their ships to avoid them being taken and for their own safety."

"What did you think of the General?" I asked him. John in a thoughtful tone answered, "His men greatly respect him. He is agreeable and seems like a fair man. The people there trust his judgement in a military and personal matters. In talking with him, his intelligence is undeniable." John added, "I think if times were different, he would be quite jovial. He received the prisoners and raised a committee as to decide on their fate. The General sent me back with orders to sell the cargo and return the Unity to its owner, John Langdon in Portsmouth."

John's expression turned quite serious as he added, "The General also sends his caution to Gloucester with information he received that Captain Linzie of the British ship Falcon, was quite angered at his loss and is vowing retaliation. The word is that British Admiral Graves is plotting something." I told him, "We have shored up defenses here. The women here have given up more of their silverware to melt down into musket balls and a lot more men have arrived to help defend this town." We started eating and John informed me, "We were able to bring back supplies with us to take to Falmouth which included gunpowder and some more ammo. Washington is also sending us some men."

Daniel nudged John saying, "Tell him about Arnold." John was finished eating by now and pushed his chair back saying, "General Benedict Arnold has been planning to take Quebec. General Schuyler in New York will travel up by way of Lake Champlain. Arnold intends to sail to Fort Western in Augusta and travel inland." I interjected, "That's not the easiest way to get there." "No.", he responded and went on. "He will ask the Penobscot to guide his troops through the wilderness. I will be there ahead of him with these supplies and pass the word on. Daniel will take charge while I'm gone."

There didn't seem much more to discuss, so we bid each other good night. John left the next day. He was gone a little over a week. On his return, I was anxious to hear any news. I followed him from the ship to his tent to put his things away. "Well, tell me", I demanded. "Not much really", he said. "I didn't waste any time finding Andrew Gilman and we hurried to see Orono. I explained to him about the upcoming arrival of Arnold. Orono listened quietly and when Gilman was finished translating, Orono assured us that the Penobscot would consider the request." "That was it?", I asked in disbelief. "Yes. You must remember we want their help but we cannot make them do something against their will. It would certainly turn them against us if they were forced to harm their own people." I nodded remembering, "I forgot that members of their tribe extend to the Quebec area." John assured me, "Orono is not foolish. His decisions are based on what is best for his people. He will meet Arnold and make his decision at that time." "What is your opinion of General Arnold?" I asked. John answered, "I like Chief Orono better."

In the following days, I learned that John honestly admired Orono and the other Chiefs. It bothered him that the Penobscot may be swept into something they did not agree with. I could understand John's caring about the Penobscot and his frustration at not being in attendance when Arnold arrived. He was confident that Gilman would make sure that Chief Orono was informed well. Gilman himself was in love with a woman from the tribe. John's orders were to remain with us.

We got word around October 21 from Falmouth. Five Penobscot and St. John Indians went along with Arnold as guides. They had left on their journey the last week of September.

Once more, at evening supper, we had been discussing General Arnold. Daniel started the conversation with, "Arnold thinks this expedition will only take 28 days." John said, "Good luck to them. The maps he has are not very good. It's not even a charted route." I thought about that for a second and added, "He has no idea of what that river holds with waterfalls and fast water." John agreed, "The worst of it is the way it is charted, the mileage is underestimated in my opinion." I nodded and said, "What of the Penobscot who will be going with Arnold?" John said, "A few will be going as guides but I'm not sure which of them will go." I was suddenly tired and told them I was heading to bed. John then informed me, "You're on watch tomorrow, Jabez. Take who you need and plenty of supplies." Being overtired, I snapped, "By God, I think I'm going blind constantly looking out to sea." Both Daniel and John looked surprised at my outburst but Daniel only cracked back at me, "Let's hope the sea and sun is all you see tomorrow." I went to bed feeling sorry for myself and glum about snapping at John but I would rather be looking at my wife and children this evening, not their sorry faces.

The following weeks, our watches from shore produced no sightings of British ships. The weather was getting cooler and without the sun beating full force on our faces, it felt good to get the men moving and not sitting idle.

Toward the end of October, John called his company together. "Falmouth has been attacked. In fact, the town was set on fire." He let that sink in with all of us. Ephraim Sands spoke up, "What happened?" John said, "I'll tell you what I know. Five ships entered Falmouth Harbor on October 18 and sent boats ashore. They gave the townspeople two hours to evacuate. The townspeople begged for mercy. The British Captain Mowat said he would agree if the people gave up their arms and swore allegiance to England. The townspeople in response evacuated the town." "Dear God", said John Lines and the rest of the company began to mutter. Daniel was visibly agitated at the disruption and spoke loudly to John, "Tell us the rest." When the men quieted, John went on, "The ships began to fire on the town at 9:40 and it continued until the evening. The Captain not being satisfied at the damage he had done, sent a landing party ashore with men to burn anything that still stood. A small group of brave men resisted the British and a few Brits were killed." "What about the families?", I inquired. John responded, "A thousand people were left homeless. There are troops on the way there to help them with some kind of cover for the winter."

The story now told, John said, "We are to increase our watches. Word is that the British vessels have left Falmouth and appear to be heading south." "Our company is to patrol south of here first thing in the morning." "Aye.", I answered. John spoke to us all, "We don't know if they are planning any other outrageous attacks like this anywhere but we are a likely spot."

Our company was out on patrol almost daily but there were no sightings. A few weeks later, John told the company, "We learned the British ranking officers were disgusted about what happened in Falmouth, Admiral Graves and Captain Mowat were sent back to England. They have been disgraced." Moses spoke up saying, "I hope they get punished severely for it."

In November, we stood on the shore again as Captain Manley of the USS Lee brought in a British ship called the "Nancy" laden with munitions for the British troops in Boston. It was brought into Gloucester harbor. We stood on shore, ready for whatever might happen while Glover's men boarded and found that there were 2,000 muskets, 8,000 fuses, 31 tons of musket balls, 3,000 solid shot for 12-pounders, a cannon, 100,000 flints and much other military supplies. Everything was loaded onto wagons and brought to George Washington Headquarters in Cambridge. Daniel was excited as he announced, "This is a gold mine!"

None of us were to accompany the wagons to Cambridge as our enlistment was up. John called up the company to inform us. He began, "You've all done a good job here. Foster, himself, is pleased with us all. There is another company coming up to take over here. Clean your quarters to make ready for them. Captain Elden is still in Boston with his company. I would like to go to Boston to help but, I believe we have earned the right to go home for a few weeks to our families. Let's go home, get some rest in our own beds and good food. I plan to leave for Boston the beginning of January. I would like for you to join me but, that decision is yours. So, let's pack our things and head home tomorrow morning. We will meet the day after Christmas and discuss plans." The company was cheered at the news and John dismissed us. Daniel and I were ordered to make sure that the barracks were cleaned accordingly. I would have cleaned them myself if it got me home to Sarah any quicker.

Coming home to Buxton was more joyous than I could have expected. It just seemed like we couldn't get there fast enough. The word had spread unimaginably fast that we were arriving. The company spread out as each man headed toward their homes. Here and there women and children were rushing down the road to find their man. I was about a half mile from home when I spotted Sarah running down the road toward me. She was carrying Jabez and had Samuel in tow by the hand, his chubby little legs trying to keep up protesting all the way at her speed. As soon as I got close, I jumped down from my horse.

Samuel now caught sight of me and somehow, he managed to outrun his mother toward me. When he was no less than three feet away, he flung up his arms and jumped up into mine. I hugged him so tight, I thought I might have crushed him. "Papa!" he kept saying with his little arms around his neck. I never broke stride carrying him toward Sarah. She stopped. I could only gape at this woman holding our son who is now six months old.

Instead of saying hello, I could only say, "How on earth did you get more beautiful!". She stepped into my arms, baby and all. Samuel yelling, "Ouch". I set him up on my horse, took the reins in one hand and had Sarah snugly inside the other arm. After a few steps, she handed me Jabez and took the reins. I don't know how I got home without falling as I studied this little guy in my arms all the way home. He looked at me and smiled. I smiled back the rest of the way.

The next few weeks flew by. Jabez, like Samuel, is a happy babe and quite comfortable letting me hold him. Samuel was very proud and protective of his little brother. Sarah couldn't do enough to make me comfortable. The boys had our undivided attention throughout the day. I helped Sarah get the house settled so I could spend as much time with her as possible. Though we hadn't spoken about my leaving again, we both understood how precious these few days would be. Daniel and John, likewise were at their homes making the most of their time with their own families.

As planned the day after Christmas, we met and almost all who had gone to Cape Ann agreed to join again. We even managed a few new men. John informed us we would be leaving the first week of January which was a little over a week away. We hoped in that time to recruit more men.

Leaving Sarah again, was no easier than it had been eight months before.

5

1776

SIEGE OF BOSTON

The morning we left, we all gathered in town to leave for Boston with our families there to bid us goodbye. Sarah and my sons were there to see us off with the other women and children. Some of the women were crying but, Sarah stood there smiling brightly. I leaned over on the saddle horn and gazed back with a smile of my own. She was being so brave. This image I knew would remain with me in the many months ahead of me.

Daniel had spent the morning gathering more men for the cause. While we waited, I saw no sign of Molly and thought it odd. We all left together with farewells ringing out behind us. We had gotten a few miles down the road when Daniel came up short on his horse bellowing, "Sweet Jesus, I hadn't said good-bye to Molly." He wheeled his around saying, "I will catch up!". Watching him ride off, Ephraim Sands said, "I would like to see how he explains himself to his wife". We continued on with many jokes about whether or not Molly would be forgiving him.

We were prepared to really have a good go at teasing him on his return. Eventually he caught up and his look cautioned us to keep our counsel. He caught up to me saying, "I don't deserve that woman". "Wasn't she furious?" I asked. He replied, "No, she scared the devil out of me. I went charging into the house to find her not there. I checked around the town, nothing. Finally, I searched a few spots I know she likes to go with the children and finally found her. She was holding the baby and crying. When she saw me come up, she was trying to hide the fact she was crying. It destroyed her that I had left and not bid her goodbye. She said she was afraid she would never see me again. It took me a while to calm her and let her know that hell or high water, I would be home and we would have our lives together. I can't believe what I did. My foolishness hurt her so much."

It was a rarity for Daniel to be so humbled. This event struck him deeply. "The women have it hard, when they are left behind" I told him. They knew they only had a few days with us and don't want us to leave worrying about them. They are sturdier than you think. It's hard to hide your feelings behind a smile. That my brother, is love". I thought that would bring his usual wittiness back but it did not. Instead, his face was the most serious I had ever seen it when he vowed to me "I will never hurt her like that again". "Yes, you will", I threw back at him. His shoulders slightly sagged as he said, "I hope your wrong Jabez". Daniel was truly grieving over hurting Molly and was unusually quiet all the way to Boston.

On arriving at Cambridge, the city of Boston was still under siege. There was some confusion as to where we needed to go but, once John found a spot for us, he took off by himself. We dismounted to rest and water the horses. We were at Lechmere Point a section of Cambridge which was part of Boston. In the near distance, we could hear cannon fire. The Woodman brothers happened to be nearest to me. James said to his brother Joshua, "Have you ever seen so many men?". Joshua replied, "I already miss the space we had in Gloucester". Moses joined in, "Cheer up boys, I think the whole of Boston is looking like this." Joshua squeezed his nose with his fingers saying, "Good Lord, the smell is just awful." It was true, the smell of men's body odors and animals defecating everywhere was insult to our senses. Looking around at the activity around us, it was even more chaotic with wagons and horses trying to maneuver around the mass of men and tents splayed out everywhere. I fervently hoped we would not be told to just find ourselves a spot. This area looked pretty bleak.

A little over an hour later John returned with a Colonel walking beside him. He was introduced by John to us as Colonel Varnum. He eyed us all carefully as we did him. We were now under the command of Colonel James Mitchell Varnum. He had a friendly nature about him and was quick to approach us. His face had a flushed appearance, with dark eyes but otherwise, but when he smiled at us, his teeth were perfect and white. He had a full head of hair that was short on the forehead. When he removed his hat, he brushed his hair forward. We would see him do this quite often.

Varnum spoke to us in a formal manner, "Gentlemen, you have been ordered to my regiment under the command of General Greene. He insists on a clean camp and we drill every day. He is a good man and cleanliness is imperative. We suffered severely from dysentery this past summer and his efforts have improved the situation greatly. The men he found here on arrival were undisciplined and inexperienced. He has made great improvements with his troops and heed my warning he intends to keep this camp organized. Any questions?" John stood forward, "Yes sir, where are we to go?" The Colonel answered with a nod, "We are camped in Roxbury. I have a meeting here and then will accompany you to camp", he replied. "Thank you, Sir. The men and I will wait here for you", said John.

Varnum left for his meeting and John gathered us around to tell us the Continental Army was in the process of being completely reorganized.

Many regiments were receiving new names and others being disbanded to be absorbed in other regiments. Enlistments were being called for one-year service. Varnum's Regiment was reorganized as the 9th Continental Regiment under General Greene. John allowed us a half hour to look around and talk with people in the vicinity.

Soon the Colonel returned ready to head back to camp. As we rode, he informed us of the events and plans ahead. "The Brits have been randomly firing cannons at the city. They have also been raiding stores and homes for supplies. Even setting fire to a few. We have been deterring them the best we can so their plundering of the city is kept at a minimum. It's been a bit more difficult with the Loyalists aiding them. A month ago, Washington sent a fellow by the name of Henry Knox to Ticonderoga. We have no heavy artillery here to end this siege. Knox brought the idea to Washington that if the cannons were brought from Ticonderoga that we recently captured, we would have the artillery needed to drive the British out. Washington made him a Colonel and put him in charge of the expedition. We just received word that he is being held up because he needs snow to move the sleds that the cannons are loaded on to get through. He's young and optimistic and very clever. I believe his resourcefulness will win the day."

"How young is he?", asked John. "I believe he is only 24 years of age and a large man", replied Varnum. "In the meantime, we have been gathering up whatever cannonballs the British fire at us to build up our ammunition stores for when the cannons arrive." He went on to say "We are also making our presence known around the city to let them know we are here and growing in numbers". John asked him how the ammunition supplies were and Varnum hesitated before going on. "We are very low. We are making spears in case the British decide to land and attack". Daniel's expression was priceless. "Spears?" was all he could say. John not wanting to insult the Colonel said in a teasing voice, "Why not? After all, Jabez took the Indians on with his drum and that worked quite well". Varnum turned to give me a long hard look and then burst out laughing. "My friend, you are going to have to tell me the story!" This was my first chance to speak to the Colonel so I told it to him my story. Varnum was fascinated.

Of course, Daniel finished it for me by informing him of my picking up the rifle and quitting my position as drummer. Varnum was totally amused. "We don't have many drums, but your welcome to use them any way you wish if the British land.", he managed to get out through his laughter. The men within ear shot were infected by his laughter and were all joining in with the good humor. The rest of the ride to camp was conversation of a personal nature and we learned he is from Dracut, Mass, went to Brown University in Rhode Island and while there became a lawyer. One of the men shouted out, "Daniel! You'll be wanting to make a friend with him!" Varnum, not understanding the joke, sent an alarmed look toward Daniel. He relaxed a bit when the rest of the men went into another round of laughter. The good humor continued all the way to camp.

The ride to our destination was dismal. The camps absolutely stunk and still there were men everywhere. Most of the homes looked abandoned. There were very few women and children in the city as we rode through.

The sudden contrast when arriving at Greene's camp, was remarkable. The tents were clean and in very neat rows. The men were drilling. We got there as they were finishing and to our surprise, they went right on to the task of cleaning their rifles. Varnum took us to be introduced to General Greene. I was surprised as the man approached us. He had a definite limp but was otherwise he was a healthy, confident stature of a man.

"Gentlemen, meet Brigadier General Nathaniel Greene". "Welcome" he said to us. John stepped forward and spoke to the General. "Sir,

I am Captain John Lane. This is my 1st lieutenant Daniel Lane and my Ensign Jabez Lane." With a wave of his arm to all the men he said, "Most of us served together in the French and Indian War, Sir." Greene nodded to the group and said "It's nice to receive men with experience". I happened to glance toward Varnum and I received a wink with a huge grin on his face. No doubt the Brigadier General would be informed of the story he had just heard. Greene went on in a stern, officerly tone, "Varnum will show you to your tents. I expect cleanliness to be as important as your training. We train each afternoon. Everyone takes a turn picketing at Dorchester Heights. It looks like the harbor is beginning to freeze there. If the Brits come ashore, I believe it will be from that direction." "Yes sir, understood", said John. With that, we were following the Colonel again. I still marveled at how tidy the camp was. Tents were all in neat rows, not like the other camps we had just passed. The horses had plenty of pasture.

Once we arrived at the designated spot, Varnum began "Gentlemen, listen carefully. Last summer, the camps had a huge small pox and dysentery outbreak. Greene is strict with his rules of camp. Tents are to be cleaned and aired daily. Men are to use only the latrines to relieve themselves. Anyone caught not using them is severely punished. When you are finished relieving yourself, you are to cover it over with dirt or snow. This practice has proven to reduce sickness in camp."

We listened intently as he went on. "The men that arrived had no military training when they arrived, some had never shot a gun. Greene commanded that everyone perform drills every day. I find that the busier these men are, the more tired they are by the end of the day, which leads not only less discontent, but healthier men. Also, there is to be no card games or gambling of any kind. Understood?" The company responded, "Aye Sir". Varnum looked at us all carefully and said "I will leave you to get yourselves placed. You will begin drilling with the men tomorrow".

He turned to John and his last words were directed toward John, "I will meet with you and the other Captains within the next few days". "Aye, sir", replied John and with that Varnum was gone.

We settled into our lodgings and John was quick to get us organized and participate in these exercises. There was a lot of parading about. Rifle drills were limited as we found that ammunition was in short supply. Some men would forage the spent rounds after practice so they could melt them down and make more balls.

Our regiment was incorporated into the Continental Army as the 9th Continental Foot under the command of Brigadier General Greene. General Greene we learned was a Quaker and is 2nd in command to Washington. He is a very close advisor to Washington and we often saw them about inspecting the camps.

On picket duty, I was able to take in the view of the harbor from Dorchester Heights. There were the British ships sitting calmly in the harbor. It was amazing to see this once bustling town reduced to scarcely a soul walking about. A few British soldiers seem to be the only life on the streets below. Things were quiet. There was anticipation that Knox was succeeding in his efforts to bring the cannons from the captured Fort Ticonderoga to us here in Cambridge. This was mostly considered as impossible but hope was high.

Just a few weeks after our arrival, in came Knox with all fifty-nine cannons. Exhilaration was in the air as the news spread. The high-ranking officers were called to Washington for a meeting to decide on our next step. Greene returned from headquarters calling all of his officers, including his Captains in to go over the plans.

On the night of March 4, six weeks after the cannon arrived, John called his company together. Everyone was anxious to hear what our role would be. "We will be heading to Dorchester Heights. We are assigned with the other companies to help with constructing emplacements up there. Engineers will be assembling the cannons in place. We are to assist in anything we are asked."

No one interrupted John as he spoke. "I hope you understand it is imperative we do this quietly and quickly. Also, we are going to cut and drag a few trees with us. They are to be painted to look like cannon so the Brits think we have more firepower then we actually do. There will be no drills today, get some rest and be prepared for tonight's adventure." With that he dismissed us.

Daniel and I went over to John to have a few moments together. John had to report back to the Colonel, so time was short. Daniel said, "What a wake up for the Brits tomorrow morning". This actually made John smile a bit. "Do we remain in place once we are done over there?" I asked him. John looked toward Daniel and said, "I believe we are to remain in place, but keep the men together". Looking toward me, he said, "Make sure everyone is doing their part and no one wanders off. If we have to move, I don't want to waste time looking for anyone." I responded, "Understood".

It wasn't a very long march to the spot and once there everyone went right to their duties. It was quite a spectacle watching the cattle pulling those cannons into position. I had my first glimpse of Colonel Knox. He was a large but fit looking man. He was well over two hundred pounds in weight but he was constantly moving about. He had his men working all night. There were a couple thousand of us in one spot and I wondered at how this was to be done quietly. The answer came soon enough. Washington had ordered some of the cannons be placed at Lechmere's Point, Cambridge and at the Roxbury location and they were firing away. The noise from where we stood was deafening. So, our construction work would carry on undetected.

As dawn broke, the cannon work was all done. The log tree cannons were equally impressive. One genius even came up with the idea using hay to look like a cannon. By morning light, you could not tell the real cannon from the manufactured likenesses.

Colonel Varnum arrived to inform us to stay in place as the British were plotting to attack the defense. He sent a message through the Captains of each company relating, "You performed a good night's work. Now relax a bit until we have further information." Again, the Colonel was off to see what General Greene's next plan was for us. As we waited, a snowstorm blew in, in the late afternoon. We were all around a fire to keep warm. "I believe this storm will be keeping the Brits on their ships" I remarked to Daniel. "Aye", he agreed. He went on, "In the meantime we are freezing our 'arses' off up here on this hill.

The storm lasted for a few more days, but the ruse with the cannons worked. The Brits woke up the first clear morning and could see the row of cannons. On March 8, we were informed that an unsigned letter had been delivered stating that "The city would not be burned to the ground if the troops were allowed to leave unmolested". We were now relieved to return to our tents in Roxbury. Because of the arrival more bad weather, the British ships were not able to set sail out of Boston Harbor until the 17th. It didn't matter, the city would soon be free from siege.

No sooner had the British left, we were ordered to get to Long Island in New York. John joined the company for dinner in the evening. "General Washington believes that the British would try next for New York Harbor." He explained what he had heard. "If the British gain control of New York harbor, they would have access to the Hudson River which would give them free rein all the way to Canada. So, we must get to Long Island as quick as possible and build defenses there. Washington has sent more troops to attack Quebec to keep the British from gaining control from the North".

He was besieged with questions from everyone and he patiently answered them all. Some wanted to know if they would be able to see their families before leaving. "We leave tomorrow morning" he quietly responded. "The General and his Officers went into the city this morning to survey the damage. The Brits have looted and destroyed almost all of the homes, taken livestock, supplies and as much water as they could carry. These people will be rebuilding everything. The cannons have punched holes in the roofs and sides of the buildings. It's a mess down there."

The men were quiet as they thought about the situation of the people of Boston coming back to their destroyed homes and businesses. Ephraim Sands said, "I can't imagine my wife being removed from our home and then have to return to such a mess." John Boynton added, "Can't see my wife, Hannah, letting them in the door. She'd win that small war for sure." Those that knew Hannah knew that she was fiercely protective of her home and poor John suffered some light hearted teasing about it. John finally spoke up to all and said, "Well, we should all retire and get our rest. We have to break camp in the morning and everyone will help with the work".

The next morning, I woke up to Daniel bellowing for everyone to get their "pretty arses" out of bed. He organized men to see to a quick breakfast and while that was being done, the rest would prepare the tents and equipment that needed to be packed on the wagons. Of course, I was ordered to supervise the loading of the wagons and Daniel was off to supervise the breakfast. We were quick and organized. John had gone to meet up with the Colonel to discuss the plan for departure. He was pleasantly surprised to see everything done and the breakfast being cleared up. There was even a plate of food, although cold, waiting for him. The only thing left for him to do was to order us to mount up. He brought us to our assigned position in the march and there we waited.

Apparently, some of the other companies were not as efficient as ours. Daniel was griping about it and when I had had enough of his chatter, I rode over to John. Nodding to the figure on his horse above us I asked, "He comes with us?". "Of course," he replied. We sat there gazing at George Washington mounted on his horse on a rise above us overlooking his troops.

It was my first look at General Washington. He sat calmly above us on his white horse. There were a few others mounted with him but, the General's identity was unmistakable. "He looks to be quite tall", I said out loud. "Yes, he is", John responded. Not being able to see his expression from where I stood, it was quite obvious by his posture the man exuded confidence. John spoke in a thoughtful tone, "I have just fifty men that I'm responsible for, he has thousands. Every aspect of this war is on his shoulders. I don't envy him".

We watched as Greene appeared and took his place in front of us. Nodding toward General Washington, Greene prepared us. As he rode down the line of companies in his regiment, he bellowed, "He plans to get there as fast as possible, so be prepared for a hard march". While we continued to wait, John confided, "I like Greene as I do Varnum. Greene has educated himself well on military affairs". I asked him what did he do before the war?" "His family owns a forge and they make anchors for the ships I believe", John answered. He said with a rare smile, "I have got to check on the men. Make sure Daniel is staying out of trouble".

I watched John as he left to check on his men. We were all in marching order. Looking around, the men's chins were held high. The end of the long siege was a small victory to us. Daniel came up and continued his grumbling, "Damn I wish we would get moving. It will be lunch before we get a few steps". Agitated by Daniel's impatience, I snapped, "They are just about ready to move. Good Lord, how does Molly put up with you."

Major Crary came riding up toward me and asked, "I'm looking for the Captain". Daniel responded a flippant manner to the Major, "He has ridden up toward the front." For some reason Daniel didn't take to Major Crary and it showed in his attitude. I believe it was mutual because the Major fired back in steely tone, "The Colonel wants to see him, now".

After a while, John came riding back to us slowly. As he approached, I couldn't read his expression but knew it wasn't a happy one. "I'm being sent to Cumberland County to recruit more men", he said. "What about us?" I asked. John told us, "Major Crary will be in command for now." "Safe travels, John", said our new Ensign Moses Atkinson. I had been promoted to 2nd Lieutenant and Daniel 1st Lieutenant according to the new officer ranks that took place. Moses was now Ensign. I was quite happy for him as it was well deserved. I knew him quite well at home, but a bond had grown between us. I spent a lot of time with Moses as he was a likable fellow and performed his duties properly and promptly.

"Take care of my little brother", John said with a smirk knowing that would test me. We watched him ride off. "He always thinks of me as a little kid", I muttered to Moses. "Maybe because you're like a little puppy to him", Moses teased. He went on with his tease saying "I'm not exactly pleased he asked me to watch out for you. If something does happen to you, my legs better be in properly good working order when he returns." The thought of it put a huge grin on my face.

***

BATTLE OF LONG ISLAND

From Boston we marched to New York by way of Providence. We had set out in somewhat of a formation but ended up in scattered columns throughout the countryside. The air was cold and wet. The ground covered in frost. As the morning wore on, the frost was melting and the dirt roads became muddy in most areas. This made traveling quite difficult. The horses were slipping in the mud and word came up from behind that a few wagons were stuck.

As we went through the different towns, people would come out to see the army traveling through. The people were fascinated with the sight. The colonies had never witnessed an army of this size on the march. When we got near Providence, Greene wanted to make an impression of his home town to General Washington and ordered two of the Rhode Island companies to clean up, dress up and parade through the street of Providence as an escort for George Washington. Varnum left us to ride with the parade. John's company would not be part of it. The cheering could be heard for miles. When Greene returned, he seemed to stand a foot taller. His pride apparent.

We reached New London, Connecticut at the Thames River and on April 11th. We boarded the transports to Long Island in a blizzard. There were no conversations on that trip. The men were busy making sure the horses stayed secure as well as holding on to whatever they could, with the violent rocking of the transports. After what seemed an eternity, we landed. A lot of the men were sick from the harrowing voyage we had just taken. I looked at Moses and said, "I believe my stomach isn't where it is supposed to be." Moses didn't laugh at my attempt at humor saying, "I didn't think we were going to make it across." We stood watching the men unload the transports. Men were either carrying luggage off or bringing the horses to shore. Occasionally, I saw a man stop to empty what was left in his stomach. I said to Moses, "The poor devils. We've got to let them rest as soon as this is done.". Moses answered, "By the time everything is done, they will feel better, I'm sure."

One man coming off the transport could hardly walk while trying to keep the horse he was leading calm. I took sympathy on him and hurried over. As I got closer, I could see how white his face was. It was Benjamin Woodman. I took the rein of the frightened horse out of his hand and said, "Go and sit on shore." He looked relieved and started to say something but instead, clamped his hand over his mouth. "Go!", I commanded and watched him stumble off to find a spot.

As soon as we were settled, Daniel and I sought out Major Crary. It was no easy task with everyone scattered and the confusion of things at the moment. "Daniel, Jabez!", he greeted us. Daniel in a formal manner said, "Major, what are our orders?". The Major said, "I just spoke with Generals Greene and Varnum. Varnum is to camp near Fort Box somewhere near this godforsaken place. Get your men prepared and in line to march." Daniel stiffened up and said, "Thank you, Sir." With that he just walked away. In an awkward moment, the Major's eyes landed on me. "We'll be ready in no time, Sir." I saluted the Major and hustled off to catch up with Daniel.

Washington was convinced that the first blow would fall on Manhattan, however Greene and his aide-de-camp, Colonel Reed, believed it would be Long Island. Washington decided to play it safe and split his force. Our company, under Colonel Varnum were camped near Fort Box at Brooklyn Heights.

On July 8, General Washington ordered our brigade to Red Hook, just west of Fort Box more toward the shore. Red Hook is a triangular piece of land on the west side of Long Island. It is within the boundaries called Brooklyn Heights. The summer was spent building the fortifications and keeping watch. Those that were not on patrol or working on the entrenchments were to help with cooking food. Our daily diet consisted mostly of a pound of beef, fish or pork, a gill of whiskey or spirt and one pound of flour. Sometimes peas or beans could be rationed. We would often talk of our women at home and the meals they would have ready for us at night. I hoped Sarah and the children were in good health and eating well.

As the weeks went by, the men in camp became constantly sick due to the damp air, the ground was always wet and our diets were not enough to sustain us for the grueling work building the entrenchments. Dysentery spread and behind that came the dreaded smallpox. A church down the road was set up for a hospital and soon that became overcrowded. Idle times were the hardest for us all as we would all think of being at home with our families. We missed the laughter of our children, the warm dry beds at night and most of all the good food on the table prepared by our wives. Tempers were beginning to flare again and the stench of close quarters and low tide were beginning to get the better of everyone.

John caught up with us sometime in June. By then, Moses and I were inseparable. He was a huge help in keeping things organized. He spent a great deal of time checking on each man's health. Always after them to keep their tents aired. I followed behind him to make sure the ammo was kept dry. The constant fog and wet weather made the gunpowder useless. We did all we could to prevent that problem.

After John made an inspection of the company and got our reports, we settled in for some food. This time, Moses, as Ensign joined our supper. John informed us he had been held up in Boston due to an argument about recruits. He told us the story. "I sent Sargent Thompson on ahead with fifteen recruits to meet me in Boston. When I got to Boston, I found the recruits were reenlisted into Colonel Phinney's company by Lieutenant. Merrill. So, I went to General Ward to have the men returned. The General wanted me to take the money back. I sent a message to Varnum and he accused Colonel Phinney of violation of a General Order issued back in November regarding recruitments. At the first court martial, Varnum accused Lieutenant Merrill of persuading Thompson to burn the enlistment papers he had signed with me. I had to sit through two court martials. Merrill was cleared and I was told that my enlistment of the men was not legal as there was no proof of the paperwork." His disgust was clear on his face. He went on to say, "Varnum fought for me, I won't soon forget that." Looking for any word from home, I asked, "Did you get home at all?"

He nodded and said, "All are healthy. Sarah misses you. Samuel and Jabez are growing strong and they are surely a handful for her. I brought the children over to our house for dinner one evening. Joanna came over with her children as well as Molly. It's hard on the women without us but they are helping each other as best they can.

"What about your children?" I asked. His wife had died shortly after we left. He responded, "Sara, (who is John's oldest daughter), is struggling with the children. With the loss of her mother and me gone she is doing the best she can with them and Daniel's wife Molly and your wife Sarah come over often to help them. I spent a couple days cutting wood and doing repairs that were needed. Joanna is very helpful with the cooking. For a girl of nineteen, Sara does quite well with everything." With a smirk he said, "Seems like she's taken a fancy for Elijah." "Bradbury?", I asked. He nodded with a grimace, "Kept asking about him." With that John was rolling his eyes. I thought about this a second and replied, "He's a good man, hard worker. She would do well with him." He pondered that for a few seconds and said, "Maybe I'll put him in the front line permanently." He seemed serious, but it struck me funny. John loved his children and his daughters, (especially Sara) were sacred to him.

Who should come up to us at that moment but the poor, unfortunate Elijah. He greeted John with a huge smile. "Welcome back, Captain." John took on a steely eyed look and said, "Thank you Elijah." Elijah looked a little nervous but forged on, "How are Sara and the girls?". "Well", was all John said. When Elijah opened his mouth to say something more, John bellowed, "Aren't you supposed to be on picket duty or SOMETHING?". Elijah couldn't get away from us fast enough.

I went into a complete fit of laughter with John glaring at me. As soon as I could talk, I said, "John maybe you could use that tactic on the Brits. They would be fleeing home in no time." His temper now turned on me, "You can picket with Elijah tonight." I sauntered away still chuckling, feeling John's eyes piercing holes in my back. I was in a great mood with John back and knowing the families at home are doing quite well.

At the end of June, John and I were discussing plans for the day with the company when Colonel Varnum appeared. "John, I have something to share with you." With that he handed John the paper he held in his hand. It read:

'New York June 16. 1776

   Sir

   I am now to acknowledge the receipt of your favors of the 27 Ulto & of the 3 & 6 Instant and in Answer to the 1st think you was right in your direction to Mr. Bartlett about the Brigantine Hannah as Mr. Morris had wrote for one—The two schooners, considering their force & number of men certainly behaved extremely well in repelling the Attack made by such a number of boats, and It is only to be lamented, that the affair was attended with the death of Captain Mugford—he seemed to deserve a better fate.

   The determination of the Court of Inquiry upon Colonel Varnum's complaint transmitted in that of the 3rd, is very different from what he expected or I imagined it would be from his state of the case—Whether It is right or wrong, It is not in my power to determine, as the Evidence which was before them is not Inserted in the proceedings, which ought to have been, as I at this distance can have no other means to warrant me, either in confirming or rejecting the Sentence—I cannot but add that It seems extraordinary to me and exceedingly strange, that Captain Lane should have been at so much trouble and expense to get the men without having a right to 'em—For which reason, to discountenance a practice extremely pernicious in Its nature, of one Officer trying to take away & seduce the men of another and on account of the Imperfection in the proceedings in not stating the matter fully & the whole evidence; The Complaint should be reheard and everything appertaining to It, the manner of enlistment & particularly specified for me to found my Judgement on The Arms &c. which you sent to Norwich, as mentioned in the Invoice contained in that of the 6th are not arrived—The number of Carbines is only half of what General Putnam wrote for as I have been Informed, and It is less by three hundred than I directed to be sent in my Letter from Philadelphia of the 28 Ulto. This I suppose had not come to hand when you wrote, as you have not acknowledged the receipt of It.

I have enclosed two Letters for Major Small & Charles Proctor Esquire. supposed to be at Halifax which being wrote with a design to procure the enlargement of Captain Proctor a prisoner on board the Mercury man of War or Induce them to Intercede for a more humane Treatment to be shown him, I request you to forward by the first Opportunity by way of Nova Scotia.

I am this moment favored with yours of the 9 Inst. advising me of the Capture made by our Armed Vessels of one of the Transports with a Company of Highlanders on board—and I flatter myself If our Vessels keep a good look out, as the whole Fleet are bound to Boston which sailed with her, that more of them will fall into our hands—This is a further proof that Government expected General Howe was still in Boston.

I am extremely sorry that your health is more & more impaired and having heard by a Letter from Colonel Hancock that Mr. Whitcombe, Colonel Whitcomb's Brother, is appointed a Brigadier General, I shall order him to relieve you as soon as I am informed that he accepts his Commission and If he does you may immediately call him to your assistance before I am certified of his acceptance, this will ease you of some trouble 'till I can regulate a few matters of Importance here which I hope to do in a little time.

G.W.'

Finally, John said, "Colonel Varnum, I appreciate your defending me". The Colonel nodded, "It was the correct thing to do, Captain." The Colonel turned to me and added, "If you recruit, keep the men with you and the paperwork in your hands." With another nod toward us, he turned and left. That was the end of the matter but it did not sit well with John. He walked away from us without saying another word. With the matter officially decided, John went on with his duties here at Long Island.

In July, Daniel received word to travel to Cambridge. Varnum told John it was a special mission designed by the Continental Congress. He wasn't sure of what it entailed. Daniel, of course, always ready for the excitement, was glad for the break in what was becoming a dull routine here. He was to report to Colonel Francis. He was gone from us within the hour.

On August 10, the officers stood with General Greene at the narrows. Looking down, we could see the English fleet before us. Putting aside the fact that this force was formidable, it was an amazing sight. "This is spectacular!", General Greene remarked. "The entire English fleet is before us." We tried to do a count of the ships but they were closely packed together making it a difficult task. The final count was close to three hundred ships before us.

Once that was done, he wanted a report of the conditions in camp. The Colonel informed him of the welfare of our camp. We have had lot of sickness in camp and the Colonel suggested to General Greene that reinforcements would be welcomed. The General with his familiar limp, decided to walk through the camps with the rest of us trailing behind.

Greene himself looked very ill. He was a man who inspired me. His utmost concern was for the welfare of the soldiers and he pushed his own limits tending to the men in his command. He stopped and spoke to the men he passed. Once he was done with his limited tour, he organized the removal of cattle and the removal of the grain that had been threshed as well as dismantling of mills. The rest of the grain were to be stacked so that if attacked it would be easy to burn. His officers were clearly concerned about the General's health but the General instead, walked toward another campfire.

When the General moved away from us toward another company of men, I was standing with John when he said to Varnum. "The General does not look well at all." Varnum's expression was solemn when he said, "I have known General Greene and count myself lucky to be his friend. He suffers more than you know with asthma, pain in his joints as well as his injured knee." John hesitated and then said, "His energy is boundless. One would not know." "No" replied the Colonel. He now had the attention of all the men near us and as they moved in closer to him, he spoke to us all. "Although he does not seek pity for his afflictions, he does what he can to ensure the health of you all. This man fights for the relief of the wounded and insists that the men that are seriously ill be cared for. He fights not only the British but, for your health as well. You may not like that he is persistent in you learning your drills and orderliness of the camp but it is for a reason. He has to be forced to lie down to rest. I urge you to think twice before you complain, for his silent complaints are much larger than yours."

The men were silent as Varnum walked away. Greene was a man who was always seen visiting the different camps. He spoke to his men. He was tireless in his efforts at inspecting our tents, provisions and our neatness. The men went back to their duties with a more purposeful attitude. Varnum's words whether he knew it or not, struck a deeper respect for the General with the men. If anything, the camp was made cleaner and men got along with each other much more pleasantly.

A day later, cannon fire announced the arrival of the Hessian ships. The Hessians struck fear in a lot of the soldiers from the tales that were told to them. They were reported as close to eight feet tall with spiked teeth. They would eat babies, rape women and drink the blood from their enemies. The morning after the announcement of the Hessian sightings, the men were called up. John addressed the situation. "I hear of the tales of the Hessians. They look eight feet tall because of the tall hats they put on their heads. Better targets for you, aim for just below the monstrosities. The teeth aren't spiked, but ugly as hell. I don't believe they eat babies or drink blood. They want you to fear them. They want these stories told to gain the advantage."

The middle of August, John came back from an officer's meeting. "What's for dinner?", he asked. "Found some ham and a bit of corn.", said Moses. "Where did the ale come from?", he asked. Moses responded, "Found that, too!". John looked at me and I just shook my head silently signaling, 'Don't ask'. John shrugged his shoulders and we all sat down. He asked about what duties the company had accomplished that afternoon and we filled him in. I said, "Okay, John. I know that look. You might as well tell us." John swallowed his food and informed us, "Greene's brigade is now incorporated into Nixon's brigade. Colonel Varnum protested to Washington that Nixon was promoted to rank over him. He was insulted by this and offered his resignation as did Colonel Hitchcock." "What about you?", I asked. I knew he hoped to be promoted to Major. "There's the rub.", he said. "The position of Major is now to be done away with. So, I remain Captain." Moses saw the bigger picture and interjected, "This is not a good time for the officers to be at each other's throats and resigning. We have British and Hessian ships just below us that we know will probably land sometime soon." I agreed with Moses saying, "Let's just concentrate on keeping our company in order."

In the week that followed, John's demeanor was changing by the day. While he conducted himself in front of the men properly, I could tell he was still trying to understand the changes that had taken place in the ranks. As if that wasn't enough to bother the man, the loss of his wife and what was happening with his children weighed heavily on him.

August 21, a severe thunderstorm moved in. Some of the soldiers thought this bad luck and sure enough the next day, word arrived that the British had landed on the south side of the island. Greene had taken to bed with sickness and General Putnam, "Old Put" as he was frequently called, took over his command. The following days were used to prepare for the coming assault. It was time to burn the fields and move all livestock out.

The morning of August 27 we were woken up to cannon fire and musket shot. Moses was immediately rounding up the men. We all formed up in front of John and he quickly informed us of the situation. "Bedford Pass had not been guarded and the British took the advantage and marched right up the road through the night. They came in behind the troops led by Chester, Washington and Sullivan heading straight for us."

John positioned us on the rise overlooking Gowanus Creek. I had John Wilson on one side of me and Abiatha Woodsum on the other. We could hear the firing of guns and cannon and the screams of the wounded and dying. Soon we could see our troops being chased by the Hessians running toward us. There was a critical problem for the escaping men. They had to cross Gowanus Creek to get to us. The bridge caught fire forcing the men into the water and mud. We watched in horror as these men were bogged down by the weight they carried. There were men crying for help but, they were left behind among the chaos and we stood there dumbstruck as we witnessed their drowning. "Dear, God", Came from Samuel's lips. "Aye", responded in disbelief.

We looked down at the Bedford Road to see British troops marching this way, shoulder to shoulder. Through the whole of this panicked crossing, the men were bombed by the British with grapeshot, round shot and chain. Grapeshot consisted of smaller balls, nails or stones and rocks wrapped in canvas that would break apart and scatter, round shot was one solid ball and chain would be a chain with a ball on each end of it. Lord Stirling counter attacked at Gowanus Road in an attempt to aid the men trying to cross. From our vantage point all we could do was look in horror as these events unfolded. Those that survived the crossing fled further up the line. By early afternoon the British stopped their advance. They started building entrenchments below us. That evening it began to rain.

John met with the officers and returned with word that about twelve hundred Americans lay dead below us and there were another fifteen hundred wounded, captured or missing. "Unfortunately, we are trapped between Lord Howe's fleet behind us in bay and his brother General Howe's forces in front of us", said John. The question was asked, "What now, Captain?"

John looked at his company of men, all with strained faces and replied, "Washington has requested John Glover and his Gloucester men bring every barge and boat and get us across the river." "John", I said, "There are thousands of us and the narrowest part is a mile wide! It would be a miracle." "Pray for that miracle, brother" he said. "In the meantime, we stick together. The regiments are overrun with panic. Take shifts watching what goes on down there."

Close by, we were hearing whispers for help. Every once in a while, a form would come out of the cover of darkness and we would run to help an injured soul back into camp. A few of us ventured down as quietly as we dared to see if there might be another soul to save. We did manage to find a few. When we returned, John was there and he was enraged. His face just inches from mine he shouted at me, "What were you thinking?". Standing there, wet, muddy and satisfied that I had helped at least a few souls, I quietly said to him, "What if were me down there?". John's lips clamped together and we glared at each other for a minute before I slowly turned and walked toward the nearest fire.

It rained hard for two more days. The fog swept over the area so thick that it was difficult to see the man in front of you which was a blessing as it halted any further attacks. The night of the 29th it was still raining but the winds turned northeast. We were ordered to prepare. Crary came to us and said, "Get ready, Washington is making his move." We were then ordered to stoke the campfires the best we could and to keep silent. We were then moved up toward Fort Greene. Varnum met us there. "It is imperative you maintain your silence. The ferries have started across the river. As the next shift of ferries leave, you will move up toward the road toward the ferries. Keep these fires going so the Brits don't get suspicious. Pray this fog and wind hold up". Due to our position, we would be on the last ferries taken off the island.

That being said, he hurried on to pass the message to the rest of his companies, John was ordering us to protect our ammunition and food from the rain. Ephraim announced the obvious saying, "It's going to be a long night, boys." Eventually we were moved further down the road and the same orders stood. After more waiting, we were moved to the next spot stoking the fires while we waited for the next shift in movement.

We were finally at the ferry. Silently we climbed aboard the barges. General Washington stood on the docks overlooking the process. Once every man was loaded, the sky cleared and the moon was bright. I looked back. There stood Washington, the last man to get on board a barge. It seemed like we all held our breath at this disaster of light and the sun coming up on us. I could hear the oarsmen talking about needing three hours to get across and we would be spotted for sure. I was afraid the Brits were going to see us and we would be left behind. Looking back to the barge behind us, Washington stood on the bow of the barge looking ahead and is if he fully expected it, a heavy fog rose up from the ground behind him and spread across our side of the river. It was our break!

It took a few hours which felt like many more, the Gloucester men got us across the choppy water silently and seeing the opposite side of the river was a godsend. As soon as we landed, Varnum sent orders for us to set up camp and get things in order. The men were quiet as we worked. Our first major battle was a serious defeat. The camp was devoid of the men's usual chatter.

John spoke to me for the first time since our disagreement the other night. Uncharacteristically he seemed uncomfortable when he asked me how I was. "I'm fine John.", I replied. I would not have changed my decisions that night and didn't want to talk about it again. Instead I asked, "What happened at the officer's meeting?" He realized I didn't want to talk about the other night, it was done and over. John gave me the news he received. "Washington praised Lord Stirling and his Marylanders for their efforts. Lord Stirling was captured. Of the four hundred Marylanders, two hundred and fifty-six were dead. The rest were captured." I could only look at the ground. They had valiantly stood the ground as a decoy so the rest of us could get to safety. John added, "Varnum gave us orders to head to Harlem Heights. Washington has something up his sleeve and we are about to find out what that might be. We leave in the morning." "Alright John.", I answered. We took off together in search of something to eat.

That night the camps spoke with admiration of the bravery of four hundred Marylanders. I listened to them as they talked to each other. Looking at each man, I became concerned. We had just lost Long Island. I did not doubt their bravery or that their hearts were resolved to defeat the British but, not one man here was a professional soldier. They were farmers, storekeepers and the like. The British had us out-manned. Could these men before me stand up to the fight ahead?

It would not be long before we would be tested again by the world's most magnificent army.

***

BATTLES OF HARLEM HEIGHTS AND WHITE PLAINS

Washington had two weeks to prepare his defenses on Manhattan. Harlem Heights is where John took me aside and said, "I'm headed home. I still don't understand these promotions or why Putnam was put in place. He didn't know the men or the terrain." John was still angry at the disaster on Long Island. He was in a black mood which was not like him at all. All the challenges he had faced starting with the loss of his wife, the loss of men, the loss of a promotion and the loss of battle had finally caught up to him. Looking hard into his tormented eyes, I asked "Hang on a bit longer". The single word "No!" burst from his lips. It was final. There were many men deserting after the loss at Long Island, he would be one more. I hoped he would get his thoughts together if he returned home. I knew his desertion would be another loss to him when he thought about this in the months to come. "Right now, I feel I'm needed more at home than I am here", he said. He jerked me into a quick hug and was gone. I would be at a loss without his guidance.

The next day when we were called up to parade, John was reported as "deserted". Everyone was silent at this bit of news. My stomach knotted up tight. I stood stiffly, eyes forward and lips clamped tightly. I could feel the men's eyes directed toward me. When the company was dismissed to its duties, Moses approached me. I said, "I don't want to talk about it, Moses. Just get to work." Inside I kept thinking, John will come back.

Now, with both of my brother's gone, the weight of company fell on me. Colonel Varnum and Major Crary took me aside and asked if I was up for it. "Yes, Sir.", I responded. The Major said, "There won't be any promotions given out for a while yet." I understood what he was saying and responded, "Aye, but I want these men to stay together and me with them, Sir." The General bowed to me and said, "I understand. You are to attend the Officer's meetings when called. Keep your company in order. I have every confidence in your ability." I stood straighter at his confidence in me. I looked him in the eye and said, "Yes, Sir. Thank you, Sir."

I began to speak more with the men about tactics and the advantage of working together as a unit making it quite clear that the idea of standing face to face on a field firing at each other quite stupid. They were quite receptive to the idea of using trees, rocks or anything they could find as protection from incoming bullets. I found that they were agile, intelligent and caught on to the ideas I was trying to teach them. The men that came with me from Buxton, understood the importance of working together silently and with great stealth. We had pretty much learned them from the Indians we had fought against. The Buxton boys worked with the others in the company on how to communicate with whistles or animal calls. Even hearing them talk about what to do in certain situations. I needed to build their confidence in me and they in each other.

On September 15, Howe struck at Kip's Bay. The inexperienced Virginian militia posted there, broke and ran. Word came back to us that Washington was enraged. The men were fleeing and he on his horse was dangerously close to the enemy trying to rally them. Bullets flew all around him and he was never struck. Still the men fled.

We were still well established at Harlem Heights and Washington made preparations to meet the British there. General Nixon called his officers together. I sat with Major Crary as General Nixon explained Washington's plan. I listened carefully, learning our company would be in the forefront. When General Nixon dismissed us, I caught Major Crary studying me. I was sure I was being measured. I looked him in the eye and nodded. He nodded back and I headed toward the men to prepare them.

The company called up, I explained, "General Washington has prepared the design of this attack carefully. We will be a major factor, so, I would be pleased if you listen carefully." All the men stood still and quiet. They listened while I outlined the whole of the attack and what our part would be. There were no questions and no comments. I wished them god speed and sent them to prepare themselves and get some rest.

Early in the morning of September 16, Colonel Knowlton and his rangers began the ploy. They rode close to the enemy lines basically taunting the Brits. They were under heavy fire and exchanged shots for nearly an hour. Soon more British troops appeared and Knowlton retreated. The British seeing the retreat began to blow the fox hunt call on their bugles. To them it meant we were on the run like scared rabbits. This was an insult to our men and only served to incite anger down the line.

As planned, my Company now became the bait. We followed Crary down the slopes from the heights and engaged the pursuing British. We were to remain engaged until Knowlton and Leitch rode back in. Knowlton was to come in from behind the British but due to the fog, they found themselves flanking the Brits. We were ordered to hold our position and keep firing. Crary was constantly urging us to fire. Being under such close fire, I could see a few of the men with shaking hands trying to reload.

I went to one man who looked like he would fall due to the amount of trembling in his body. He looked at me. I fired and looked back pointedly at him. As calmly as I could possibly manage, I reloaded with him copying my every movement. I looked at him and said "Together now man." We raised our guns and shot. I gave him a quick pat on the shoulder and I left him reloading. I went as quickly as I could up the line stepping over bodies strewn on the ground encouraging the men. The pressure on the Brits continued and eventually they retreated. We had taken the field. It felt like this battle had gone on for days instead of hours.

"Damn", said Ephraim, "it feels great to walk off the field instead of run". All around me the men were crying "Huzzah!". Varnum announced, "Men, good work. We have had our first victory today. We have a lot of wounded and dead still on the field. I want the dead buried and the wounded brought in." I took a good look around. The sight before me was as horrendous as what we saw on Long Island. This time though, it was a lot of the men from our regiment. I could not take my eyes away from the bullet ridden bodies and wounded men, some were groaning and others crying out for help. The men that were not wounded were doing their best to help their fellow patriots. Moses had already taken over supervising. He picked men to carry the wounded back to the hospital and supervised a detail to bury the dead. I had to leave with the Major to report to the General. General Greene complimented us on our win. When Major Crary reported on the losses, General Greene's expression was stoic. We were dismissed. I said to the Major, "Sir, I am going back to see to the dead." The Major nodded and walked away and I headed back.

The rest of the day was spent taking care of the dead. While Moses supervised the digging, I walked around. I identified the bodies of a few men that I recognized from around the camps. Witnessing their wounds, the blood everywhere and the life gone from their bodies is more than a human spirit can bear. My gut wrenched as I am looking at someone's son, brother and/or father. I think of the family at home who will never look upon this loved one's face again. As to some of the soldiers who have fallen, I'm grateful that these families are saved the pain of seeing what atrocities had fallen on the bodies of these men they loved so much. Once the burying was complete, the men joined me in a short prayer over these departed souls.

That evening the report came in. Nixon's brigade reported casualties at seventy-five. We were the hardest hit. Not a soul from Buxton was lost but, Dennis Lines from my company was killed. Mr. Lines came from Haverhill. We lost Captain Micajah Gleason of our regiment. Also reported was the loss of Major Leitch and Colonel Knowlton. He was shot in the back and brought back behind the lines where he died. After the casualty reports were read, our regiment along with Colonel Weedon and Major Price's regiments were to retire and refresh ourselves.

Making my way back to my company, a familiar face came to me. He greeted me with, "A word, Sir?". This was the shaken young man on the field. I answered him, "Of course." He was hesitant and then spoke, "I'd like to thank you for what you did for me in the field today." I looked hard at this young man and understood his discomfort. He appeared to be shamed by his conduct. "Fighting up close like that is the worst of battle. You weren't the only guy out there with shaky hands." He seemed to relax a little. I asked him, "What is your name and where are you from?". "James Chambers from Tewksbury, Sir", was his reply. "A lot of good men from Tewksbury.", I responded. He stood in front of me looking so unsure of himself. I took pity on him and went on telling him, "I was eleven when I saw my first fight during the French and Indian War." At his look of surprise, I went on, "It doesn't get any easier.", I said managing a smile. I clapped him on the shoulder, "I'm glad to have you in my company. I'd rather a man know fear than a fool running headlong into a bullet." I let the words set in and his face visibly relaxed. Trying to encourage the young man, I added, "When the nerves get the best of you, breathe deeply. Go and get some sleep. Everyone here has earned it." The young man seemed relieved at our conversation. He left me with "Good night, Sir. Thank you, Sir. See you in the morning."

October 1, I was ordered to attend a court-martial. I cleaned up the best I could and freshened up my uniform and headed toward headquarters. On the way, I met up with Lieutenant Jemmy who was also assigned to the court martial. "Well, what do you think? I've never attended to a court-martial." he asked me. "I never attended a court-martial either", I replied. "I hear that It involves Sargent George Forbes", he said. I responded "Could be, I know he's been imprisoned. We will soon find out" as we had now arrived at headquarters.

We were brought into the room where this trial was to take place. There were thirteen of us here to attend the trial. It was held in a formal manner which spoke of the serious nature being brought before us. Colonel Weedon spoke first. "Good morning. I have been assigned President of this court-martial. The members here are Lieutenant Colonel Richardson, Captain Wolcott, Major McDonnough, Lieutenant St. John, Captain Hoit, Lieutenant Jemmy, Captain Byles, Lieutenant Lane, Captain Braccon, Lieutenant Drake, Captain Gaston, Lieutenant Clarice and William Tudor, Judge-Advocate." This court will now be duly sworn in. Once that was done, the trial began.

Sergeant George Douglass was brought into the room. Colonel Weedon spoke again, "Sergeant George Douglass, of Captain Forbes' Company you are accused of mutinous conduct, exciting a mutiny and speaking disrespectfully of the Commander-In-Chief of the General Officers of the Army of the United States. How do you plead?

The Sergeant looked at the Colonel with a defiant look about him and spit out "Not Guilty". The prisoner was seated and two more men were brought into the room and seated as well.

The first man called was Ensign Bonner. He rose and sat in a chair that faced us. Colonel Weedon began with, "Please tell us what you witnessed with regard to these charges." I glanced at the Sergeant who was now glaring at the Ensign. The Ensign looked directly at the Sergeant while he told his story. He stated, "I was officer of the Guard while stationed on Harlem Common. There were a few prisoners being held, Sergeant Douglass being one of them. I heard the prisoner say that the Generals had sold the troops on Long-Island and had brought the army up to Harlem, to sell them there. He then began singing "God save the King."

Colonel Weedon said, "Thank you Ensign, you may go back to your seat. Captain Forbes, please come forward." The Captain rose and sat in the chair that the Ensign had just vacated.

Colonel Weedon again said, "Please tell us what you witnessed with regard to these charges." The Captain sat straight in his chair and after giving the Sergeant a look of disgust went on to say, "The morning of the same day Ensign Bonner was on guard, I was walking near the quarter guard, and heard somebody singing, "God Save the King." I walked over to where the singing was coming from and found it to be Sergeant Douglass, from my own company. I ordered him to cease, he instead finished singing the song. When he finished singing, he said to a soldier standing with him, "He was his King and he would have no other King, which we should soon see.""

Colonel Weedon said, "You said that the Sergeant is in your company. What do you say of his character?" The Captain answered, "Yes sir, he is a Sergeant in my company. He repeatedly disobeys orders and has lately become mutinous within the company. He frequently insults our Commander in Chief. I believe he is in the wrong army."

Colonel Weedon said to the Captain. "Thank you, Captain. You and the Ensign may wait in the next room." When they had left the room, he said to the prisoner, "Sergeant, do you have anything you wish to say?". The prisoner did not respond and the Colonel asked the guard to accompany the Sergeant to the next room while we deliberated.

Once the room was cleared, Colonel Weedon discussed the case with us all. It was clear to all of us that the Sergeant was guilty and the discussion ended rather quickly. We then had to decide the punishment. Colonel Weedon suggested one hundred lashes. Major McDonnough argued that this seemed too much. The Colonel said, "You heard the Captain complain of his disobedience. The Judge-Advocate stepped in to say, "He is not on trial for his disobedience today. The charge is for mutinous conduct." The Colonel argued, "Isn't it one and the same?" After some debate, a number was settled on and the Colonel documented the sentence.

The prisoner and witnesses were brought back into the room. Once everyone was seated in the room. Colonel Weedon cleared his throat and addressed the room. Sergeant Douglass, the prisoner is found guilty of mutinous speeches and speaking disrespectfully of the Commander-In-Chief. You are sentenced thirty-nine lashes on your bare back for said offence. To my surprise, the Sergeant didn't react to this. He didn't flinch at the words nor did he say anything. The guard escorted him out, followed by the witnesses. It was now our duty to witness the prisoner's punishment.

The rest of us filed outside and stood talking among ourselves for a few minutes. We felt that the punishment was justified. Captain Byles seemed a sensible man and said, "We just can't have this behavior among the ranks. It will spread like a disease and our cause will be lost." Major McDonnough said, "His enlistment is up very soon. Even if he wanted to re-enlist, it will not be accepted. The man shows signs of madness descending on him. In the meantime, Captain Forbes will have to do his best to deal with this problem."

Colonel Weedon then came out with the Judge-Advocate and we all proceeded over to where the punishment was to be carried out. Captain Forbes' company was already there. Without any delay, the

Sergeant was stripped of his shirt and put against a pole and the punishment was carried out. My teeth ground with every lash to his skin. Although this punishment was justified, I could not help but feel for the man. After serving in the previous war and seeing men killed and wounded, I had also seen the terror that drives madness into a man's mind. Visions of the bodies of your brother soldiers after a battle, tending to their burials, carry a man's mangled body to a doctor for help or the noises in the night as well as not knowing exactly where the enemy may spring from at any time, will taunt a man's sanity.

When the punishment was completed, I left to join the company. I tended to my required duties, returned to my tent, poured myself some rum and I prayed that the men in my company and both of my brothers would get through this war with our bodies and minds intact. I didn't much care to gather with the men that night. Moses came into the tent. He knew about the trial and punishment. He kept his thoughts to himself and went directly to sleep.

We rested for a few days and were then ordered to New Jersey. Our destination was Kings Bridge. General Clinton's brigade marched out first and then Nixon's brigade second. Behind us was General Roberdeau. We crossed the Hudson and settled in at the Westchester side of King's Bridge. It was a quiet area, mostly farm land. It was thought to be where the British would enter to try another attack. We were to defend the area and build barracks. Unfortunately, to do this, farm fields ready to be harvested were destroyed. Trees were felled to build obstructions for the British. The property owners had taken their families and gotten them to safety.

Moses and I watched the work being performed. Moses with a pained voice said, "It pains me to see these farms and homes being treated in such a manner. What are we were doing here to our own countrymen?" I understood the necessity of it however, it didn't make me feel any better about it. In response I said, "This is just a part of the injustice of war when it is in your homeland." Moses shook his head in disgust, "It doesn't make me like it any less." Moses walked away stiffly. Ephraim came up at that moment and said, "What's wrong with Moses?" Gruffly I returned, "He doesn't like what we're doing here." Ephraim stood quietly with me a moment before he spoke, "No, no. It's awful what we are doing here to these people's farms. But Sir, imagine if the Red Coats were standing here. Do you think they would treat this any better?" I shook my head no. Ephraim added, "I'm thinking they wouldn't have even given these people a chance to run to safety. They would have brought the buildings down around them." I looked at him and he was studying the scene around him intensely. Finally, when he spoke, it was with humor, "By God, if they tried this with Elizabeth home, I'm sure she would have taken on the whole British army and sent them off." I watched him walk away, glad for the humor but, realizing we all had our thoughts on home.

Washington arrived at the middle of October and held a meeting with his officers. After that meeting, we were informed that the British forces were at Throg's Neck, which was close by and had us outnumbered. The decision was made to hold the defense until they arrived. The troops were ordered that on the British arrival, the barracks were to be burned and the bridge destroyed. This would give Washington sufficient time to get to White Plains and reinforce once more.

A week after Washington left, the British showed their faces. As ordered, the barracks were burned and the bridge planks were ripped apart to prevent the British from crossing. They would have to find another way to enter the city. We on the other hand were ordered to White Plains. Before leaving, Major Crary called all the officers to report to General Greene. General Greene had a sense of urgency when he spoke. "A large number of firearms and ammo are still here. Your orders are to obtain as many wagons as you can gather, load them up and bring them with us. Let's get this done as quickly as possible. If the British get their cannons in place, we will be doing this under their fire. Dismissed!" We all took off running.

Once I returned to the company and explained the situation, a few men managed to find wagons and our company worked together with the other companies to get the equipment loaded. It was a chaotic scene, due to the need to get moving quickly but everyone worked together and everything was loaded much more quickly than expected.

We followed Nixon to White Plains without having to combat the British back at the bridge. Moses was even less pleased to see us destroy everything we built. I let him be for the time being. I was less than happy myself.

On October 28, the Battle of White Plains took place. Our company was there but did not participate in the frontal action. This time we were behind the front lines. At 9:30 in the morning, General Howe's forces started firing their cannons on us. Shortly after, that they come directly at Washington's army.

At one point, a soldier reported that Hessians were trying to flank Washington. This is the side that our company stood. As if by magic, Moses was by my side, "Sir?", he said. With a sideways glance, my grip tightened on my rifle. "Gather the men". Moses' answer was, "Begging your pardon, Sir. They are right behind you." Turning around to them, "Are you ready!". Their response was a loud roar. I turned and we ran toward the enemy mass coming toward us. Looking to my right, I saw that the other companies that had been standing beside us were doing the same. A surge of confidence made us run faster toward our objective.

Once more, the retched sounds of bullets passing over our heads challenged the men to keep their wits about them. I stopped the company when we reached a stone wall thinking it would be suitable cover. Immediately the men were firing, reloading and firing again. I stopped from shooting to look over and see one of the new men in my company standing while he reloaded his rifle. I screamed at the top of my lungs, "Get down to reload those guns!". Apparently, I was heard over the roar of cannon fire, bullets whizzing by and the screams of the wounded, because when I looked again, the man had taken cover as commanded.

By mid-afternoon, we could not hold the defenses any longer and orders arrived for me to pull the company back. The signal was sent down the line and as a group we ran back. The battle continued on until late afternoon when heavy rain and winds forced a halt to the action. The reports that evening were three hundred men dead from each side. Washington considered this a draw.

As I always did at night, I walked around to check on the men in the company. Most were huddled around a campfire. I stopped to talk to them. My nephew, John Woodman offered me his mug and said, "Rum, Sir?" I took a sip and handed his mug back to him. "Thank you, John." I couldn't help but realize he had my sister's eye color but otherwise he was the image of his father.

To the men I spoke, "You did well out there today. For the men that are new to the company, I don't much care for the tactic of standing in the line of fire. If you have the chance to take cover while fighting, do so." One of the new recruits spoke, "Sir, at the drills, we are taught to stand like men, as they put it." I responded, "Standing men are targets. Men behind rocks and trees, live to fire another shot. Do their damn drills but, you will fight in my company according to my instructions." Looking around at them, most of them were nodding their agreement.

I stepped into the circle and looked into each of their faces as I spoke, "We have so much ahead of us. As you have already seen, war is ugly, seeing our friends die is ugly. I don't want to lose anyone else. Let's do it my way, cover your asses out there. Work together. Let's all get home to our families." A few seconds passed as each man looked the man next to him. Finally, I could hear "Aye" as they responded one at a time.

Phineas Towle spoke up saying, "The next time you find yourself standing in line of fire, think of what we might be having for breakfast, then get your pretty arse down!" Ephraim Sands bantered back, "With the food they are sending, I just might stand!" The banter brought a lot of laughter from the men. I had to laugh myself and said, "We are marching in the morning, so if you want your 'BREAKFAST', you might make sure you get up and moving. Good night all."

Before I stepped away, however, I asked James Chambers for a minute. He got up and we stood a few feet from the men. I looked him a second and smiled. "You did well out there today, James." What he said next and the excited manner in which he said it, just about took my legs out from under me. "Thank you, Sir. I did A LOT of breathing!". The laughter just bubbled up from my stomach. The men looked over in bewilderment. James at first was surprised my laughter, but then he found the humor in his own words and his giggles joined mine. I clapped his shoulder firmly and left to get some sleep.

My last thought that night was about the men. They did in fact do quite well today. There was no hesitation in any of them as we charged toward the enemy. Hopefully, they heard my words tonight.

The next morning, we were marched North of the city. Howe had intended to attack us but found we were gone. Howe had turned back to New York City and this allowed Washington to march his army to New Jersey. Howe had the advantage yesterday. Why he did not follow us to finish us off I think was a mistake on his part. Had Howe followed us on our retreat, he could have possibly taken Washington's army.

***

BATTLE OF TRENTON

From White Plains, we marched a short distance to Castle Heights and once again new defenses were to be built. Our company was officially merged into General Greene's Brigade and I was officially made Captain receiving a Captain's sword. I received a lot of congratulations and while I was humbled that the men had such faith in me, it was not really a happy occasion for me. I felt I had obtained it from John's leaving.

That evening, I had my supper with Moses. We went over the day's events and plans for the following day. We ate a few more minutes before Moses said, "What's bothering you.". I took a deep breath and said, "I'm honored to be Captain, but I do feel some irritation towards John." With his fork half way to his mouth, he inquired, "How so?". I went on, "I understand his reasons, but I didn't want to become Captain under these circumstances." Moses mulled over my words for a few seconds and replied, "Yes, we could use John here. Yes, he is needed at home. However, you became Captain on your own merits." I started to speak but with a wave of his arm he went on, "You are just as good as him, if not better. Not to disrespect John but, he has to deal with his family for a time at least and get his mind straight about the politics of war." I stared into the fire and muttered "Thanks" to Moses.

He sat for a minute and prodded, "John isn't the only reason here, best to voice it." "It's hard to put into words. I have no problem going into battle but, ordering other men to do so comes much harder, especially, after Harlem Heights. I keep seeing the men on ground dead, dying or wounded. Could I have done something different?" When I finished speaking, Moses was thoughtful. "You gave orders that you were ordered to give. It wasn't your fault when Knowlton came from the wrong direction. These men think well of you, Jabez.

You stand strong and brave and they follow that. Not one man ran from the fighting or left our company. Share your doubts here but, don't ever let them see it." I looked at him. He made sense and I felt better for voicing it. Moses, as if sensing my thoughts, stood. "Get some sleep Captain." With that he left me to my own thoughts.

November 6th, Washington called a council of war. The discussion was lengthy and a lot of discussion regarding where the Brits would go from New York City and what might be done about it. Washington's decision was to leave three thousand men at Peekskill, New York and the passes to the Highlands. Washington himself was going to New Jersey with troops. Nixon's brigade was assigned to Major General Lee's division under General Heath. Nixon's brigade contained the regiments of Thomas Nixon (brother of General Nixon), Varnum, Hitchcock, Little and Lippett. General Nixon himself and those that were sick or wounded remained in Peekskill.

The brigade was now split and my company was now under the command of Hitchcock. We crossed the Delaware River into Pennsylvania. The British remained on the Jersey side. At our officer's meeting, we were informed that Washington had sent orders to General Lee to reinforce his position north of Philadelphia. The rumor among the officers was that Lee was upset with Washington and in the following weeks Lee had not arrived. Among the Captains, I learned it was obvious Lee was dragging his feet on Washington's orders. He resented Washington as Commanding General and thought he, himself should be in charge. He was obviously going to hinder Washington as much as he could.

General Hitchcock called his officers together and after greeting us, we were informed of the latest news and Washington's next plan. His report was: On December 12, General Lee fell into British hands. Approximately two thousand of the remaining men hurried here to join Washington. At Washington's meeting of officers, the subject of

Enlistments expiring the last week of December was discussed. If Washington is to use this force, he would have to do so before the enlistments expired on December 31. He proposed his plan to strike by surprise at the Hessian garrisons at Trenton and Bordentown on Christmas night, when the troops might be expected to relax their guard for the holiday. He has proposed the first force which he called the main force would cross the Delaware at McConkey's Ferry which is north of Trenton. Washington then suggested the army will then march in two columns by different routes meeting at the opposite end of Trenton's main street. Sullivan would attack from the south and west and Greene and Washington from the north.

The second force, under Colonel John Cadwallader is to cross below near Bordentown to attack the Hessian garrison there as a diversionary tactic. There will be a third force under Brigadier General James Ewing, which is to cross directly opposite Trenton. The purpose of this would be to block the Hessian route of escape across Assunpink Creek. With that, the other Captains again voiced to Greene about the enlistments that would be ending. Greene said that Washington is considering his options.

After the meeting with Greene, I rallied the company together. I was careful in my words, as I knew these men wanted to go home. They were homesick, cold and hungry beyond words. As I looked at my ragged company I began, "Washington has asked that the Captains relay these words from a pamphlet written by Thomas Paine, a fellow Patriot." I cleared my throat, because the words were so poignant at this time. I read to them,

"These are the times that try men's souls. The summer soldier and the sunshine patriot will, in this crisis, shrink from the service of their country; but he that stands by it now, deserves the love and thanks of man and woman. Tyranny, like hell, is not easily conquered; yet we have this consolation with us, that the harder the conflict, the more glorious the triumph. What

we obtain too cheap, we esteem too lightly: it is dearness only that gives everything its value."

I let those powerful words sink into the men's minds before I went on, "Washington plans to take Trenton. He further relays to all the men, 'God bless you all. Thank you and Good Luck'". I let those words drift over the men for a few minutes. Joshua Woodman spoke, "What are his plans?" "We are going to attack Trenton on Christmas night. He is hoping the Hessians will be celebrating the holiday.", I answered. Now James Woodman spoke, "How does he plan we get there, Sir?" I took a deep breath to prepare myself for their reaction, "We are going to cross the river. John Glover is bringing his boats to take us across." Ephraim Sands went apoplectic, "It's ice! Sir!" His explosion raised grumbles from the rest of the company. To calm them and myself I suppose, I said, "Glover thinks he can get us across at night so we won't be seen. If he got this far to us, then crossing a river won't be a problem." Comically almost, the groans and complaints went to expressions of, "That's true." And other comments such as "He got us off Long Island, didn't he?" I finished the meeting with, "The plan is set for Christmas Eve. Hopefully the Hessians will be drunk and/or sleeping. In case we are separated, Washington's password is "Victory or Death. I would advise you all to stay close to me, as we know how fast things can change on or off the battlefield."

Two days passed and in those two days, John Glover arrived with his Gloucester men. Some of the men in my company were acquainted with some of Glover's men, so I allowed them to go and greet them on their arrival. I went myself to see the General. He saw me coming and waved. I was pleased he should remember me. "Good day, General.", I called to him as I approached. His smile was huge on his face, a face much weathered from so many years at sea.

He came forward and stopped me from saluting and instead shook my hand. "No formalities, please. I should congratulate you on your rank of Captain." I replied, "Thank you. It's not as grand as General and I congratulate you for that." He sobered his expression for a minute and said, "I'm sorry to hear that John headed home. I know you will do well." "Thanks." I answered. "He asked, "Where is that other, brother? Daniel, isn't it?". "Yes, it is and he is somewhere in New York the last I heard." He shuffled his feet a bit, and added, "I hope you hear good news from him soon." I thanked him again.

Changing the subject, I told General Glover of his legacy with my men. "They heard it was you taking us across. They are convinced you are the only one who could do it, as do I." He stood a bit taller and said, "Thank you for the praise but, it would be all of my men who did the hard work. I am fortunate to have such brave men under my command." I smiled wide and said, "I feel the same way about my men. I have seen these men do the unthinkable." The General with a wave of his arm toward the men around us said, "I no longer let the youthful faces fool me. They dare to do more than I had thought of in the last war." I agreed with him and responded, "This time we are fighting a professional army instead of with it, like we did in the last war." We went off to find a pint and spent a while talking about more pleasant things.

Christmas night was cold, windy, and snowing and the Delaware River was filled with blocks of ice. We boarded the boats commanded by John Glover and his Gloucester men. I felt confidence in the man after the heroic efforts of he and his men made getting us across from Long Island. They were efficient and fearless in what they did. This would be another test to their skills as the river was flecked with ice, some the size of boulders. As we were crossing the heavier snow arrived. The water was rough and made rougher with the chunks of ice hitting the boats. Each time a piece of ice hit our boat, it would throw a spray of water at us and I worried a few times that it would shatter the boat and we would drown. We had no protection from the freezing cold water spraying up at us, the snow coming down on us or the wind as we traveled across. It felt as if we were in slow motion.

By the time we were halfway across, my clothes were soaked and I had no more protection from the weather. The cold had now reached into my bones. Everyone was silent during the ride across, each deep in their own thoughts and fears of getting across. Joanna's son, John Hancock sat beside me in the boat. When he did speak, he said, "Captain, I don't think I have ever been this cold. Do you think they will give us a rest on the other side to light some fires and warm ourselves up a bit and perhaps get a little dry?". "It's not likely, John. This crossing is progressing slower than planned. We need to keep moving if we are to be successful with the element of surprise. Fires may alert the enemy of our whereabouts." John just muttered, "They should have issued more rum to warm our insides and less of the cold food." I couldn't stop my laughter from erupting when I replied, "Thinking the same thing myself, nephew." I went on to say, "This attack must be successful. The morale is so bad and enlistments are up. I fear we will lose our army if we fail." John's humor was in full stride when he said, "I will be re-enlisting and anyone in our company that packs his things, I will be right behind him kicking his arse down the road." Those that heard him chuckled with a hearty "Aye!". John became thoughtful after everyone's laugh and said, "I think Washington's password this night, 'Victory or Death' has put a spark in some of the men. We will rally. I want to go home a free man."

It felt good to have talked to him. Pushing starving, half clothed men beyond their endurance was not sitting well in my mind. I never had a problem taking the orders but now, their welfare was my responsibility and it sat heavy on my heart. As if he heard my thoughts, Phineas Towle who had been listening behind us yelled to me over the wind, "Captain, we will hold our own. I won't be heading home unless you are leading the way." I twisted around as best I could to clap him on the arm and answer him with "Thanks Phineas." I looked at the faces around me and the ones that had been within earshot were nodding their heads in agreement. Most of them had come with me from home. As we were now reaching the shoreline, my thoughts were grateful for the men I had come so far with. I wanted them all to get home.

We landed and had to wait for the rest of the troops to arrive. It wasn't until 4 AM that we were able to begin our march. Our company followed Greene and Washington up the road. The horses did not come across with us so we had to walk eight miles to get to the northern part of Trenton while Colonel Cadwallader marched to the south of the town. As first light of day rose above us, I looked down at my feet. In the trodden snow from the men ahead of us were blood from their poorly covered feet. I looked toward Moses Atkinson and he was looking at what we were marching over. I was horrified. His expression was emotionless. Before we set off on our march, he came up with some rags of cloth and had done his best to wrap the men's feet and their hands enough to be able to use their muskets. As we marched, Washington on his white horse passed us a few times. He encouraged the men to keep going and would stop once in a while to speak to a man.

It was 8 in the morning when we reached Trenton, well behind schedule. Greene's brigade was ordered to attack and we ran in. Knox's cannons were hitting the Hessians hard on one end of the town and the Hessians withdrew to a field just outside the town. Even a few blocks away, the booming of the cannon caused repercussions in my chest. We chased the Hessians still firing on them out to a field. We took cover in houses and battled for another hour. We only killed forty but the number of captured tallied over nine hundred. Washington's counting on them to be resting for the Christmas holiday proved true. I learned from another officer that Ewing did not make it across the river with his troops. They had in fact, turned back. This meant the bridge was not blocked and an estimated four hundred Hessians had escaped that way, running for Bordentown.

We suffered four dead and four wounded, thankfully our company, one of the first to run into town was untouched. The troops were elated, the victory we needed had arrived. The Hessian leader, Colonel Johann Rall had been shot in the side and was brought to one of the homes in the town where he later died. I gathered my company together to await further orders.

While we waited, the men's conversation was energetic. I spotted General Greene with his familiar limp walk among the men. He still cared deeply about the health of the men and in true form, was amidst the crowd of men himself to check. I noticed that his limp was worse with the cold but it was amazing how it never slowed him down.

Ephraim and Phineas were jostling Moses. Moses was busy attending to the hands and feet of one of the men. Somehow Phineas had gotten hold of a Hessian hat and had it on. As he was a small man, the hat looked ridiculous on him. Ephraim grabbed it off of him and stuck his hands inside for warmth. He then went behind Moses and was poking him in the back with the tip of the hat. Moses was in such a good mood; he could only laugh at their antics.

The women in the town started to come out on the street and they offered what blankets and food they could. I heard one of the men, William Andros say, "Sorry about your house Ma'am." She gave him a hug and said, "I can go back and sit on my porch without fear now. You did a good thing this day."

As I listened to their conversation, I was surprised at what I heard her say to him. He was asking her about the Hessians and a few men became interested in their conversation. William said, "Did the Hessians treat the people well here? They must have been a handful celebrating the Christmas holiday?" "Actually", she said. "They were not celebrating. They have been harassed nightly by the local militia. The militia would attack the pickets or sneak into town, fire at them and then disappear into the night. I heard that Colonel Rall gave his men orders to sleep on their weapons so they would always be prepared. They are weary from lack of sleep the last few weeks. A picket did not go out this morning because of this blizzard."

Colonel Crary finally arrived and filled me in on what was going on. I shared what the woman had told us with him. He remarked how that helped us get into town so easily. He left just as abruptly as he came. I called the men to muster and filled them in.

"I want to share what Colonel Crary just related to me. Washington has been informed that the Hessians had planned on attacking Philadelphia, so he is going to accommodate them and parade them through Philadelphia as prisoners." A cheer of "Huzzah" went up through the men. Raising my arms up to quiet them, I went on, "We are to get back in the boats and head back across the river". I had thought this order would bring about a riot but, the men took it in stride. While we waited to board the boats, Benjamin Woodman and I took a quick walk around. "Ben, look around you. Do you see what I see?", I asked him. All around me, these men, clothing and shoes falling off their bodies were talking, smiling and animated. "Sir?" said Benjamin. I answered him, "An army Ben." Benjamin looked around and said, "I see men in rags, covered in snow." I turned his shoulders to look at them again and said, "Look at the men, not their clothing. We are all exhausted, yet they stand straighter." Benjamin nodded realizing what I had just pointed out to him. He said, "The black moods are gone for now. We needed this boost in morale. I'm thinking Washington just might receive some re-enlistments." "Aye.", I agreed.

It wasn't until the next morning that we all got back across the river but, it seemed easier to get across this time. The blizzard had let up. We were assuredly tired, cold, hungry but most definitely elated. Fires were quickly built and the men were huddled around them enjoying a pint of rum. The conversations were all about the day's victory and heading home in a few days for the comfort of home. I warmed myself for a while by the fire with them and then went to lay down in my tent. The men were soon finding their own places to rest.

When I woke the next morning, it was cold inside the tent. So cold, my mind objected to the idea of going outside. Eventually, I got up and went to check on the company. Moses informed me that many of the men in the brigade were very sick but our company only had a few men slightly ill. This was good news. After a few bites of a tasteless breakfast, I left him and joined with the other captains for Washington's next orders.

Crary informed us that the Cornwallis has left Princeton to attack us. "Washington says he will not fight on their terms. He is not waiting for them to get here. He intends to re-cross the river and meet them at Assupunk Bridge. When he was done with relating Washington's plans, I spoke. "Colonel, most of men in my company are ready to head home. Their enlistments are up. I'm not sure I can persuade them to stay". It was echoed by the other Captains in attendance.

From behind me, the familiar voice quietly spoke, "I would like a word with the men". I turned, there stood General Washington looking me right in the eye. His next words were to all of us. Captains, please bring your men to parade. I would like to speak to them. He nodded in my direction and walked away. I hurried to my company and ordered them all to stand parade. "Washington himself wishes to address us." The men hurried to their positions alongside the other companies.

Moses lined up the men and fussed, "Stand up straight! Chins up! Washington is coming to address soldiers, not sloppy farmers." Once he was satisfied with the look of them, he turned to me with a wink and a "Ready, Sir".

While we waited, I looked hard and long at each one of them. I was quite proud of them. Realizing I had never told them this, I broke the silence, I mustered up the words, "You have all done well and suffered so much. I could not choose a better group of men to be with. It is my honor to stand here with you." With that I turned and faced front, standing as tall and straight as I could to show my pride for them as we waited. Moses leaned over and whispered, "I enjoy your eloquent speeches, Sir." I managed a quick grin at his snarky comment. I never liked to express my feelings or talk much in front of the men as a whole.

Washington, on his horse, followed by drummers advanced in front of us. He began with "Men, your services are greatly needed. You can do more for our country then we ever can at any future date. I am entreating you to stay." The regimental commanders then asked "All who would stay please step forward, the drums beat for volunteers." Not a man stepped forward. One Captain addressed his Colonel saying "My comrades are worn down with fatigue and privations. Their hearts are fixed on home and the comforts of their domestic circles."

We watched as Washington wheeled his horse about and rode in front of the regiment. He spoke again. "My brave fellows," Washington spoke in a louder voice but, without anger, "You have done all I asked you to do, and more than could be reasonably expected; but your country is at stake, your wives, your houses, and all that you hold dear. You have worn yourselves out with the fatigues and hardships, but we do not know how to spare you. If you will consent to stay one month longer; you will render that service to the cause of liberty, and to your country, which you probably can never do under any other circumstances."

The drums rolled again. The soldiers felt the force of the appeal and began to talk among themselves. I could hear one man, "I will remain if you will." Another said, "We cannot go home under such circumstances." A few men stepped forward, then several others, then many more and "their example was followed by nearly all who were fit for duty in the regiments, amounting to about two hundred volunteers."

These were veterans who understood what they were being asked to do. They knew well what the cost might be.

I had stepped forward and could only wonder at who in my company behind me did. When I turned to look, I felt more pride than ever in my company. To their honorable credit, every man in my company re-enlisted for another six weeks.

6

1777

BATTLE OF ASSUPINK CREEK

Immediately after all had signed their enlistments, we were back in the boats crossing the river yet again, dodging the floes of ice that were constantly harassing the boats as we crossed. This time, the horses and wagons were brought over after the men were taken across. As soon as all landed, we marched toward Assupink Creek. Once we were there, we secured our positions on the high ground south and east of Trenton. Our company was positioned over the lower ford. Knox quickly got his cannons in place. Surveying the area, Assupink Creek was running high and could only be crossed at a few fords and a single bridge. Moses and Ephraim came to join me.

Moses informed me. "Sir, I have found a spot for the horses to graze nearby." Ephraim looked at the river below, "Do you think they could get their horses across this?" I pointed out to them a few spots that seemed to be shallow. "Maybe in these spots." Ephraim exclaimed, "I'm glad it's them trying to get across here. I'm perfectly happy to stay on this side." I turned to Moses, "Would you please bring the company over here?" He nodded, "Yes, Sir", and was off. Ephraim stood beside me silently while I thought the situation through.

Soon the company appeared. Addressing them as a whole, I shared the plan, "This is the area we need to hold." Pointing to the place I had been concerned about, I explained, "See these points? I believe they may be able to get across there so concentrate on keeping the Red Coats away. Now, we need to make cover for some protection. Let's get some trees down and build a wall. There are boulders and rocks around. Let's move what we can over here. To Ephraim I said, gather up some food. Fill whatever you can with some fresh water down there." Thinking I might have everything voiced, I ended with, "We must do this as quickly as possible so, get started. They set to work right away. I helped out with moving the trees by using my horse to drag them to where I wanted them placed.

The project completed, we sat behind the walls to rest a bit and chew on fire cakes. They weren't very appetizing. On top of being tasteless, there was even less nourishment that we badly needed but, they would fill our stomachs and we could chew on them as we marched. Food was getting scarcer and with these quick movements and supplies were having a hard time keeping up. Fire cakes were made by mixing water and flour and tossing them into the fires. As a result, this was fast becoming part of our diets. Daniel Boynton received a particularly burned and hardened fire cake and in a disgusted tone said, "If we run out of bullets, we could hurl these at them." Ephraim tried to act as if he was hurt by Daniel's opinion of his cooking, retorted, "You're welcome to make the next batch." Daniel absolutely hated cooking as he burned most everything. The men started groaning, "No, not that" and "We will die!" which was followed by laughter. Done eating and taunting each other, we studied the other side where the British would possibly take cover or try to come through. Until the British arrived, men would take turns watching the area from behind the placed trees for the British arrival.

Two days later on January 2, Cornwallis arrived. He sent troops toward us across the fords but Knox and his cannons fired heavily on them and quickly sent them back. Cornwallis now sent the Hessians across the bridge. Once again, the cannons were booming and the Hessian bodies lay strewn across the bridge. Behind them came British troops with the same results. We kept up our volleys as here and there Hessians and Brits made three attempts to cross the ford. Along the fords and on the bridge, there were volleys of shot keeping the British at bay. We kept vigilant and held off each wave coming at us. As darkness fell, Cornwallis stopped pressing his attack. The wall we had built, had served us well.

As things quieted down, one of Greene's men came to us at the ford and gathered the Captains together. He confirmed what we already saw, the British and Hessians suffered heavy losses. Washington had sent word of "well done". He relayed from Washington that fires were to be built high. It was ordered to tie rags around the horses' feet and the artillery wagons and once that was done, under the cover of the blazing fires, we maneuvered behind the British flank headed toward Princeton. Absolute silence was ordered to carry out this plan.

In compliance, each Captain went back to his men and supervised carrying out these orders. While some were fixing the rags to the wagons and horses, some were helping the injured and sick. Our wall was dismantled and set fire to. I helped out with the work and observed the men. I realized we were becoming particularly good at organizing what needed to be done and do it efficiently.

Once again, Moses appeared. I smiled at him, "The men did quite well out there today." "Yes, Sir", he responded. He added, "It was good to prepare them beforehand. It was a boost of confidence." I asked him, "Do you need anything, Moses?" He quickly answered, "No, Sir. Just checking to see if you desired anything else." I answered him with a slight grin, "I desire to be home with my family sitting beside my nice warm fire." Moses grinning back at me returned, "I'll see to that right away, Sir".

After a minute, Stephen Whitney appeared before me with a concerned look. He was usually a quiet man. It was quite clear he wanted my attention. Moses stepped away with an excuse to see to the men before Stephen spoke, "Sir, it's Lemuel Rounds. He appears to be quite ill." "How ill?", I questioned. "Definitely has a fever. He will be quite angry I told you because he wants to stay with the company." "Where is he?", I asked. "I sat him over by the fire while I did the cooking. He's quite weak, Sir." "Go on back to him. I'll be along in a minute." Stephen hesitated and to ease his thoughts I offered. "Say nothing, I will do what I can for him." Stephen responded. "Thank you, Sir.", and took off. Once I was satisfied with the progress of our preparations, I wandered over to the fire. Stephen was tossing the last of the fire cakes into bags and handing them to Lemuel to tie the bags securely.

I raised my hands over the fire to warm them saying, "How are we doing here?" "Well, Sir", said Stephen as he cast a worried glance toward Lemuel. At that moment, Lemuel began to cough. "Lemuel how are you feeling?" He looked terrible but he bravely answered, "I'm doing quite well Captain, looking forward to our stroll this evening." He glanced at Stephen. Before he could say anything more, I sat down next to him, "Lemuel, you sound awful and up close here, you look worse." He plead "Please, let me stay with the company."

His face held a look of determination and I didn't want to disappoint the man. I am certain he didn't expect my response and the look of shock on his face confirmed it when I spoke to him. "We will be marching through the night. I'm putting you on my horse." He started to argue but I cut him off. "You're ill. You can stay with the company, but I won't have you lagging behind slowing us up." Turning to Stephen I ordered, "Get my horse, quickly." Stephen hurried off and I grabbed the last bag of food to secure it. Lemuel whispered, "I'm sorry, Sir."

"It's okay, Lemuel", I responded.

Stephen appeared with the horse. "Help me here, Stephen." We each took a side of Lemuel and heaved him up. Stephen wrapped his blanket as well as Lemuel's around the sick man's shoulders as best he could. My order was to Stephen, "You stay with the horse and see that Lemuel stays on top of it." Stephen, still fussing over Lemuel answered "Yes, Sir" as I started to walk away. I had gone a few steps when I heard Stephen chiding Lemuel, "No one would think badly of you if you went home." Lemuel's ragged reply stopped me in my tracks, "I will not be returning to Buxton without my Comrades."

Walking away from them, I felt a knot of pride toward the company and offered a silent prayer that Lemuel would revive.

***

BATTLE OF PRINCETON

All that night we marched to our new destination. We managed to circumvent around the British soldiers without being detected. I would have loved to seen Cornwallis' face this morning when he realized that the whole of Washington's army had crept by him in his sleep. Washington had left behind a couple hundred men with pick axes to make noises that would make the British think that Washington was digging in. Before daylight, they were to leave and catch up with our troops. The route we traveled was icy and the horses stumbled quite a bit. A few men fell through some icy ponds we had to cross.

Intelligence had reached Washington that there was a stretch of road that was hardly used and would lead us right into the town. This is the road he chose to take.

We arrived at dawn of the next day, January 3, two miles outside of Princeton. We were once again, behind Washington's proposed schedule. Washington wanted to delay Cornwallis so he sent Brigadier General Mercer to destroy the bridge at Stony Creek. Further down the road Washington turned us onto the unused road on the right. My company was assigned to Hitchcock's brigade. The first in the column was General Sullivan's division. In that division was Isaac Sherman and Arthur St. Clair's brigades. Behind these brigades came John Cadwallader's brigade with Daniel Hitchcock's bringing up the rear. The shots from the bridge reached our ears and Hitchcock and Cadwallader were following Washington in that direction. Cadwallader's men got there first. His men fired one volley and started to flee. Washington on his horse was right in front of us with the Virginians. He signaled us to go to the right side of the field and we hurried to our position.

What happened next, was not to be believed. Our orders were not to fire until he gave the signal. By now the Brits had moved their troops out of range of the artillery fire. Washington motioned the men to advance and went ahead of them. When he was just a couple dozen yards away from the British, he turned his horse and we all heard "Halt!" and then "Fire!". The Americans and British fired simultaneously. The field filled with smoke and there was no visibility. Had I just watched the end of Washington? After a few moments, the smoke cleared to a haze and there sat Washington on his horse, neither of them harmed, waving his men forward!! I was stunned! Every man on our side of the field rallied. We were cheering loudly as we ran as fast as we could toward Washington.

Hitchcock took charge at that moment ordering us to fire at the British flank. We advanced on them slowly picking them off. A British officer, named Mawhood ordered a retreat and we kept charging. They were in such a hurry to flee they left their cannon behind. Washington yelled to the retreating Brits, "It's a fine fox chase, boys!". This brought on another cheer from the men who were at the Battle of Harlem Heights and had heard that obnoxious bugle call. In unison, our regiments surged forward after the Brits. We continued to chase them until nightfall killing some and taking some prisoners. At last, Washington called off the chase and we rode back to Princeton as darkness enveloped us.

Walking into Princeton, it was another chaotic scene. I found myself near Colonel Thomas Nixon who took a few minutes with me. I saluted and he grinned, "Captain Lane. Another good day." I grinned back, "Yes, Sir. What is happening here?" We both stood there taking in the scene. The Colonel said, "While we had been on our chase, Sullivan had evidently had his hands full as British regiments took up a position outside of Princeton, across a ravine. The British sent their troops to take down Sullivan but he cut them to pieces. After making a brief stand, the British retreated into the town in a building called Nassau Hall. Alexander Hamilton with three cannons blasted away at the building. Finally, some Americans rushed the front door to which the British hung a white flag out of one of the windows. Sullivan allowed them to walk out of the building and lay down their arms.

In front of me, the rest of the American troops began to loot the abandoned supply wagons and whatever they could in the town. Washington quickly sent orders to the troops that he wanted to be on the move quickly. There's no time for celebration, it was just a loot and run." I was more than happy to get out of there. I spotted Moses a few yards away and said, "I best get my company prepared to go." He stood beside me as Moses approached.

Moses came near and I informed him of what I had just learned. "If you would get the company together, I would appreciate it." He smiled and pointed and there they were, all ready to go. "Thank God, they listened when I said stay together.", I smirked at Moses. Moses grin was wide when he said, "Told them I would shoot them myself if they wandered off. I'm a soldier, not a babysitter." If I knew one thing about Moses, becoming an Ensign, he learned the value of order and he followed it to the most minute detail. Moses went back to the men to inform them. Colonel Nixon nodded toward Moses who was bellowing at the men, "He runs a tight ship." Watching Moses in action, I gave the Colonel my measure of the man, "He understands the importance of order but more importantly he understands their needs. It is him who sees to their wounds and their bellies. He cares deeply for them and they know and respect it. In return, they do as he bellows." The Colonel responded, "Crusty on the outside, soft on the inside." I looked at him quickly, "Yes, Sir. We just don't let him know we have him figured out."

Washington led his army out of Princeton. We, under Moses' hollering, assembled and followed the Commander to Morristown.

On the March, Colonel Nixon rode up beside me. "Captain.", he said. "Colonel.", I responded. When he didn't say anything, I asked him, "What should we expect ahead of us?" The Colonel was happy to relay what he knew saying, "Washington had sent men weeks before to build huts in Morristown. Hopefully all if not most, will be ready when we arrive. It's where he plans to spend the winter." I replied, "It will be good to let the men rest a bit, Sir." "Agreed", he replied.

On our arrival we found that they were still working on this project. Instead of cramming men into already crowded huts, our tents were pitched, trench latrines dug and the sick were grouped again to a designated site. I checked on Lemuel and found him in the tent that my nephew, John directed me to. He seemed much better and so, I was happy to not send him off to the church that was designated for the sick. Lemuel was still pale but was insistent, "Sir, what are my orders?"

"I need you to rest for at least another day", I said sternly. "I feel much better, though", he argued. Smirking at him I answered firmly, "That's an order. Do I need to have you guarded or should I send Moses in?" Giving up he answered, "No Sir, Thank you, Sir".

The next day, help was needed to get more shelters built to get men out of the cold. This is where Ephraim Sands excelled and at my request, he enthusiastically ran to the call along with a few others from the company. At home his skills as a hewer were unmatched and here, they proved unequalled. As worn out as these men were, they were in a big hurry to get warm in these huts so they were built quickly. He worked tirelessly and accurately much to the men's admiration.

When the huts were finished, I had Ephraim summoned to my hut. In he came, he was obviously tired but looked concerned as to what I might ask of him. "Sit, Ephraim". He slumped into the chair and said with a sigh, "Thanks Captain." I clapped him on the back and plunked a cup down in front of him. "For your hard work these past days." He saw the rum and said "But aren't these your rations, Sir?". Now it was my turn to sigh, "Tonight you are Ephraim and I am Jabez, two friends." I pulled out another cup and said "Here, we will both have a drink." He smiled and said, "That I can do, Jabez."

We enjoyed our drinks for a few minutes in silence. Moses came in and seemed surprised but happy to see Ephraim sitting there. He grabbed his own pint and sat down with us. Ephraim asked me if I had heard any news of Daniel. "I heard he is near Peekskill but that is all. With the re-organization of the army and us to be headed there in the next few months, I'm hoping at least to see him". I went on, "It seems to be quiet without his antics around camp." Ephraim nodded his head and with a grin and said "Aye". Moses grunted and joined in saying, "We have Phineas Towle and Ephraim here keeping things lively."

I had no idea what Moses was talking about but, felt that as long as I didn't have the arguing in camp and these men worked so well together,

I didn't need to be informed. Moses filled us in on the company news. "The men are settled in their huts. The horses have been put over in a field nearby where they can get some grass. The townspeople have sent over some hay as well. A hunting party was able to bring in some meat but it's not enough to fill all the bellies we have here." Ephraim asked, "How's Lemuel?". Moses filled us in, "Much better. He was able to help out a bit today gathering firewood. Stephen wouldn't let him go very far.", he said with a chuckle.

"Have you heard from home lately?" I asked Ephraim. "No, I haven't" he answered. "I miss my Elizabeth. I worry about her but I know the children are there to comfort and aid her. They are old enough to help her with the farm, thank God." "You've been married a lot of years", I stated. "A lifetime" he responded with a smile.

My thoughts were on Sarah and our two young boys. As if reading my thoughts, he said, "Sarah is sweet natured but, she is a good, strong woman." Moses nodded in agreement and questioned, "It's two years now. How much longer do you think this war will last?" I shrugged, "I have no idea. I fear if we lose, the British will be harsher with the Colonists. Ephraim, took a mouthful of rum before he spoke, "Aye. It started out as a protest about taxes without a voice. The money they took from us was being sent to another country with no benefit for the Colonists who worked so hard to earn it. I want my children to learn to work hard for what they want. How can I teach them that if much of what I earn is taxed to support someone else? I want a better future for my children." "Yes" said Moses, "We want our freedom from them."

Ephraim became quite thoughtful. "We talk about this at night. When we win this war and rid ourselves of this tyranny, we will be bringing home to our children a new world. They will have the freedom to become anything they work hard enough to do. Think of it Jabez, we will be handing to them a country that they will be the future of and in control of. They will determine their future because, they will command it. The government they design for themselves will be decided here, on this soil, not from across an ocean."

Moses and I let his words sink in. Ephraim was rarely serious in his comments, yet his words were inspiring. I said, "The guilt I feel of leaving my wife and sons sometimes smothers me. I can't walk away now. I know I'm fighting for their future. When It was time to re-enlist after Trenton and Princeton, I wanted to throw the pen and run, just run all the way home. I just couldn't do it. I want to go home free of England's rules but, moreover I couldn't leave all of you behind. All I could think of was Lemuel Rounds, as sick as he was, still moving forward to the fight." Ephraim nodded and said, "The men talk at night about the same things, my friend. It's what keeps our spirits up and remind ourselves of why we suffer this war."

I was looking at Ephraim in a new light. "You know Ephraim? You aim your words as straight and true as your axe." The three of us chuckled at that. He tipped his cup back, finished his rum and said, "Thank you for the rum and friendly conversation, Jabez." He headed toward the door and looked back at me. "G'night Captain" and with that he was out the door.

That first night, in the hut that I shared with the officers in my company, out of the cold was a luxury to me. There was a small fireplace inside and the warmth was a welcome sensation to my bones. We had many days and nights without rest or food. Some nights without a cover over our heads. I drifted off to sleep in my cot thinking of what Ephraim had said. It was the first good night's sleep I had had in a long while.

The next morning, I rose early and used the time to look at our surroundings. It was easy to see why Washington had picked this place. It is surrounded by hills. It would provide us some protection from the cold winds. I had climbed to the top of a hill and below me the views were beautiful. On the other side of the river, the British camps could be seen. Washington had men on duty up here keeping an eye on what the British were doing. I stayed for a while enjoying the peace and quiet that I rarely was able to enjoy and thought more on my conversation with Ephraim.

It was true that the men we had left home with had built a bond. When one man had a task, another would step up and help him. Of course, being huddled together surrounded by a mass of other soldiers, with lack of food and proper clothing in the bitter cold and long endless marching, followed by illness and fatigue brought on bad tempers and arguments. Luckily in my company arguments were short lived. At meetings with the other Captains, I found some men were stealing food, and whatever they could get away with from each other, including clothing. There were some serious fights and a few short mutinies which resulted in court martials. If found guilty, the punishments were severe including up to one hundred lashes on the back or their service terminated. In severe cases there had been a few executions. I constantly talked to my men about this and tried to deliver fair justice to their complaints so as to keep our troubles within the company. I prayed my company of fifty would stay true. My thoughts were broken as I looked below at our camp starting to stir. It was time to head back. I needed breakfast.

As I sat down to eat, Moses appeared. "Captain, there is to be an officer's meeting in one hour." "Thanks, Moses.", I said between bites. Samuel Brooks who was usually very quiet spoke up, "Sir, how long are we here for?" All eyes were on me. "Not sure but, I wouldn't mind staying in a small, warm hut for a few weeks." "Aye" the men responded in agreement. We went over the plans for the day and who would be doing what for chores. That settled, I left to attend the meeting.

Washington himself informed us at the meeting. "Varnum has been promoted to Brigadier General and has been sent home to recruit more men in order to build another regiment. Colonel Hitchcock has died, Colonel Angell is now put in charge of Hitchcock's Rhode Islanders and Colonel Christopher Greene, cousin to General Greene now has command of Varnum's old regiment." He followed that with re-assigning some of the companies to different regiments. Our company was now put under the Colonel Thomas Nixon of General John Nixon's command. I looked over to find Colonel Nixon's eyes on me. I nodded with a smile. I liked the Colonel very much. I had met his brother John, the General many years ago. He and his brother had arrived at Crown Point just two months after my father died in 1756. The General was a Captain during the French and Indian War and well-liked by those in his company.

When the meeting concluded, the Colonel had requested my atten-dance so I immediately went to him. He welcomed me and invited me to sit. With a smile he said, "My brother, the General remembers you as a young lad at Crown Point. He also tells me your brother; Daniel is with him in New York." Eager to have news of him, I interrupted him, "How is he?" The Colonel replied, "He's well and the General thinks highly of him. I'm told he is a hard worker as well as a steadfast soldier." I nodded and said, "Thank you, Sir. He is." I added, "John is also a good man and was a great Captain but he had one argument too many with the army and went home." "Yes", he nodded. "There has been shall we say, "struggles within the ranks".

After a few uncomfortable seconds, he went on, "I remember John quite well, I know losing your father at the time was hard on all of you, but your brother kept control of himself and his surroundings which was quite remarkable for a young man of his age in that position. I wish I could have more men like him in my command. I'm sure your father would be very proud of all of you." I had a lump in my throat at his kind words and thanked him for saying so. "What about you Jabez? Have you your own family?". I told him of my beautiful Sarah and the two small sons at home. He listened to me with a wistful smile while I talked.

I was becoming comfortable with the conversation and said, "I have heard the stories of your bravery at Breed's Hill in Boston." He only shrugged and said, "The company fought bravely, we were also the last to leave the hill. It was my brother, the General who was wounded in Boston." "I'm sorry, Sir. It was his leg if I remember correctly.", I interjected. The colonel said, "Yes, but he is recovered now and waiting for us in New York." he replied. I asked him about his family and a look of pride clearly showed in his face. My children are well and growing. As a matter of fact, my son, Thomas Jr is a fifer here in the regiment." "Very good.", I responded. He spoke with fatherly pride regarding his son.

He looked at me with a questionable expression, asking me, "What was this story I heard about you and a drum in the last war?". Being at ease with the conversation, I didn't mind related the story to him. His laughter was genuine and he joked, "So, the drum beat out the tomahawk?". I chuckled and nodded at his quip.

After a few moments of silence, he took on a serious tone, "We are to stay put due to the winter weather. In the meantime, we will be monitoring the British." I asked him, "What do you think our next move will be, Sir?" "Not sure.", he answered, but went on, "I believe we are going to be trying to hold on to the northern territory in New York. We must maintain control of the Hudson River and keep whatever Brits that are in Canada, in Canada." I quickly responded, "I agree, Sir." He stood up and shook my hand and said, "Let's hope our Generals agree with you and I. It was nice speaking with you, Captain." He released my hand and I saluted him and hurried back to my company.

The next few months were the coldest of my life. If not for the huts we had, I fear with the scant clothing (which I was still requesting) and the huts we had been using; we would surely have died from this blasted cold. If the men were not on work duty, parade or patrols, they were in their huts keeping themselves warm. Dysentery had become a common plague through all the camps, along with smallpox. Our company was no exception. I worried constantly about the men's health.

Colonel Nixon called the officers in for a meeting. He greeted each of us as we came in with "Shut the damn door!". He was sitting closest to the fire and as each man filed in, he took the next chair closest to the fire. Captain Toogood leaned over and said, "He doesn't sound happy. Is it the cold or are we in trouble for something that might have happened?" Captain Harwood replied, "Can't wait to see what this is about.".

The Colonel cast his eyes toward us. Fearing we had been overheard, we sat quietly and waited. Finally, he stood and addressed us. "The small pox situation has become so dire that Washington had ordered every man be inoculated. The church nearby that has been set up for a hospital, is overflowing with the sick and dying. You are to see that every man complies." The room was completely silent. He then asked for reports from each Captain as to their company. Each Captain had the same complaints which were; the rags the men had for clothing, shortage of food and illnesses.

The Colonel's irritation was quite clear but it was not directed at his officers. "I understand the situation and have been aggressively making requests." He went on, "To make matters worse, we have a lot of men leaving and heading home. General Washington is clearly distressed and is sending to Congress for more. Trust me, we are trying to get aid here as best we can. In the meantime, let's see what we can do from here to get these men comfortable. Scouting parties must continue, they will hunt for food as well. When these men come in from patrol, the men here are ordered to make sure there is a fire and food ready for them." The Captains nodded their heads in understanding.

Before he let us leave, he informed us, "I will personally be walking around the camps. I would like to make sure huts are clean, the latrines are properly taken care and check with the men myself. Good day, men."

Outside, I stopped and had a short conversation with Captains Holden, Toogood, Buckmaster, Spur and Harwood. Captain Toogood said, "Guess the men are going to be unhappy with us in the next few days.". Captain Spur replied, "If it keeps me from getting sick, that's fine with me." Captain Toogood added, "I've heard the inoculations themselves will make you a little sick." Captain Holden offered, "Maybe we should keep that part quiet until the inoculations are done?". Captain Harwood ended the conversation with, "It's cold. I'm off to get the men together and inform them." We all said our quick good-byes and headed in our different directions to camp.

The Captains under Thomas Nixon were likable. I learned they had been together a while. They shared each other's concerns and offered advice to each other. I hoped the winter with them would be amiable.

I was surprised to see that inoculations began the very next morning. I made sure the whole company complied with the order. The inoculation in fact, did make us all ill for a week. Moses openly cursed and railed at me when we were in our quarters but he had really gotten ill from the inoculation, so I let him be. It was the first time I witnessed his temper. His temper because of his illness did not diminish my respect for the man.

Not long after that, supplies came in. It included much better clothing for the men and they were happy to receive it. Some supply wagons came through and we were able to get some hearty dinners into us but, with thousands of men in camp, the food supply obviously got thin pretty quick. The morning after we had received the clothing, Moses was about to open the door of the hut to leave when I yelled, "Good God! What is wrong with your legs?" He looked down at his legs and a huge grin split across his face. "Warmth Captain. I never planned to be an example of fashion." With that he strode out. Instead of discarding the old, worn-out rags, he stuffed the old stockings inside the new ones. He was left with lumpy looking legs.

When the company was called up for parade, I had in front of me a company of lumpy legged soldiers with idiot grins on their faces. I made no comment on it, they did their work and they did it well. They had the right to find warmth in whatever way they could. When the Colonel arrived to inspect our camp, he was pleased with the look of the huts. He stopped to talk to the men and seemed quite pleasant with them. I waited off to the side until he finished. He strolled over, rubbing his hands for warmth. He addressed me, "Captain, I'm pleased to see the camp is clean and neat. I see the men are clean as well." I replied, "Thank you, Sir." That was it. He just walked off toward the next camp. He never said a word about their "lumpy legs", he also did not comment on their neat appearance.

Toward the end of April, orders were received and we followed Colonel Nixon on the march to Peekskill in New York. The past few months were quiet and the company was in fairly good health. The idleness had started to wear on them as their thoughts were turned toward their families at home. I understood how they felt as my daily thoughts were on Sarah, the children and the rest of the family back home. The idleness brought on some bickering between them. It was a relief to march away from Morristown. I had hoped once the march to Peekskill began their moods would improve. This was not the case at all. It started to grate on my patience with the men constantly grumbling and sniping at each other. I had had enough of this.

One morning, after hearing one comment too many the night before, I called them to reveille. They all stood before me. I began with, "Men, we have been tasked with a dangerous mission. It is quite likely you may be caught or killed. For this I will need ten volunteers." I looked at fifty men standing before me, with confused looks on their faces. Only weeks before, their biggest complaint was of their idleness and questioning why they were not fighting Brits. I stood patiently for a few minutes keeping my composure.

At last, Phineas Towle stepped forward and right behind him, William Andros. My temper got the better of me and I addressed them all. "I requested ten and only two have stepped forward?Last night, all I heard were complaints about boredom. The two men I have heard the least from, stand in front of you." I ordered them back and forth in front of the company. "Take a good look the rest of you. These are bravest men in the company. Take warning, you will be seeing more Brits soon enough. Do you already forget the battles we have fought?" As I looked around, I could see on their faced that my words had touched them. My temper now somewhat softened and finished with, "My greatest wish is that we ALL get home to our families when this war is over. We are more than soldiers. We are friends and family. We all have the same dream. Once we get to Peekskill we are going to be in the thick of activity."

To my surprise, the men started cheering. My ruse to stop their bickering, actually had rallied them together. I heard not one more word of complaint the rest of the march toward Peekskill.

Part way through the march the weather turned, so we stopped our march for two days. The Colonel took advantage of this and called his officers together. He asked the Captains about each of their companies. All reported things were well until Captain Toogood pointed toward me and said to the Colonel, "Perhaps you should ask Captain Lane how he handles disgruntled soldiers." Colonel Nixon said, "Please tell us your method, Captain Lane." I could only glare at Captain Bigmouth Toogood before I spoke. I told the Colonel and the other Captains (most of whom had already heard the rumor) about the imagined assignment.

The Colonel stood there staring at me, mouth agape. "Whatever possessed you of the idea?", he inquired. "Well.", I stammered, "They were complaining of being bored and I decided accommodating them would be much better than yelling at them to buck up." The whole room erupted in laughter when I wasn't trying to be funny. To my defense, I yelled, "Well if I stood there yelling at them, they wouldn't see my point." The Colonel looked like he was trying to maintain a serious composure and after a few moments, raised his voice over the laughter to settle the officers down. "I find that quite clever. He gave the men something to think about."

With that he turned to his aide, Captain Buckmaster, and with his voice just a bit louder said, "Why don't you come up with ideas like that?" Captain Buckmaster sat grinning back him stating, "I'm not that smart, Sir." This sent the room into more laughter.

By the middle of May we arrived at Peekskill, we were assigned to Major General Putnam's Division. During the march there, the Captains spoke quite a bit to each other. They used their conversations to help solve problems that may be occurring in their companies, help each other out and exchange ideas.

Captain Buckmaster turned out to be a good friend to me and well-liked by the other officers. He came from Framingham, Massachusetts, the same town as the Nixon family. Once we arrived at Peekskill, I, along with the other Captains, reported to General Nixon immediately. After informing where our quarters would be. General Nixon said, "Jabez, when is the last time you saw your brother?" Thinking something wrong, I was hesitant when I said, "About a year sir." The Colonel smiled and said, "His quarters are about a mile down the road. If your men can handle setting up your quarters without you, you have my permission to head down there to see him. I'll expect you back by tomorrow night. In the meantime, I would like to visit with my brother the Colonel." In my excitement, I almost forgot to salute him.

"Thank you, Sir!" I couldn't get out fast enough.

I actually jogged back to the company and gave them the news of Daniel's company. "One of the Boynton's asked, "When will we be able to see them?". My words rushed out of me, because I wanted to get going, "I'm headed over to Daniel's camp now. We will set things up so you can all see each other as expediently as possible. If I can arrange it, a few will come here, while a few of you will go to his camp. We need to coordinate this so there will not be any trouble." Moses gave me a nod saying, "Get going, Captain. If we can't figure out what things needs to be done here after all the other camps we've had to set up, God help us." I knew he had things covered. I thanked him quickly and went to get my horse. The ride down the road was a bit tricky so I had to slow down and maintain my patience. It is springtime and with that comes a lot of rain and snow melt. Add a few thousand men marching back and forth and you have a total mud pit to maneuver.

I got to Daniel's quarters and as I got down from my horse, the door burst open and out ran Daniel. Not known for any physical endearments, his huge embrace separated my feet from the ground. "Jesus man, I think you got taller!", he said laughing. One of his men, took my horse and Daniel had his arm around me hurrying us inside. It was the happiest feeling I had had in a long time. He quickly poured rum for us. I asked him, "Have you any news from John or home?". He began, "Not much but I know John and his sons are taking care of our farms the best they can. Everyone is well. My son Isaac left home with William Hancock, found me and joined up in January." I told him, "John's son, John Jr and Joanna's son, John Hancock are still with me and have become efficient soldiers. I'm sure the cousins would all like to see each other." Daniel said, "I expect the men from both our companies want to see each other. We are going to have to arrange that." I agreed with him on that. He listened to my idea and we formed a plan as to how to make it happen.

His expression became quite serious. I have some bad news. He informed me of Ebenezer's Redlon's death. One of Ebenezer's sons, Ebenezer, Jr., was in my company and I was quite sure he didn't know yet. I asked that he be called here immediately. Best he received the news from Daniel and not idle gossip. Daniel sent for a man from his company and I gave him directions on how to get to my company. Daniel gave him strict orders to not let Ebenezer know why he is being sent for. Daniel told me the story. "He had become quite ill due to exhaustion and fatigue. One day he could go no farther. We found a barn to shelter him. His son David and another man stayed with him until he passed. They buried him there beside the barn." I was sorry to hear the story. I liked Ebenezer as well as his two sons. He was a good man.

Daniel introduced me to his Lieutenant, Ebenezer Peabody who came from Boxford, Massachusetts. He was a genial man and even gave me his bed for the evening. He brought in some hay and made himself a bed in a corner of the room. My blanket was brought in and we settled in while Daniel looked in on his men. Lieutenant Peabody and I finished with the bedding for the evening and we went out to greet the others. It was good to see the familiar faces from home after a year. Being so far from home, everyone was anxious for any news that could be shared. I met some of the other men from other parts of Massachusetts including his Sargent, John Dain. I had met him a few years back while we were stationed in Maine. He was very happy that I had remembered him and we chatted for a few minutes. The Sargent then introduced me to Ensign William McKendry also serving as Quartermaster in Daniel's company. He was from Stoughton. He was a friendly fellow and it was obvious the men in Daniel's company got along quite well with each other. They spoke how protective Daniel was of his men. I had to ask, "Does he still portray himself as Alexander the Great?" The display of eye rolls confirmed it.

The conversation ended as Daniel came toward us. I looked over Daniel's shoulder with a nod and Daniel turned to see that Ebenezer's son had arrived. I looked at Ebenezer, Jr. who looked so much like his father, quite tall, broad-shouldered, and muscular; light hair, gray eyes, and ruddy complexion. We took him inside Daniel's hut and quickly informed him of his father. Daniel poured him some rum while he let the news set in. Daniel spoke, "He was much loved and admired in the company. He was good with chipping in and helping AND very brave." The boy remained silent.

He then related a story to Ebenezer about his father. "Let me tell you about our first battle. When the shells started whistling around him, he ran like a quarter horse some twenty rods, stopped short, ran back to the ranks and fought like a tiger through the remainder of the battle. That night at camp, the question was asked 'Uncle Ned, what in the world started you off? We thought the devil couldn't scare you.' He was all excited and started his stammering and said, "Well, y-e-o-u s-e-e, them shells went to which-on-em, to which-on-em, to which-on-em, and I thought they meant me, so I got out o' the way.'" It was quite true that when his father got excited, he stammered. Ebenezer smiled at that and thank us for informing him. His brother David had come in just then and the brothers embraced without a word. I offered my condolences to them both and David turned to Daniel asking for permission to leave. As they walked by, I reached out and gave Ebenezer a gentle tap on the shoulder. The young man's face was filled with sorrow and I felt for him. "Daniel and I watched the young man walk away to grieve with his brother.

We sat alone together and Daniel said, "Glad you're here. The men have been a bit cranky lately". I laughed and told him my story of what I did to the men on the way here. His head went backwards laughing. After a few minutes he gained some control and said, "No doubt your men will be telling my men, so I won't be able to try that ruse myself!".

I told him, "It's bound to happen. Being away from their families for so long, close quarters, lack of food sometimes and then when things are quiet, the idleness sets in. Their minds wander off to their homes and they become agitated."

Daniel agreed with me and then asked about where I had been and what the company had seen. I filled him in on our adventures over the past year. He went on to tell me his story, "I reported to Dorchester Heights. Spent a lot of last summer recruiting and then back to Dorchester Heights. I was a 2nd lieutenant under Captain John Wentworth in Colonel Ebenezer Francis' regiment. After a short time, we were transferred to Colonel Aaron Willard's regiment. By the way, Colonel Willard is a clockmaker. I hear his clocks are quite remarkable. In September, we left for Ticonderoga to support General Schuyler. Other than patrols and keeping our eyes on a few Loyalists and Indians, we were ordered to hold in readiness. Now we have Colonel Alden and have been placed under General Nixon's command."

He asked "What is your opinion of Colonel Nixon?" I replied, "I like him. He seems to be a good man and the other Captains like him." I looked up, "What of Colonel Alden?" Daniel shrugged his shoulders, "I just do as I'm ordered." I left it at that. I got the impression he wasn't fond of the man nor did he totally dislike the him.

Daniel and I talked about the news that the boys brought with them from home. Even though John had quit the army, he had gone home and was quite involved with the town militia protecting the town. What Loyalists lived in Buxton, had fled and the news was they headed to Canada. We agreed that the women and children we left behind would be much safer without their presence.

By the time we had finished talking about the news from of home, we were well into the rum and by the time my head hit the bed, I was sound asleep. The next morning, Lieutenant Peabody had coffee made and had cooked up some bacon he had wrangled out of someone somewhere. Daniel came in from outside with a half dozen eggs and the Lieutenant asked, "Ah! Great! Where did those come from?" Daniel with a devilish grin said, "Found em". Once again, I was laughing at his antics. "This is the best breakfast I've had in a long time", I remarked as I stood up. We went outside into the heat of the morning and started walking. "Brother, I'm glad to have had a day with you. I've actually missed you and the family so very much", I managed to say. Daniel put his arm over my shoulders, leaned in and said, "Me too, little brother, me too". I smacked him in the chest and taunted him with, "What my big brother can actually say something nice?" He was surprised and answered with, "And it will be another year before I share any concern for you, little brother." The rest of the day, went just as amiably. He introduced me to some of the men and we even ran into Colonel Ichabod Alden, his commander. After salutes and pleasantries, the Colonel left us with, "Good Lord, two Lane's in the same brigade. God help the Brits!" Daniel and I took a quick glance at each other and Daniel being Daniel, yelled after the departing Colonel, "Have you met our brother John, Sir? How about the nephews and my son?" The men around us were amused and the Colonel kept walking with a wave back at us.

I left in plenty of time to get back before dark. My mind and body were in a much better place. I was determined that the men would see their relatives camped here. The next day, as planned, Daniel had sent some men to me while I sent a few of mine off to him so they could visit with their relatives and friends. It worked out quite well and the men went back to their respective companies very happy. It was good to know that we were now in the same brigade.

Ephraim came to me and I asked him how Ebenezer was fairing. He glanced over his shoulder and said, "I'm not sure, Captain. He is unusually quiet but we're giving him space to come to terms with his father." "Keep an eye on him.", I said. "Will do, Captain.", and he was off. Low and behold, not a day later, Moses came running up to me while I was tending to my horse. "Captain, you better come quick. It's Ebenezer." I let out a "Damn", and took off with Moses. We came upon the men in a circle and they moved aside to let me in. Two men were holding Ebenezer and another two men were holding my nephew, John Hancock by their arms. Both boy's faces and hands had blood on them.

"What is going on here?", I barked. Neither one would answer. Still trying to not get angry, I said, "Should I just punish you both?". The expression on both boys now showed a bit of fear toward me. Ebenezer spoke first, "I told him to leave me alone and he just wouldn't do it." My poor nephew stood there looking at me. "All right then. John, you come with me.", I said crisply. John followed me to where I could have a quiet conversation with him. Once we both seated, I said, "Tell me what happened." John's words came out in a rush, "He's not speaking to me at all. He was airing out his blankets and cleaning his tent and I thought I would give him a hand with it. He did tell me to go away but I persisted and took one of his blankets to take outside to give it a shake. He followed me out and the next thing I know we are throwing punches at each other." I understood his wanting to help his friend. They were both the same age and were often seen together.

I sat there for a few minutes looking at him. He was obviously concerned about his friend. "John, he's grieving. I believe his anger is that he wasn't near his father when he died, not at you." John said, "Am I in trouble?". I thought for a second hoping I was handling this situation correctly, "Not as far as I can see. Let me have a word with Ebenezer. Go tell the men to send him to me and get yourself cleaned up. In the meantime, give Ebenezer his space for now. Can you do that?" The young man jumped up and said, "Yes, Sir", as he took off in a jog.

In a few minutes, Ebenezer came toward me. His feet dragging on the ground with a tired and sullen look on his face. "Sit down.", I barked. His expression changed to worry as he had never been the subject of my anger before now. "Okay", I said, "Tell me your side." Now he squirmed a bit. He had just attacked his best friend and the anger he had directed toward his friend seemed to have drained from his body. "I'm sorry, Captain. I shouldn't have done that." Still trying to maintain a stiff composure so he would grasp my meaning I said, "No. You shouldn't have. For Christ sake, you're best friends. You know as well as I, had he gotten angry, without a doubt he would have gotten the better of you!". We sat there for a few seconds so my words would sink in. I could see his eyes moisten a bit. He choked out, "You don't understand, Captain. That was my father.".

I softened my words when I said, "I understand better than you think, son. You are twenty years old?". He nodded his head yes and I went on. "I was twelve years old when I lost my father in the last war. I didn't know my father well growing up as he was always off fighting somewhere. Then, when I became a drummer boy in his company, I finally got to spend time with him. Even then, he was busy trying to run a company. I watched him die and I still mourn the loss of him. I was lost and didn't know how to come to terms with it but, I had two brothers who looked over me." Ebenezer's attention was intent. I went on, "You have a young man over there who thinks of you as his brother and he's doing the same thing MY brothers did for me yet, you chose to abuse him. He opened his mouth to say something but I waved my arm and continued, "I will also point out the older men have been keeping an eye on you too. I also know you have been sneaking over to see your brother at night yet I never said a word." Now his expression showed shock that I should know.

Feeling I might have gotten through I addressed him with, "Now, how shall you be punished for this?". He hung his head down and said, "I don't know." I let out a big sigh and nodded toward where John was standing, "I hope you have not lost the friendship of a very good man. I would have pummeled you right into the dirt, if it had been me. If I find out you have let your anger out on anyone else in this company like that again, I shall beat you black and blue myself. Now go and finish your work. When your done with that clean up. When I see you on parade in a few hours, you had better look shiny. No more sneaking out of camp!" He was stunned that this was the end of it. "Go!", I barked.

Ebenezer ran like a gazelle from me. I sat there watching him. As he neared John, he stopped and slowly approached him. What was being said, I could only guess but Ebenezer stuck out his hand and after a few seconds, John grasped it and brought Ebenezer in for an embrace. Then, the two of them headed toward the tent they were sharing. It was humorous to observe the rest of the company that had been standing around to see what would happen. Grown men who always maintained a 'devil may care' attitude had been really concerned with the episode. As Ebenezer and John walked away, there they stood quite pleased that the situation was resolved. At least, I hoped it was.

The first week of July, we were called up to an Officer's meeting. Colonel Nixon greeted us when we were all settled and informed us, "This regiment along with Ichabod Alden, John Greaton and Rufus Putnam are now assigned to Major General Israel Putnam's Division. We have received information that Burgoyne and Howe are planning an invasion from Canada. They should be coming by way of the lakes and travel south on the Hudson River. We have been ordered to sail up the Hudson to Albany and to support Schuyler." "When do we leave?" asked an officer sitting behind me. The Colonel replied, "We have only a few days to make ready. Best get to it men."

On July 8, we boarded our transports. Daniel was there to see us off. "Word has come in that Ticonderoga has fallen to the Brits", he told me. I had heard the news. He looked so serious and I slapped on the arm saying, "We'll go get it back while you take a nap." He lightened up with a wink and said, "My company is leaving here in a few days to join you. We'll probably get there before you as you will probably get lost on the river. We will be out scouting for Brits. If I find you, I'll try not to wake you from your sleep." We both laughed at the thought. We stood there quietly as the men and equipment boarded.

Once all was aboard, I was the last one to climb up and as I did, Daniel shouted up at me, "Watch your backside, little brother." I shouted back at him, "You as well." As an added measure, I threw out to him, "When you arrive, we will have had everything taken care of. Don't feel under any obligation to rush!" As the transport moved out on the open water, he had his hands on his hips and his head was thrown back with laughter that carried over the water to us.

We arrived at Albany four days later, on the twelfth of July. The Colonel was not happy when he gathered the officers together. He informed us that Schuyler was not happy with Nixon, he thought Nixon was too slow in getting there and didn't think that we had enough men in our regiment. There was some protest from the officers at that bit of information. However, the Colonel went on speaking, "We are to immediately head north toward Fort Ann. It's on the eastern side of Lake George. Intelligence has reached Schuyler that General Burgoyne has taken Fort Ann and is making preparations to head toward Fort Edward." Captain Japhet Daniels spoke up, "What is our role in this, Sir?" The Colonel looked across at us and replied, "We are to hinder his progress as best we can. We are to destroy any bridges we come across." He cleared his throat and went on, "Washington has sent us axes to bring down trees onto roads and any river passages we come across." There was silence at this bit of news. This was going to be grueling work. The Colonel spoke again, "General Washington has also ordered that should we be obliged to retreat, not to lose the axes. These axes are all the army has for supply. That's all for now."

With that he abruptly left us. He usually liked to talk with everyone for a minute or two. Captain Harwood left with me. He said with a chuckle, "Don't lose the axes?" Captain Buckmaster chimed in saying, "I wouldn't lose mine. That's a mighty handy weapon".

On our march out of Albany, we passed Daniel and those men that were arriving. I yelled over to Daniel, "Sleep too long?You're late!" He grinned and tossed back, "We'll be right behind you, brother. My company will catch up to yours and we'll see who can bring more trees down. Phineas Towle bantered, "Nah, Captain. We'll not only bring more trees down, but be able to catch a nap ourselves!" Both companies laughed and this brought on some more bantering between the men as they passed each other.

Within a day, Daniel's company caught up with us and was participating in the work. The bantering continued while they worked which brought on a small competition between the two companies. Each night, there would be a friendly argument as to who did more that day. Daniel complained to me, "It is completely unfair as you have Ephraim Sands." "I could give Ephraim tomorrow off, if you would like", I offered. "Of course, a good day's rest would have him ready to go the following day." Daniel countered, "How about if you use Ephraim but send two of your men to my detail to even out things better." I shot back, "Then it is no longer a competition if my company has to help yours". I could see I was getting the better of him and added, "You might as well forfeit." Daniel's response was without words, he abruptly stood up and left my tent absolutely enraged. He barely had the covering of the door shut when I actually clicked my heels in the air.

Working our way southward, the two companies chided and taunted each other as we continued to block roads and rivers. Even Daniel lightened his mood and had fun with it. We eventually made it to Fort Edward as tired as ever, however, scouting parties were immediately sent out. One to patrol the east side of the river and one to patrol the west side watching for British troops. Our scouting parties were harassed with hit and run tactics daily. It was crippling us but it further fumed the men's anger toward the British each day.

On the 19^{th,} around two thousand Indians attacked the Block House. We were able to send them off with cannon fire. Burgoyne was now coming directly at us. Daniel took a party of about thirty-five men on a scouting patrol. The next day, five of the scouts returned, one of them a Corporal. They were from Daniel's party! The Corporal said, "We were attacked by a large body of Indians near the House this side of the Fort. I'm afraid your brother and his men were taken captive." Fear struck me that the Indians had him.

My experience from the previous war taught me that prisoners were not treated well. The Corporal added, "Your brother's horse was left in a pasture up the road. He was clearly spooked and we could not handle him safely. He's there and hopefully calmed by now." I got permission to head out to find the beast and left with a small group of men. When I got to the pasture, the horse was gone. I came up on some men and asked if they had seen the horse. "Yes, Sir. It was taken by Major Whiting. You best head back with us, Captain. They have decided to abandon Fort Edward." My mind was screaming, "What about Daniel and his men?" As soon as I returned, I found wagons being loaded and the men and women getting ready to march. As soon as I got the company organized and ready to go, I found Major Whiting and inquired about the horse. He informed me that it was put in the service of the Continental Army. He made it quite clear there was to be no further discussion on the matter.

I reported back to Colonel Nixon and arrived in time to hear his orders for the regiment to line up. We were heading south for Stillwater. With the axes…

At Stillwater, we learned of a lady by the name of Jane McRae, who had been murdered by the Iroquois. Seems that she was traveling to Fort Ticonderoga to join her Loyalist fiancé. She was staying at the home of a friend Sara McNeil in a village near Fort Edward. The Indians had raided the village and the two girls were separated. Sara had been brought to Burgoyne for a reward. However, Jane's captors had a quarrel over the reward for her along the way. They killed her and took her scalp. Burgoyne didn't punish her murderers fearing that he would lose his support from the Indians. This outraged Patriots and Loyalists alike. This seemed to harden the resolve of the soldiers as the story quickly spread. In the meantime, I questioned everyone coming in for news of Daniel. All I learned was that he had been taken to Burgoyne and was a prisoner there. I prayed for his safety and the others that were with him.

We spent the month in and around Stillwater, we captured some British and Hessians. The month was heavy with rain. If not for the warm weather, we would have been totally miserable.

On the 16th of August, there was a battle in Bennington, Vermont which was approximately forty miles away from us. The Germans were completely surrounded and the Loyalist and Indian positions were overrun. Stark who led the battle and his militia were tending to the prisoners, were surprised with the arrival of more troops. As Stark and his men began to retreat, another group led by Warner arrived to reinforce Stark. Another heavily contested battle broke out and both sides disengaged when the darkness fell. The German's retreated and had lost a significant amount of men. It was a victory that roused the Patriot troops when the news was heard.

Less than a month later, September 9, Colonel Nixon's called his officers in for a meeting. Colonel Nixon, got right down to business with us, cutting us off from our usual banter before our meetings started. "Gentlemen, I'm here to inform you of changes in the higher command. General Gates has now replaced General Schuyler. This

I hope will relieve some of the tension in the higher ranks you have probably heard about in camp. General Burgoyne and his army at this moment marching toward us. Plans are being formed and I will keep you posted as to what is expected of us. In the meantime, make sure your men are prepared. We could move within days or weeks. That is all, thank you."

He was brief and obviously wasn't in the mood to discuss any more than that. We all rose and filed out. Captain Buckmaster gave me a signal to wait for him so I waited outside talking to the others while I waited. It didn't take long for him to record the very brief meeting and he joined us outside within minutes. We chatted outside for a few minutes before Buckmaster turned and said to me, "Share a pint?" I nodded and we took off to his quarters.

We sat down with our ale. Richard took a swig of his ale, "I'm glad that they aren't splitting up our regiment, Jabez.", he began. "I feel the same way", I answered. I took a swig and added, "I would have a hard time leaving the area until I hear word about Daniel." Richard sat still before he answered, "I honestly believe he will be alright. He's smart and knows when to keep his silence." He saw me roll my eyes and with a chuckle, "Jabez, he didn't come this far being reckless. But he sure does enjoy getting under your skin." I had to laugh at that because it was true. I told Richard, "When we were young, I was always quiet. Everyone was older than me and Daniel was louder. My father instructed me as a young boy that I would learn a lot about men and war by listening to *what* men say they will do and then watch *what* they do. Sometimes it is not the same." Richard nodded, "That is a wise way to measure a man." Nodding back at him in agreement, "With my brothers, what they said, they did and in return the men have trusted their leadership. I have never forgotten that advice from my father." Richard thought on my words before he said, "It's called honor, Jabez."

The conversation turned toward the Generals Gates and Schuyler.

"I heard about the tension between the two of them", I shared. Richard replied, "Aye, it has been frustrating. Schuyler is furious. He doesn't think much about the troops, so I'm not sure why he would want to command it." "Ego", I interjected. Richard leaned forward, "No matter. Gates seems to care more about the men and their welfare. He is cautious with his actions. Add to the animosity between those two Generals, General Arnold has been in a flap as he believes he should be in command." I said, "I heard those rumors, too". Richard rolled his eyes and went on, "General Nixon has been frustrated with these higher ranked Generals because it is affecting his command. Maybe now, with a decision of leadership made, there will be a lot less tension in the camp."

I voiced my concerns to him, "Gates was an English officer and is now a Virginian. I never liked the English officer's attitudes toward us in the last war and I don't like the Virginian attitudes toward us New Englanders. The Virginians consider themselves aristocracy and their snobbish behavior is a bit much to take at times." Richard heaved a heavy sigh, "That's true. They consider us clods and the officers can be quite uppity at times but, for the most part, the men within their companies are quite easy to get along with." I nodded because he was right about that, "In the meantime, I avoid them." I finished off my ale, "It's about time I got back to the company. Thanks for the conversation and the ale." He rose from his seat as I stood to leave, "Have a good day, Jabez."

I wandered back to the company. It was good to be friends with Buckmaster. He was smart and had a good ear and eye on what was going on in our regiment.

A few days later, on the 16th, I had just come back from a scouting party and received news that Daniel was in camp. I couldn't believe what I heard. Isaac had sent word as to where he and his father were and I went directly to them. I was directed into the tent where Daniel's men were all standing about outside. I entered and found Daniel lying on a cot. Both of his sons beside him. Isaac greeted me with "Uncle! Can you believe it!". The pure joy on this young boy's face tugged at my heart. For the moment, just knowing he was sitting with his father was all the remedy the boy needed. "How is your Dad?", I asked him. "He's very sick", he responded. The doctor said we were to let him sleep. He had a fever when they rode into camp. He pointed over to the other cot and said, "Captain Watkins came in with him. He's very ill, too."

We just sat with him while he slept for a while and finally, I got Isaac to come out with me. I had to get back to the company and persuaded Isaac and Daniel to get something to eat and sleep. I promised them both I would be back in the morning. As I mounted my horse, Daniel's men were walking the boys away and I knew they would care for the boys as well as they had been these past few weeks.

The next morning, after calling up the company and getting duties for the day assigned, I headed back. As I was coming up to Daniel's tent, there stood Daniel's Lieutenant, Ebenezer. He greeted me with "Welcome back, Captain". We shook hands and I inquired about Daniel and Captain Watkins. "They are both awake now, Captain", he said. On the ground by the door were blankets rolled up. I asked him, "Why are there were perfectly good blankets on the ground?". He shook his head with a grin and said, "Late last night, one of the men realized Isaac wasn't around, so he walked here to check and found the boy sleeping on the ground outside the tent here. So, he walked back to grab his blanket and a few of the men handed over theirs as well. They walked back, piled them on the ground and lifted him onto the pile. The boy never woke up." I clapped him on the shoulder and said, "Please pass my thanks to the men for taking care of the boy." "Yes sir", he said. He grabbed the pile of blankets and said he had to get back to the company. With that, I went inside. Daniel was awake and it scared me to see him so uncharacteristically still and quiet.

He was happy to see me and Isaac's joy was contagious. "How are you today?", I asked him. Obviously, he didn't look well and seemed irritated to be laying there. "Damned sick", he grumbled. I couldn't wait to hear his story, "How in the world did you get back here?" His answer was, "I simply asked the General for permission to go home being I was so sick and to take care of affairs at home." Captain Watkins in the other cot who was awake and had been relatively quiet, said derisively, "Burgoyne had had enough of him. Your brother disrupted things at every opportunity. Insulting comments at anyone that went by, especially the officers. Burgoyne even put us on horses and gave us escorts to make sure we got here!". I glanced at Daniel who just laid there smirking. I wasn't surprised at the man's story. After all, I had grown up with him and knew how well he could instigate. All I could do was laugh and told them both I was happy they made it back.

We visited for a little while and of course I had to get back to the company. Isaac had to get back to his duties. We left together. While we were outside saying our good-byes, along came Colonel Alden and the surgeon. The Surgeon spoke to Isaac, "How is your father this morning?" Isaac with a huge smile said, "He's awake and acting more like himself but he seems very sick". "He is a very sick man", said the Surgeon. The Colonel spoke, "We are going to send him home to recover. Burgoyne's army is marching toward us and we expect a battle in the upcoming days. Our Surgeons will be very busy tending to the wounded." He looked hard at Isaac and said, "I will let you go with him but, you are sorely needed here as well. I leave the choice to you." He answered Isaac's questions on how his father would get home and after Isaac seemed satisfied, he informed the Colonel he would stay. My admiration for the boy grew at that moment. He had the wisdom of someone beyond his years. The Surgeon went in the tent to tend his patients, Isaac went off to his company and I asked the Colonel for a few words.

Colonel Alden and I stood there for a few minutes. I said, "Sir, the story is remarkable. Why would Burgoyne release them?" The Colonel related what he knew, Daniel had in fact persuaded Burgoyne to release them but had sent a letter along with the escort. "The letter had conditions, we have his doctor, Dr. Wood. Your brother and Watkins were released in good faith that we would send back Dr. Wood. The other condition is that they would return to their homes and fight no further." "They are in no condition to fight at the moment", I said. At the Colonel's nod, I stated, "We both know he will be back to fight as soon as he is able." The Colonel nodded. "Your brother is a good Captain. He is a fighting man for sure. I prefer a man that stands by his convictions. We have been at odds with our opinions him and I, but I would welcome him back when he is better. I will for that day." Our conversation having ended, I went back to my duties. That night I wrote a letter to Sarah for Daniel to bring back with him. Once I finished it, I sent it over with John, Jr. I knew he would like to see his uncle before he left. I had suggested he write to his own father and mother, which he did. A few others wrote letters to send home and I was glad to see that John Hancock wrote to his mother. I knew Joanna would be relieved to hear from her son. The next morning Daniel was headed home.

Shortly after Daniel's departure, orders came down to prepare the usual two days of provisions ready to go and each man allotted half a gill of rum. The tension in camp was palpable as the men got themselves prepared to move. I had a moment with Captain Buckmaster and he passed on to me, "We are definitely going to face Burgoyne. The General says Burgoyne must be stopped." We were headed north.

September 19, a battle occurred at Freeman's Farm west of Lake Saratoga. We were near the battle and put on reserve in case we were needed. I was agitated to sit idly by. Hearing the cannon fire and musketry in the distance, I felt useless with orders to stand by. We could hear the noise until darkness came down on us. When Colonel Nixon met with us the next morning, he gave us the news. He started with "As you all could hear the battle was long. We lost about two hundred men to the Brits' six hundred men. The decision was to withdraw our troops from there. We are to continue south to Bemis Heights as Burgoyne's army is headed that way. Burgoyne wants to get to Albany and he will have to use the road through Bemis Heights to accomplish that." One of the officers asked Colonel Nixon, "Does that mean Gates is still in charge?" The Colonel nodded his head in the man's direction. He never gave his opinion on the politics of who was in charge. He went on to say, "He will be riding with General Nixon to Bemis Heights. Keep your companies sharp and in line. No one is allowed to leave their camps without permission. Unless on a scouting patrol at night, your men should be getting rest." We were dismissed and the officers were immediately off to see to their companies.

I managed a few private words after the meeting with the Colonel and asked about Daniel's company. I knew they were part of the front line. The colonel said, "I think they only lost a couple men but feel free to go check on them." "Thank you, Sir. Do you have any knowledge of my nephews?" "I sure do!", he said quite pleased. "They were both at the General's side during the battle. Kept their calm and gave the proper signals." Relief washed over me. I thanked him again, and left him.

***

BATTLE OF BEMIS HEIGHTS

About a week later, October 1, at Bemis Heights we saw our first signs of Burgoyne's army. There were small skirmishes daily. Gates kept the main troops behind the fortifications that week. During that week the Colonel gathered his officers together. He went over the duties for the day and informed me that I was to take my men and go out on patrol. When the meeting was over, he said, "Captain Lane, if you would give me a moment." "Yes, Sir.", I replied.

Once all the officers had left, he spoke. "Keep sharp out there, Captain. In addition to the British parties scouting us, there are colonists arriving to aid us. Don't be shooting at the wrong targets." I responded, "I understand, Sir." His composure was quite serious as he gazed at me. He went on, "Don't fire your weapons unless absolutely necessary. You will be giving your position away to any nearby Brits and trust me, they are nearby. I'm sending your company out because they can get through the woods so quietly." It was true, on every patrol we employed that tactic and were quite successful at it. "Understood, Colonel.", I answered. I dared to ask the Colonel about the arguing between General Arnold and General Gates. His expression became irritated but he answered my question. "I'm sure it is all over the camp and I can tell you, it is true the two of them have been quite hostile. Just this morning Gates has relieved Arnold of his command." At my shocked expression he added, "Gates prefers to lead with more caution while Arnold would run headlong into what I think might be a disaster. However, that is my opinion. He has been excluded from the commanding officer's meetings." My response to that was, "I hope it doesn't cause any significant chaos within the troops here. I'm sure there are men still loyal to Arnold." With a grin to the Colonel I added, "Glad I'm out of the fort for the day. I've had enough of the bickering." The Colonel nodded agreeing with me, "Aye. We can only hope Gates' plan will be successful against Burgoyne." Not wanting to waste any more time, I saluted the Colonel saying, "Aye, Sir. With your permission, I will get the company moving." Looking defeated, he returned the salute with, "Dismissed Captain. Good luck and exercise caution out there." I nodded and said, "You're welcome to join us, Sir." The Colonel grinned and said, "I might enjoy myself too much." Grinning back at him, I left to gather the company.

I chose about twenty men and the others wanted to go but, I needed the best and a few so as not to be spotted. The more I took, the more chance of noise we would be making. Moses wisely made sure each man had a bayonet and a knife before we headed out. The company was more than happy to get outside of the fort. I chose to leave heading away from the direction of where the Brits were camped. Once we entered the woods there, we turned toward the outskirts of Burgoyne's camp. After about an hour of moving from tree to tree, I heard a familiar bird call the men used as a signal coming from my left. I raised my hand to the men that could see me to hold their position which they passed on down the line. I moved over to where the signal came from.

There was Abiatha Woodsum and Elijah Bradbury with a Brit standing in front of their bayonets. I looked around me for signs of anyone coming to this man's aid. Seeing none, I spoke very quietly to him, "If you so much as sneeze, it will be your last sound on this earth." The frightened soldier nodded his head that he understood. Continuing on in a low tone I asked, "Are there any others close by?". He just stood there. Irritated Elijah nudged him with his bayonet. The man quickly pointed over his shoulder to his right. "How many?", I growled. He held up three fingers.

I directed Elijah to move this man toward the rear of the company and stay put. He was to direct ten men toward me. Elijah nodded he understood while Samuel tore fabric from the soldier's uniform and wrapped it around his mouth, tightly. The man's eyes bulged. Samuel whispered fiercely, "Your very life depends on how quietly you walk right now." The man was terrified, frozen to the spot. Elijah growled, "Move, Red Coat!". They brought him to the back of the company while I pondered the situation.

When Samuel returned with the requested men, we worked our way to the area the soldier had pointed toward. We soon found the three men sitting on the ground talking between themselves. They were so absorbed in their conversation, they never heard us circle around them. I stepped up to them. One made a move toward his rifle and I said, "I'm not alone." My company stepped out from the trees and the three of them instinctively put their hands up in surrender. We bound their mouths and marched them back. "Elijah", I commanded. Elijah stepped forward and said, "Yes, Sir." My order was, "Go with Samuel and take a quick look around. Meet me back with the men." I was quite sure there was no one about but wanted to make sure. Once we all regrouped, we headed back to the regiment.

Colonel Nixon met us as we entered camp, quite pleased. He addressed the whole group saying, "Good job, all of you. Take the prisoners to General Gates, I'm sure he would like a word with them. I will be right along." I dismissed the group and walked with the Colonel towards General Gates tent. "Did you see anything else out there?", he asked. "Yes, Sir. We came upon some men headed here to join us so, we gave them direction. I hope they arrived without incident." His answer was, "Yes, they did. They told us of a company of men they had spoken to." I went on, "As for activity around Burgoyne's camp, it's surprisingly quiet. We were quite close to where he is supposed to be and only came on these four men." The Colonel listened intently to what I had to say and said, "Thank you, Captain. Go and rest. We will be sending out another patrol shortly."

Elijah and Samuel had come up to us at that point and I bid the Colonel a good day. On our walk back, Elijah and Samuel were quite chatty. It was very common with the men coming back from a stressful situation. I asked them, "Was the General pleased with his gift?". "Oh yes, Captain. Quite pleased. When he questioned the prisoners, he was informed they never heard us come up on them.", said Elijah. Samuel added with a laugh, "Must have been Lane's company and he asked if that was so, which I proudly told him 'aye'." I chuckled with them and said, "We have been ordered to rest so we should get right on that."

During that week, thousands more men arrived to join us. My company was ordered out on another patrol but it was uneventful. I hoped something would happen soon as the camp was filling up and I worried about the sickness that accompanies so many men living so close. The company by now was quite adept at keeping close together but I did remind them of the idea. One could almost feel that something big was about to occur and I constantly badgered the men about keeping their equipment clean and the rifles on them at all times. Arnold was still in camp and Gates still had him locked out of conversation. There would be no reconciliation between them that I could see.

October 7, Burgoyne's forces attacked the left flank. Our regiment was on the right. At the beginning, we were not in the major battle but, we were involved in heavy skirmishes that came our way. Soon we were involved in man to man combat but we held our ground. We were so involved, I had but little time to check on the situation with the men around me. What I did see was each of them together as a group always pushing forward. After what seemed like hours, the fight drained out of the Brits and they withdrew. Our position was held but with cost. The company knew to come to me and once we were altogether, Moses reported, "We've lost two good men and ten are injured." I looked at the men in front of me, all were covered with blood. I turned and acknowledged Moses with a brisk, "Thank you.". To the men I spoke, "You all did well. Those that are hurt, get your wounds tended to. The rest of you are to tend to your weapons and take a quick rest but remain here. We need to remain on the ready. I do not know for certain if this is just a reprieve in the battle. I should be back shortly."

I found the Colonel quickly along with the other Captains. I joined the group and waited for the Colonel to speak. He wanted to know the status of our companies and each company captain reported. The Colonel then addressed us, "I'll tell you what I know so far. We have won the day." There was a murmur among us but the Colonel held his arm up to silence us and continued, "It was a bit confusing on the field. When the British advanced, Arnold against orders from Gates entered the field. It caused some chaos among the Generals however it was the marksmen from General Morgan's brigade who identified a British officer and shot him down. It took the fight out of the Brits and they have retreated." Captain Buckmaster asked, "What are our orders now, Sir?". The Colonel informed us all, "Get your companies in order and stand ready for the moment." With that we were dismissed and he left us.

I turned to head back but Captain Buckmaster requested a minute from me. "Sure.", I answered. He said to me, "I received word that one man from Daniel's company had been killed." I held my breath and asked, "Who?". "Ebenezer Dain", he replied. I remembered meeting him once at Daniel's camp. I realized Captain Buckmaster was waiting for my reaction and I obliged him. "I met the man once. Likeable man. I believe he came from Lewiston." I thanked him for the news and we began walking.

Captain Buckmaster changed the subject saying, "It was quite surprising to see General Gates deciding to confront the enemy in the open fields." "Aye. He is usually a lot more cautious in his plans.", I responded. By now we were where Buckmaster's men sat and my company was just a bit beyond them. Buckmaster sighed and said, "It feels good to 'win the day', mimicking the Colonel. He was spot on in his miming of the Colonel, I laughed and waved good bye as I walked on.

***

FISHKILL RIVER

Five days later, on October 11, Gates received a report that it looked like Burgoyne was in retreat. Gates ordered an attack. We, under Nixon were to be at the head of the army with Morgan's men behind us. On reaching the Fish Kill River, the water was shallow as we crossed but, the fog that was so dense I had a difficult time seeing who was next to me. The air and water were cold that time of year so when we were ordered to halt and stand, I couldn't help but mutter a few expletives. Nixon was already across and climbing the slope. As we stood there, the fog quickly lifted and there in front of us was the Burgoyne's army and his cannons glaring down at us. I saw Nixon turn back toward us. I wheeled my horse around shouting at the top of my lungs, "turn and take cover!". At the same instant, the canons started firing. We could hear and feel the wind of the balls whizzing by. On queue the company, stayed with me and we crossed back behind trees and rocks. For the minute, the company was in a relatively safe position. However, Nixon's rear guard took the punishment. Several of his men went down. Seeing Nixon coming toward us, I thought maybe he had been shot as he rode rather awkwardly toward us. By the time he reached the woods, he had slouched even more. Dread took over as we watched a man take the General's reins and run him deeper into the woods out of sight.

My concern was confirmed when one of Gates' aides finally arrived with orders. General Morgan wanted all the officers to report within the hour. As I approached the Colonel, I voiced my concern about the General, "Was General Nixon hit?" The Colonel spoke loud enough for us all to hear, "No. When the General was riding back, a cannonball flew so close to his head that the repercussion had affected his ears and eyesight and at the moment he cannot hear anything. He is quite dizzy and is being tended to now." Every man went silent. The Colonel further explained, "A few of the men near him were shot. I do not have the specifics on that yet." When he hesitated Captain Spur offered, "We wish the General a speedy recovery, Sir.". It was clear the Colonel was distraught over what happened to his brother, the General. Captain Harwood said, "We understand if you want to be near your brother." The Colonel nodded and went on saying, "Thank you. Before I hurry off, let me fill you in on what we know. I learned that Glover's men had captured a British soldier and when questioned, he informed Glover that the British that had been waiting on the slope for us. The General had already started to cross and Morgan immediately dispatched a man to get word to the General to stop us. The General had already turned back moments before the cannonade. Had it not been for the warning, our conversation would be quite different." We left the Colonel to meet with Morgan. Morgan gave us orders to stay put until further word was sent. Colonel Nixon and was tending to his brother and we would take direction from him in the meantime.

I shuddered at the thought of what the outcome had been if we had continued on. The British were uphill from us so, we would have been destroyed had we fallen into their trap. With the Colonel gone to his brother, every officer around me was deep in thought as we silently returned to our companies. I related what I knew to the rest of the company. The men were silent while I spoke. He was well liked by those under his command.

We stayed where we were. As luck would have it, we had Burgoyne's army surrounded. For the next week more troops arrived and we had Burgoyne completely boxed in. It took a week but finally on the morning of October 14, Burgoyne sent a flag of truce offering his surrender to General Gates. It would be another week before the formalities of the truce were worked out.

On that final morning, we were on the field collecting the rifles from the six thousand surrendering British. Burgoyne and his officers were marched to General Gates' tent for a formal surrender. I was told that Burgoyne handed his sword to Gates as was the formality but in a show of respect, Gates handed the sword back to Burgoyne.

The army marched the prisoners to south to Albany. There, a detention camp was set up. Our company was fortunate to be billeted at a house. Some of the men used the barn behind the house we secured for a barrack. Most of the rest of the regiments were able to find a secure roof over them. I was sitting with Moses and Ephraim when Colonel Nixon called on the Captains for an officer's meeting. As I stood to leave, Moses said, "Pray we don't have to suffer the role of prison guards." Ephraim's response was, "We all have our turn at Guard." Moses' tone was almost a whine, "But there has to be over six thousand of them! There could be a lot of trouble." "Relax." I snapped. "You won't be alone with them. There are multiple companies guarding them at a time. You make sure the company is alert when on duty." Moses clamped his mouth shut but his look was defiant. I turned and headed toward the Colonel. I could not voice my concern over the matter as I agreed with Moses. He most of all, didn't like being idle and waiting for something to happen made him edgy. On the field, he was the best I had. Off the field, he was even better at tending to the company.

Colonel Nixon began the meeting with "General Bracket's brigade is to take the prisoners to Cambridge. There will be a few companies chosen to escort the prisoners to Boston. The plan is to move them as soon as possible." Captain Spur interjected, "That's a relief, Colonel." Peter Harwood asked, "And how is the General's health, Sir?" The Colonel responded, "I believe he will be deaf in one ear for the rest of his life. He is having terrible headaches. He has applied for furlough and is waiting on a response. In the meantime, I will decide who from this regiment will escort the prisoners." A few of the captains, myself included, volunteered our services. "Thank you, I will inform you all in the morning."

The next morning, the Colonel summoned me. I entered his hut and greeted him. He stood and said, "Captain! Thank you for being so quick." I responded, "Not at all, Sir. I wasn't far away." He cleared his throat and said, "I appreciate you volunteering your company yesterday but, the truth is, your company is needed more here as they are best scouts I have. You know the area better than most. Not to mention the fact that you and your men have so much experience." "Thank you, Sir." Inwardly I felt good about not telling the men they had to make another long trek to Boston. He continued, "With that said, I'm assigning you to go out on patrol today. Take your men North of here. There was a report of some Indians spotted. See if you can find them and round them up. Maybe they can offer some information to us." "Aye, Sir." With that I left him, gathered the men and went off to patrol.

On patrol, all had been quiet for a few miles. William Andros and John Cole alerted me to a noise to our left. The men instinctively hunkered down keeping their silence. I motioned for Daniel and Isaac Boynton as well as Phineas Towle to come with me. We crawled up toward where the sound was coming from and found a group of six Indians engrossed in a conversation. I motioned for the men to split and circle around. Once all were in position, I stood up and fixed my rifle on them. They looked up in surprise ready to sprint. That was when my men stood, rifles fixed as well. With a motion from the rifle,

I directed them back toward the company. After trying to question them, they either didn't or wouldn't speak English with me. I didn't waste time with them, didn't care to. We walked them back to Camp.

We handed them over to the guards and I reported to the Colonel who's first words were, "Good work, Captain." I answered, "Thank you, Sir. I couldn't get any information from them." "Sit, please." He ordered. "Are you aware of Washington's lifeguard?" I responded, "Yes, Sir. Washington's lifeguard is his personal protection detail. They are considered the elite of the army." "Correct", said the Colonel. He went on with the subject, "He is looking for men to serve him. "He is requesting four men from each brigade. Should I have the choice, I would recommend your whole damn company but, he's not getting that.", he said with a chuckle. "However, per his requirements which I will read to you. Must be at least 5'8" tall, demonstrate cleanliness, honor, intelligence and sobriety is of utmost importance." I looked at him with a chuckle and said, "Not sure I'm qualified on the last point." He acknowledged my humor with a short chuckle and went on, "I have been observing the men for myself. One that commands my attention is Samuel Woodman from your company." Stunned but quite proud, I replied, "Samuel is a great man, Sir. He has a quiet demeanor and carries out orders perfectly. I would also offer he is my brother-in-law." I hesitated at the last comment. The Colonel's response was, "I was not aware of that. However, you confirm my opinion. I would like to recommend him and send him to his Excellency." I said, "Although he would be a loss to my company, I believe he would be a valuable asset in Washington's Guards. Shall I inform him, Sir?" He nodded and said, "Yes, please. Have him report to me and I will give him his papers. Oh, I would be pleased if you would inform your company that the decision was difficult for me. Every one of them are all worthy of the recommendation." I stood and with a "Yes, Sir." I jogged back to gather the company together.

Once all the men were gathered, I informed them of the news. To Samuel I announced, "Samuel, the request for you to join the Life Guards will be a loss for me. However, this will be a great opportunity for you. I will be proud to know that one of my men is worthy of the appointment. Before anyone speaks, the Colonel also asked me to pass on to all of you, that you are all worthy of such an appointment.

With that I congratulated the stunned Samuel." The rest of the company swarmed around Samuel, congratulating him. James and Joshua, his brothers, were visibly proud of their brother and couldn't resist teasing him. "You're in trouble with Sarah now. She told us to stay together.", said James. Joshua laughingly said, "Now there will be more room in our barrack." Samuel quipped, "It will be the Captain in the most trouble with Sarah!" We all shared in the laughter but I felt that familiar pain in my heart from missing my Sarah. After the congratulating was finished, Samuel went off to get his papers. When he left for headquarters, I stood with his brothers to see him off. We were all pleased for him but I understood their feelings watching their brother ride off. The Woodman boys meant a lot to me. I left them standing there with, "He will do well boys."

In November, at Colonel Nixon's officer's meeting, Captain Harwood stood first and asked, "Begging your pardon, Sir. How is the General's health?". Colonel Nixon responded, "Thank you for asking. The General, has been granted furlough and will probably be absent a number of months. The General needs to tend to his family and his health. He still suffers greatly from headaches." He looked at each of us before speaking again. He cleared his throat and began with, "It has been brought to my attention that there is a delicate matter at hand for us right here. For those of you that have not heard, it is being called the 'Conway Cabal'. I will tell you what I know. It was started by a letter written by Brigadier General Thomas Conway. He believes that General Gates should replace General Washington."

Some of us had heard of it and the room was silent as he went on. "There are other names attached to this scandal such as; Richard Henry Lee, Francis Lightfoot Lee, Benjamin Rush, Thomas Mifflin, Johann DeKalb, Samuel Adams, John Adams, and James Lovell. I do not know the truth of it with these men but, I am informing you myself. While I respect Gates, I stand with Washington. With that said, I will allow you speak freely here in this room."

Captain Barnes rose and addressed Colonel Nixon, "Sir, we have heard this news and have spoken among ourselves. Our opinion is in line with yours, Sir." The Colonel looked around the room at all of our nodding heads. "Thank you, Captains. I had feared disharmony between my officers on this issue." Captain Barnes spoke, "Sir. What is your recommendation when it is spoken of among the Camps?" To this the Colonel answered, "Thankfully we have been assigned to General McDougall who is a supporter of Washington. He is quite disgusted by this. I would request that you carefully stray away from any such conversations and your companies do likewise. It should be left to those Generals and Congress to resolve the issue." Captain Barnes and said, "Agreed" and the rest of the officers including myself acknowledged the Colonel's request with, "Agreed". The Colonel concluded the meeting with the orders for the day and dismissed us.

Walking back to our companies, I was with Captain Buckmaster and Captain Barnes. Captain Barnes spoke first, "What a mess this could turn into." Captain Buckmaster said, "Aye. At least the officers of this regiment are in agreement. I hear there are some nasty arguments occurring in the other camps." At my silence, Captain Buckmaster directed his words at me, "What do you say, Jabez?" I stopped walking and they stopped a few feet from me and turned to look at me. My answer was direct, "General Gates did win a marvelous victory however, I don't believe it merits upsetting the entire army. Washington has done an excellent job at pulling us all together. He took thousands of ordinary men and somehow created an army. He doesn't command any man to do anything he wouldn't do. Always the first in the field and the last off of it. He's earned this country's support and loyalty. Let the Generals and Congress take care of the matter. They can shoot each other for all I care." Captain Buckmaster slapped me on the shoulder saying, "Well said, Jabez." Captain Barnes said to Captain Buckmaster, "Why do you look so surprised?" Buckmaster with a huge grin actually said, "I don't think I have ever hard Captain Lane say so many words at one time." Captain Barnes responded, "Well you must admit, it was worth listening to."

We continued on toward our camps. Captain Barnes slowed his pace and said, "What you say is true. Personally, Gates I believe has higher aspirations when this war is over should we win." "As do I.", I responded. He said, "You know, if hadn't been for Schuyler's work and Arnold taking the initiative on the field, I don't believe we would have been successful with Burgoyne's capture." In agreement I added, "Gates took full credit for the victory, but I have not heard him speak of what the other officers did to aid him." We had now reached my camp and he left me with, "Washington I'm sure will prevail."

7

1778

January found the Conway Cabal still upsetting the men in the ranks. General Nixon was still on furlough. I had thought the previous winter was cold, but this one was worse. The temperatures were even lower than the winter before and there was no reprieve from the wind and snow that was constantly assaulting us. I had to suppress my agitation with everything around me. All of the men were miserable and took I pity on them seeing their lack of clothing. The cloth on my own attire had become tattered and thin. The men were hungry. We were weak from the hunger and the cold.

I had a chance conversation with Colonel Nixon when he was making his rounds. He greeted me with "Captain Lane! How are things today?" "Fine, Sir.", I answered. "How about yourself?", I asked. He shrugged his shoulders and said, "I'm very pleased to be under McDougall's command. The behavior of our esteemed Generals is ridiculous. It is best to avoid the conversations." I responded, "I would prefer that Gates and Washington handle it between themselves. I believe that Conway has stirred up a hornet's nest. It would serve us all best if they would concentrate on getting us food, clothing and supplies." "Aye", said the Colonel. He went on, "I should think this will be resolved soon. In the meantime, Gates and Conway are doing everything possible to annoy General Washington." I was uncomfortable with the conversation, so I changed the subject. "How is your brother the General? Has there been any news?" The Colonel shook his head and said, "I don't believe he will be back any time soon." It seemed he didn't want to talk about that either.

The topic was changed again when he asked, "How are the men in your company?". "Fine, Sir. They are cold and hungry." We need clothing, Sir, or there will be no army here by spring. Dysentery and the common fever struck a few but, on the whole, they are holding up well. They prefer being on patrol rather than in Camp. The marching warms them but they are weak from hunger. We manage some hunting along the way to fill our bellies." The Colonel said, "Aye. I heard your men even managed to bring some meat into the camp." He grinned and said, "I believe I have been a recipient of some of it. My thanks to you." "Not much, Sir. Mostly pigeons. Sorry we could not do better." The Colonel flashed a wide smile and replied, "Better than those damn fire cakes. Am I not correct?" I answered him with "Most definitely, Sir." The Colonel hearing the agitation in my voice, looked me in the eye, "Captain, I understand your mood. I am constantly begging for the supplies." With that he was off to check on the rest of the camp. I watched his retreating figure and thought of him. I wondered at how he managed to keep his composure with the ever-changing jostling of commanders and the constant complaints of the men. I'm sure he missed his brother quite a bit and was concerned about the General's health.

One morning, late in January, a very young man rode into Albany. The officers were gathered and introduced to General Marquis de Lafayette, who was now taking charge of Nixon's Brigade. I was fascinated with his accent, though he spoke English quite well. He took the time to greet each one of us and immediately got involved with the duties before him. He informed us that his orders were to invade Quebec. To his surprise, and ours, we had not been informed of his coming or any such invasion. He found that we had not been paid in months, were ill clad and even more ill equipped to undertake such a task. In the gossip that the men shared, Lafayette soon realized that this would be a fiasco and that the communications that Washington had received from his Generals here were a fraud.

At our officers meeting, Nixon informed us that Lafayette was frustrated and that he had written Washington informing him that, he believed he would be laughed at and his reputation tarnished if he proceeded under present circumstances. Captain Daniels asked the Colonel, "Is it true that Washington himself had requested our regiment to accompany Lafayette to Quebec?". Nixon nodded and said, "That is true. If Washington decides to follow through with this invasion. It will be our regiment to assist him." Captain Harwood spoke up, "We should be honored that the Commander has personally recommended us to the Marquis." The Captains as a whole liked Lafayette. He did not speak down to us as the British always had. His affections were directed toward freedom for the American people and his only goal was to help us achieve that. He had nothing to prove here and he showed it in his behavior.

Captain Buckmaster stood, "Sir, we desperately need clothing for the men. They barely manage patrols in the cold, how in God's name would they manage an expedition." I thought Buckmaster's words had surely angered the Colonel when in a steely tone he sharply replied, "I possess two eyes, Captain. I have sent one request after another for what we need." Now he eased his tone and went on, "I have also voiced my concerns about this proposed expedition. Lafayette is against it. If Washington heeds his friend's advice, we will not be going." I could feel the wave of relief as it washed over the officers at the Colonel's words.

Heading back to our companies, I found myself in another conversation with Captain Buckmaster. As our friendship developed, I found he had a sharp mind and an easy personality. He began, "Jabez, I'm thinking I like this General Lafayette. I feared that with his young age, he would be over anxious to put us in harm's way. From what the Colonel just said, I think he sees the overall picture of what can and what cannot be done." "Aye.", I replied. I added further, "I think in some ways he emulates General Washington." "How so?" asked Buckmaster. I was careful with my words, "He may appear boyish in some ways, but he roams the camps and speaks to all of the men, not just the officers. He listens to their opinions. Washington does the same and his decisions are made after he views the men, not just take the advice of officers. I see that happening here as well." Buckmaster agreed with me, "That's true, Jabez. He has in fact been seen sitting with the men." I added, "Also, I believe he will be in front, like Washington, if we have another battle to fight." Buckmaster said, "Do you really believe so?" I responded, "I will let you know later. He will be accompanying us on our patrol today." Buckmaster stopped short, his jaw dropped and his expression stunned. That's how I left him heading back to the company.

As the men prepared and mounted, Lafayette joined us. He arrived unaccompanied by his aids. I watched him greet each man as he rode through them toward me. There was no air of arrogance about him. I mounted and he rode up and positioned himself beside me. I sat there looking at him, quite uncertain. Did he expect me, a Captain, to give orders to a General? He quickly solved my dilemma saying, "Captain, I am here to simply to observe. It would be foolish for someone who does not know the area to direct someone who does. If you please, take charge." I nodded to the General and directed the men forward. I explained to him, "Sir, we are headed North of the camp as there have been a few Indian sightings reported." "Very good", he replied with his strong accent. I hesitated a moment more but added, "Sir, once we leave, we keep silent. We prefer to use signals to communicate as much as we can." "I have heard of this before but never have I seen it performed. I look forward to seeing this used", he responded. Ephraim let out a snort and received a glare from me. "Would that be a demonstration?", the General asked. "Yes, Sir", came from Ephraim.

Once we neared the area of the reported sighting, we dismounted and two men were to remain with the horses as we set out on foot. The General walked beside me. The sound of metal hitting metal came from his person and I stopped short to look at him. He quickly realized my concern and removed the embellishments off his uniform and tucked them in his pockets. I nodded my approval and we moved again, quietly. We walked for about an hour before we heard noise and turned toward that direction. We came upon a house that a group of Indians were obviously ransacking. We were less than fifty feet from them. The company crouched immediately and in unison the men knew what to do. The left side of the company skirted around the house, while the right side did the same. I waited for them to get in position.

At my signal, as a whole we stepped out from cover. We got about twenty-five feet before they realized we were there. One let out a war whoop, hatchet raised running toward us. We all had our rifles raised and I said, "Ephraim." Ephraim took the shot and the Indian thudded to the ground just a few feet in front of us. The remaining group of Indians looked around them. Once they realized they would suffer the same fate, the hatchets were dropped. I stepped forward, gun raised and motioned them to line up away from their weapons. Quickly, Moses and a few men were tying them up. I nodded toward Ephraim who with a few men went inside the home. After what was more than a few minutes, Ephraim strode up to me and quietly said, "No one in there, Sir. House seems abandoned." I acknowledged him with "Thank you, Ephraim." With that done, we headed back to where we had left the horses. Once there, we mounted up. Some rode in front, some beside and the rest behind, preventing the Indians from trying to escape. We continued to remain silent and Lafayette followed suit.

We finally neared the camp and the men began to speak to each other. I looked over at the General and he was looking intently at me. I smiled, quite pleased with the accomplishment and relieved that a General had not been harmed under my watch.

In the days that followed scouting parties continued. More men came into camp to join us and were schooled in military exercises. The Marquis ventured out with other patrols. I had supper with Captain Buckmaster and Captain Spurs at my tent during this time. The conversation was light and we talked about our families. Then it strayed on to military matters. Captain Spur said, "Lafayette went on patrol with us today." Captain Buckmaster said, "Went with our company a few days ago. I understand he had an eventful first patrol with you Jabez." I grinned, "Yes. I thought after that he would either stay in camp or never come out with my company again." Both men laughed as they already knew the story. I went on, "Actually, he earned my respect. He never hesitated or became a hindrance." "Same with us." both men stated.

Captain Buckmaster added, "The young man is always in good spirits. Your nephew, Isaac, is often tagging along with him in his free time." Captain Spur offered his explanation, "Makes sense, they are close in age and the two of them are anxious to observe everything." I spoke up, "It won't do Isaac any harm. Making a friend in the higher ranks may be to his advantage one day." Captain Buckmaster teased me with, "Or an advantage for his Uncle's company." I took the teasing in the tone it was meant. Buckmaster did not possess any bad feelings toward anyone. He was intelligent and because of that, he was also Colonel

Nixon's Adjutant. He never betrayed Nixon's confidence and for that reason, I felt confident in speaking freely with him.

I changed the subject and complained, "Is it me or this winter more severe than last?" Buckmaster was obviously in a light hearted mood or maybe the ale we were consuming prodded him to say, "No, Jabez. The cold weather is more severe the older you get." Spur thought that was quite funny and added, "Pretty soon the men will call you Captain Grandpa." I tried to sound mean and returned with a smile, "I'll the blow the first man's head off that dares to call me that." The three of us enjoyed the joke and the room filled with laughter. Buckmaster rose from his chair and picked up my blanket and tossed it over my shoulders saying, "I've got to get some sleep." Spur cocked his head toward me and said, "Now that, my friend, makes you look old." "Get out, both of you!", I yelled which only made them laugh harder as they walked out. Grinning, I stumbled over to my bed and went directly to sleep.

It was Isaac that brought the Marquis to me a few days after my supper with Buckmaster and Spur. When Isaac approached, I was surprised to see him. I greeted him, "Isaac, what are you up to?". He had a small group of men behind him and I recognized the Marquis directly behind him. My first concern was he might have offended the man. Isaac stood at attention and with dignified formality, spoke to me, "Captain, the Marquis de Lafayette has asked to speak with you".

The Marquis stepped forward offering his hand which I took hold of saying, "It is very nice to see you, General." He responded, "The pleasure is mine, Sir. I thank you for allowing me to patrol with you and your men. I have learned of the many accomplishments attached to your company. I very much admire what I hear." I chuckled and directed my gaze toward Isaac saying, "I believe Isaac may be overdoing it in his remarks about us, but thank you." "Not at all", said the Marquis.

He went on saying, "Actually, I had heard about you from the ranking officers. I just asked Isaac this morning if he might be related to you or your brother, Daniel." I relaxed realizing there was no trouble and responded, "Aye, I'm the lads Uncle. Daniel is his father. A few of Daniel's men are here with me now." The Marquis said with a great deal of empathy, "I was sorry to hear of all he has been through. Pray God, he will be healthy soon." I responded, "I believe he is on his way back, General." Isaac gasped as he had not heard the news yet. The Marquis slapped Isaac's back saying, "There lad, I told you he would be fine. Men with your father and Uncle's reputation don't stay down long." I said to the Marquis, "Thank you for your kindness toward Isaac. He is a good lad. I believe he will do well with his life." The Marquis looked at me as if sizing me up. I think he realized I didn't like to talk about myself and said, "The pleasure is mine, Sir. He has been quite helpful."

We both stood watching Isaac talking animatedly to his cousin, John Hancock. The Marquis breathed a heavy sigh and spoke to me, "Alas, young boys leave for war. They come home hardened men never having the luxury of enjoying youth to its fullest." His words struck a chord in me as Isaac is the same age I was in the last war. I looked at the Marquis saying, "Let's hope this war is the last one that young boys enter." "Agreed, Monsieur. Well I must be off. The decision was made to abandon the Invasion of Quebec. I am leaving to see if I can recruit the Oneida to our cause. If I am successful, I will bring them back to Valley Forge with me to meet with General Washington. I will be pleased to inform him his words were true about this honorable company." I was stunned at his last sentence and it must have shown on my face as he winked and said, "The General pays attention to everything. Adieu, Compatriot." With that he walked away with the small contingent he brought with him.

I stood there watching him walk away and had not noticed Moses walk up to me. "What was that all about?", he inquired. "He wanted to say hello.", I responded. We stood there for a few seconds before I said to Moses, "He called me Monsieur, I hope that was a compliment." "Of the highest kind.", said Moses. Glancing at Moses, I could tell by his expression, he didn't have a clue either.

In March, Lafayette left with a few companies to meet with the Oneida Indians. He received pledges from the Iroquois Indians and succeeded in recruiting fifty Oneidas. They left for Valley Forge with him.

Shortly after Lafayette departed, I was sent to Boston to acquire clothing for the men and supplies. I brought Ebenezer Redlon and John Hancock with me. Their friendship was as strong as ever. The two of them bantered the whole way and it reminded me of the banter that I used to share with my brothers. They certainly made the trip at lot less tiresome. Traveling was slow due to the spring thaw making the roads muddy again.

At one point my horse slid under me. The two boys came up to either side of me asking if I was okay. "Of course, I am!", I snapped. Seeing the concern on their faces, I immediately felt bad about it. I cleared my throat and said, "I don't know who was more startled, me or the horse." Neither one of them realized my attempt at humor so once again I cleared my throat and said, "Thank you boys. Wouldn't want your Captain to be covered in mud, would we?".

This last remark lightened up the mood and we rode on a way before John spoke, "Uncle, I mean Captain." I interjected, "Uncle is fine here on the road John." Then I looked at Ebenezer and said with a wink, "Captain to you son." Ebenezer's face was blank and John continued. "Now that the army has pretty much control of the North, do you think we will get home someday soon?". I answered him the best I could, "I have thought a lot on that myself. At this point, we need to keep what British troops in Canada, in Canada. Unfortunately, the British have stirred up some of the tribes in the area and the towns need all the protection we can give them." Ebenezer chimed in, "I don't mind fighting the Brits, but the Indians scare me." John added, "Aye, they are massacring the men, women and children in the towns." I joined in saying, "Yes, they are fierce. You must remember, most of them fought with us in the last war. Most have chosen to remain loyal to England. I can't help but wonder at what their lives would be like had we not moved in on their lands. You should remember, most of their homes were destroyed and their families butchered because of us." John returned saying, "I had not thought of it in that manner." Ebenezer added, "Like we did to the Indians that live around us."

I nodded and enjoyed the intelligent conversation with them. I said, "That's right. They just want to protect their lands and their way of living and it has been taken away from them, little by little." Ebenezer thoughtfully said, "What could we do to improve things?". Looking straight ahead I said, "We could go back to England and give them back their lands." They were silent thinking about that for quite a while.

We finally arrived in Boston. It was recovering from the Siege but very slowly. Instead of British soldiers swarming all over it was Continental uniforms everywhere. The people of Boston were out and about and were very receptive when we arrived. We found a kindly woman who allowed us a room in her home to stay. Once we dropped got our few belongings into the room, I turned to Isaac and John. "I will probably be quite a while, so if you two can manage to stay out of trouble, I will meet you back here for dinner." They two of them were excited about having an afternoon to themselves. Before they left, I made sure they had coins in their pockets.

Once I found my destination, I asked for the required goods and was disappointed to hear it would be at least a week before I would have them. I had desperately hoped to try to get home for a glimpse of my family. I could have sent for Sarah but having two small children, I wanted them all safe. Feeling dejected and sorry for myself, I spent the afternoon wandering around the city. I made it out to the wharfs and sat there for quite a while breathing in the salty air. When the hour grew late, I headed back to the house to meet the boys for dinner.

Mrs. Smith, the owner of the house, let me in. "Captain Lane! Those two nice young men arrived only minutes ago." "Thank you, Mrs. Smith. I will go fetch them." Mrs. Smith informed me, "The three of you are skin and bones. I've made a nice beef stew with fresh bread. I hope you don't mind but I would appreciate pleasant company at the table." My mouth began to water at the thought of a home cooked meal and said, "That is so kind of you. Let us get cleaned up." A huge smile lit her face and she beamed, "Ten minutes, if you please." "Yes Ma'am", I said rushing up the stairs.

When I got to the room, both of them were scrubbed clean, I mean faces shining and their hair was actually neatly combed. They had beaten the dust out of their clothes and looked quite presentable. I found myself smiling when I said, "I see you spoke with Mrs. Smith about tonight's feast?" Both of them went into action. They took my jacket and shirt and shook it out while I washed as much of myself as I could with the basin she had brought into our room. Ebenezer decided he would dust my pants and I promptly discouraged him from doing so while I still wore them. I assured him I would handle that myself. I let him take my boots so he could clean them up. John had a comb and made me sit down. "Ouch!", I yelped. "Your ripping the hair out of my head!" John kept on with his work saying, "Sorry, Sir. You should comb your hair more often." At a glare from me, he became gentle on my scalp and continued on with his work.

Once the devils were done, I stood ready to head down stairs. It was John's look that made me say, "What's wrong now?" "Nothing!", he snapped back. With a devil in his eye he said, "You almost look as good as we do." "GET MOVING!", I barked although neither one of them looked the least bit afraid of me.

Mrs. Smith had set the table with what looked like her best dinnerware. She was hustling about getting the food onto the table. John jumped up and took the heavy bowl of stew from her and brought it to the table. I was proud to see him show gentlemanly manners toward this woman he did not know and reminded myself to inform Joanna of the wonderful son she raised.

The food was heaven to us and we enjoyed every mouthful. We learned from Mrs. Smith that she herself was a widow having lost her husband in the war. Ebenezer asked her, "Do you have children?". "Why yes.", she beamed. "He is off fighting this war like you men are." "Where is he?", I inquired. "Honestly, I do not know. It's been a while since I have heard anything." John said, "I pray he gets home safely to you." She smiled at him and spoke softly, "Thank you, dear. I'm afraid he will have his hands full with repairs when he returns." By now we were finished with dinner and thanked her wholeheartedly for the wonderful food. She was quite pleased and said, "Breakfast will be ready when you awake." I quickly spoke saying, "You need not bother. We don't mean to cause you so much trouble." She let into me with a reprimand, "It's no trouble. I would like to think that somewhere out there, another woman is treating my son just as kindly." The boys were staring at me and I said to her, "It would be an honor to have more of your wonderful cooking. I thank you and I think I will get some sleep." I didn't get away from her without her giving me a brief hug. She quickly did the same to John and Ebenezer. "Good night, Ma'am. Thank you for dinner.", I heard them say behind me.

I slept fitfully through the night having laid in a nice soft bed. I woke up to the sound of hammering and the boys were gone. Coming down the stairs, the smell of bacon and fresh bread filled the air. I forgot about the hammering and followed the pleasant aroma. Hearing my footsteps, "Good morning, Captain!" came the cheerful call of Mrs. Smith. The kitchen door flew open and in she came with plates in both hands. "I'll bring the tea right out to you.", she said as she hustled back into the kitchen. "Where are the boys?", I called out. The kitchen door swung open again with her carrying my tea. "That would be all the noise you hear outside." "What!" I bellowed and ran for the door with poor Mrs. Smith hanging onto the back of my shirt trying to stop me shrieking, "They only mean to help, Captain." It sounded like they were destroying something, not help something.

Rounding the corner of the house with Mrs. Smith still attached, I found them. I stopped short in my tracks. John on the roof and Ebenezer on a ladder on the side of the house. Both of them repairing loose and broken shingles around the house. John saw me first and greeted me with, "Morning, Captain." I was speechless. These two could have spent their time enjoying the city and instead, were repairing the leaks and holes in this woman's house. Mrs. Smith, thinking they were in trouble said, "They insisted, Captain." I patted her arm and felt sheepish saying, "I'm sorry if I alarmed you. I thought they were breaking something." Together we walked back into her home and I finished breakfast amazed at the thoughtfulness John and Ebenezer had in them.

Once I was done with breakfast, I told the boys I would be checking on our supplies. They asked if they could finish their work there and of course, I told them they could. After checking on our supplies and confirming it would still be a few days, I headed back toward Mrs. Smith's. I came upon a store and went inside. I bought as much as I could carry and found my way back to the house. Mrs. Smith was surprised to see my arms full and quickly relieved me of one of the bundles.

"What have you done?" she questioned. I started unwrapping the bundles and informed her, "I picked up a few things and some food." She gasped, "You didn't have to do that!" I gave her a devilish grin and returned, "I know. Unfortunately, if you will allow it, we will need to stay a few more days. The food is to help supply your kitchen. I would like to help the boys with your house."

The woman's eyes filled with tears. Her voice caught with her answer, "Of course you can stay. It's been a long while since I've been treated so kindly. My thanks to you." I put my arm around her to comfort her saying, "Thank the boys. It was their idea." "Yes, but you allowed it.", she whispered. I turned her to look at me, "Mrs. Smith. Those two lads gave me a lesson regarding kindness this morning." The smile she gave me took ten years off of her face. "Yes.", she said with a wink, "They did, didn't they?"

We spent the next two days, inspecting Mrs. Smith's house. We repaired what needed to be repaired. John cleaned and got her garden ready for planting the best he could. Ebenezer found the paint I purchased and went right to painting the front of her house. Then he worked his way around the sides to the back until the paint ran out. All the while, Mrs. Smith cooked and cooked and cooked. Each meal was wonderful and between meals, she baked cookies and cakes. It was a pleasant few days and the boys adored Mrs. Smith. It brought the pleasant memories of home to me; sleeping in a house, tinkering with broken things and delicious meals cooked by the woman of the house. The sounds of the two boys giggling and chatting away was a bit of medicine to my heart. Finally, our supplies were ready and we had to return.

The night before we left, she insisted we leave with breakfast in our bellies which we obliged her wholeheartedly. Mrs. Smith said, "Thank you for everything you have done here." To this we thanked her for her hospitality. John bless his little heart said, "Mrs. Smith, back home my Mother is the best cook in the county. People come from everywhere to the Tavern she runs with my step father, just for her cooking." He looked at her quite seriously saying, "Your cooking and hospitality is just as wonderful as hers." I smiled and joined in with, "Mrs. Smith, you have just been given the highest compliment you will ever receive. My sister is in fact the best cook around and I agree with my nephew." She took it in the light it was meant and patted John's forearm. "My dear, I hope to one day meet this wonderful woman." Ebenezer surprised me saying, "I believe you two would be best friends. She is as nice as you." Seeing the moisture appear in her eyes, I immediately said to the boys, "Head up to bed, I will be up shortly."

They did what I requested and Mrs. Smith appeared with two cups of tea. She sat down with me and as I took a sip of tea she smiled and said, "Those boys are amazing. Your sister sounds like a wonderful woman." "Yes, Ma'am. She has not had it easy either. My father took us with him in the last war when I was but eleven. He died on the road to Crown Point. When we returned home, my mother died a month after our return. Joanna had been caring for her and our home by herself. She married a man shortly after and had two wonderful children with him, one of them being John." I pointed upstairs to where John was and said, "When John was just a toddler, his father was killed in a lumbering accident. Instead of coming to live with one of her brothers, she used her cooking skills and sold to a tavern keeper in town. She did quite well with it and a year later she was married to its owner John Garland. Together, they both run the tavern and keep up with an inn."

Mrs. Smith was fascinated with the story and asked, "Does she have a happy life now?". "I believe she is quite happy and has had five beautiful girls with him." I paused and went on, "Joanna still had the time to keep a watchful eye on me." Mrs. Smith wanted to hear more and asked, "What about your life? What is it like where you live?"

The woman was sincere in her questions and I obliged her curiosity, "I married Sarah only six years ago. We have two boys. My youngest was born while I was stationed at Gloucester. I've only spent but a few short weeks with him." She was astonished, "You have not made it home in all this time?". I shook my head no and went on, "I had hoped to maybe steal a few days to get there on this trip but, the supplies are held up here. Our town is set in the wilderness. I would not want her traveling with two small boys. It would be too dangerous." "I understand.", she whispered.

She sensed my sadness with the situation and brightened and took a stern tone saying, "You wait one second if you please." She hurried into the kitchen and I could hear pottery being moved around. In under a minute she plopped a bottle on the table. Taking my tea from me, she poured some of the contents into it. She managed to say, "It's my husbands. Perhaps this will help you sleep. I've managed to keep it hidden." She pushed the cup toward me and I couldn't help but ask her, "Why must you hide it?" She quickly explained, "Not everyone that takes a room here are as considerate as you and the two young men you brought. Some arrive on furlough and spend their time drinking. I've woken up to men sprawled on the floor because they could not find their beds. There have been a few arguments. One man thought he was going to bring a harlot into my home and I would not have it. This is no brothel!" Stunned at her words, I inquired, "Doesn't this frighten you?" Her face turned quite pale as she said her thoughts aloud to me, "Yes, very much at times. Mostly when a man returns drunk. I retreat to my room and hope they don't try to harass me there. One tried, but as soon as he opened the door, he was greeted with my kitchen knife." I gasped at her words thinking, who in the world would try to harm this kind woman. But then, seeing the drunkenness at camp, men did things that were inconceivable."

We sat in silence for a moment longer. I had finished the rum she shared and thanked her. I stood and informed her, "I have an idea. We will take care of it in the morning." She became confused and said, "Don't you have to leave at first light?". I winked at her and answered, "We will have time."

The next morning, as usual she was up and cooking breakfast. I instructed the boys as to what I wanted done. They accomplished it quickly and before we sat to eat. They took her out of the kitchen to show her what they had done. I followed the group to her bedroom. The boys had installed wooden hooks on the inside of the door and beside it rested a long board. All she needed to do was place the board into the hooks and no one would be able to open the door from the outside. The woman was delighted with their work. I could not tell you how many times she said thank you while we stood there. John informed her, "Now you can sleep through the night confidently."

We were whisked downstairs and fed immediately. When finished, I wanted to get moving and directed my comment to the boys, "Let's go men before we are listed as absent without leave." She gave us yet another firm hug and yelled, "Oh! Wait. I almost forgot something! I will need help from one of you for a second here." Ebenezer followed her into the kitchen and the two of them came back out armfuls of bundles. "For your journey back." I leaned over and said, these are the nicest smelling bundles I've ever been given. Thank you."

We packed Mrs. Smith's bundles with the other bundles we needed to bring back and mounted up. I looked back at her, standing in front of her newly repaired house. The boys turned back and waved one more time. I prayed silently for her son's return to this good woman and she would be okay in the meantime.

When we were but a few miles away from Mrs. Smith, I could see Ebenezer had something on his mind. "Out with it", I ordered. Ebenezer stammered, "You know the rifles we are bringing back, Sir?". I froze, "Of course. What about them?" Still stammering he managed, "Well Sir. We lost one." Feeling my temper rise and before I spoke, I noticed John looking back. I realized the boys had supplied Mrs. Smith with further protection. I let them squirm for a few minutes before I spoke in somewhat of a stern tone, "I hope some ammo and powder managed to get lost with it." Neither one of them answered me, but the idiotic grins on their faces confirmed my suspicion. I turned my face toward the road and decided to end the matter there.

I returned the last week of April to Albany from Boston to find Nixon's brigade was still under the command of General McDougall and sent to West Point for defense. Daniel had returned while I was in Boston and rejoined Alden's Brigade. Isaac and the rest of Daniel's company headed out with Daniel. They were somewhere north of here and I was sorry to have missed seeing him. We caught up with the regiment at West Point.

I went to see Colonel Nixon immediately on my return. "Captain", he greeted motioning me to a chair. The Colonel started with, "I'm pleased you were successful in obtaining supplies. I saw your brother Daniel before we left to come here." "How is he? Did he look well?", I questioned. "He looked quite well and was quite anxious to see his sons." "Very good", was my response and added, "Any word from your brother, Sir?" The Colonel shrugged, "He's doing well but the hearing on one side is no better. He has every intention of getting back to the brigade." Smiling I spoke, "It would be nice to have him back."

The Colonel was anxious for any news, "How are things in Boston?". I was happy to share my experience there, "Fairly well, Sir. Those poor people are still recovering. We managed to find a room with a very sweet woman. While we were there, the boys used their time to do repairs on her house." The Colonel's eyes opened wide, "Really? I would have thought they would be off enjoying the city." Laughing I returned, "Her cooking was remarkable. I think they were afraid of missing a meal with her."

The Colonel laughed with me, "True. Our diet has been more than awful." I thrust out one of Mrs. Smith's bags, "Perhaps you might enjoy something from Mrs. Smith." The Colonel opened the bag and the smell of her cookies wafted out in front of his nose. "Ah!", he said with pure delight. He offered the bag for me to take one but I pushed the bag back to him and rubbing my belly said, "I feasted on a bag with the boys on the ride back here." I stood watching him stuff one treasure in his mouth. "Sir, I should get back to the company." "Yes, of course", he said between bites.

On my way out, Captain Buckmaster was just coming in. We exchanged a few pleasantries before I shoved a bag in his hand. "What's this?", he asked. "From Mrs. Smith", I smiled and went out the door. He followed me to the doorway yelling, "Who?". Walking away, I was quite pleased with myself.

The months of April and May were quiet at West Point. Patrols brought back a few Loyalists and Indians who were interrogated for information. In June, General Nixon returned to the Brigade. Colonel Nixon informed us that General Nixon was preparing for General Washington arrival at West Point.

In July Colonel Nixon called in his Captains. "We are to leave immediately to White Plains.", he announced. There was an Indian massacre there and it is expected there may be more trouble. Washington wants us there as quickly as possible." "What sort of trouble asked Captain Buckmaster?" The Colonel apprised us of the situation. "The Brits are trying to regain control of White Plains. The Stockbridge Indians met them at Kingsbridge and they were massacred by the Red Coats. We should remember their Patriotism. Washington is there and is requesting our support should the British force strengthen and try to push toward White Plains." Captain Heywood said, "I will have my men ready within the hour." The Colonel announced, "I would like all companies ready within the hour." The Captains as a body responded, "Aye, Sir." We rushed towards our companies and the Camp was immediately in action making preparations.

We arrived at White Plains within a day. The baggage arrived shortly after nightfall. We, with Colonel Nixon, were placed on Valentine Hill. The Captains were assigned their duties and patrols were out within an hour of our arrival.

We spent a few weeks there. All remained quiet at White Plains and so Washington ordered Nixon's Brigade to Albany. Moses Atkinson as Lieutenant was constantly by my side. As we marched back to Albany he said, "Captain. What are we to expect in Albany?" I answered him with, "I don't know. The war seems to be more toward the South at the moment other than trying to keep the Indians at bay here. The Colonel said, Washington is concerned that the British are instigating the Indians."

Moses asked, "Who is this 'Brant' that the men talk about?" I told him what I knew, "All I know is he is a Mohawk Chief who grew up somewhere in New York near white settlers there. He has a sister Molly who lived with a William Johnson. Johnson was a successful British merchant. He saw to it that Brant received an education and even brought him to England. He came back here and remained loyal to the Brits. He supposedly is with Captain Butler." Moses said, "I hear him called 'Monster Brant'." I responded, "Aye, I've heard that as well. He has burned more villages than I could possibly count. Believe me Moses, he is a dangerous man. He led the massacre at Cobbleskill under Butler. The Mohawks reputation for fighting is formidable." Moses nodded and said, "Aye, I have heard a great deal about Cobbleskill." I said, "He appears with not much warning and his attacks are bloody and ruthless." Ephraim who had been listening added derisively, "Sounds like a wonderful man, Sir. Can we not stop to eat?" Moses who always appreciated Ephraim's humor shot at him, "Good grief man, didn't we eat yesterday?" I chuckled at the banter between the two of them. The men were always humored hearing their verbal assaults. John Jr. yelled from behind us, "No, Sir. That would have been two days ago."

We marched on toward Albany. Thank God for some humor. The miles of marching back and forth were monotonous to me. The summer heat and sun beating down on us made the travel much more difficult and slowed us down a bit. We dismounted and walked with the horses to help ease their discomfort. I learned there were considerable arguments and complaints in the other companies. Our company did have its complaints but, the men clearly had an unbreakable bond. I did enjoy the humor while other Captains thought it was a lack of discipline. After all, these past years, they ate, slept, fought and marched together. They tended to each other's wounds and sicknesses. They watched their friends dying on the battle field and then buried them. They had seen things testing the strength of any man's stomach or mind. They suffered lack of food, clothing and sleep. If they could still find humor in each other and what was around them, then it was good medicine for their souls.

Once in Albany, we continued with patrols and capturing any Indians sympathizing with the British. Most of the action was now taking part in the Southern states with the British. There were very few reports on the whereabouts of where Brant might be but it was rumored that he was in the area. So far, we had seen no sign of him.

I was becoming quite tired and in September became quite sick. I think I had a pretty well secured flu and I spent a week in bed. Colonel Nixon came to see me. "How are you, Jabez?" he inquired. "I'm doing fine, Sir. Will be plenty glad to get out of this bed." He looked at me gravely, "Your men are quite worried. They aren't used to you lying around." I chuckled and said, "At least they have something to think about." He smiled and said, "You've got yourself a great group of men." Then he had a questionable look on his face when he said, "Do they ever turn anything down?". "No, Sir. They are tired, hungry and sick but they stand together. I think their attitude is 'Let's get this done so we can get home.'" He nodded. "Your always out in front with them, never behind. I'm concerned for them without you. I will not be sending them out if you're going to be on your feet soon."

I wasn't sure how to respond to his praise. It made me uncomfortable.

He ignored my silence and thoughtfully said, "I would like to go home someday soon thinking my men respected me as much as they do you." I answered him, "Thank you, Sir. I have been lucky to have leaders that set the example, my men follow me, like we do *you*." With a stern look to him I ended, "Know *that*, Sir." Now it was his turn to be uncomfortable. He cleared his throat and said, "Well I'm glad to see your doing better and look forward to seeing you about." He was off. I thought of him after he left. He was a good and fair man. He tended to his responsibilities better than most Colonels I had seen.

Within a week, I was up and about and back to doing patrols and other camp duties. In October, General Nixon again requested another furlough due to family issues.

In October, I finally received word from Colonel Nixon, that Daniel was still with Colonel Alden and they were now at Cherry Valley. They would be there through the winter.

It was on November 14, Colonel Nixon while meeting with his Captains informed us that there was a massacre at Cherry Valley two days prior. The words sent a shock wave through my body. "Sir!", I all but yelled. The Colonel understood my anxiousness and said, "Captain, your brother's name was not mentioned on the 'reported dead' list but, Colonel Alden has been slain. "Stay strong, Jabez.", said one Captain. I could not tell who said it as my thoughts were racing. The Colonel addressed me, "Captain, I promise to get word to you as soon as I hear it." "Thank you, Sir.", was all I could muster. Captain Harwood said, "We all know Daniel. He will be fine. I'm sure of it." With that, I got up and walked out of the meeting without asking permission. Captains Harwood and Buckmaster came to me afterward. They told me the Colonel 'completely understood' why I had walked out. They stayed with me a little while and then went to the men in the company to relate the news.

It would be another week before the Colonel called me to him. I was greeted with a smile and felt at ease. I certainly hoped that meant the news was good. He put formality aside and said, "I found out that Daniel was alive and well, along with most of his men. They had been behind the fort's walls when the attack occurred." I asked him, "Would you know anything of my nephews?". "Both are fine, Jabez.", he confirmed. I asked about the rest of Daniel's company and he supplied me with the information he knew, "There are none listed killed in action, however, 5 of his men were taken prisoners." He shuffled through the papers on his desk and produced one reading the report, "His men that were taken prisoner by Brant were: Samuel Proctor, Joseph Smith, Charles Hudman, Andrew Garrett and Samuel Woodsum." Hearing the last name, I swore "Goddamn". The Colonel looked up and I quickly said, "Sorry, Sir. Abiatha Woodsum in my company is his brother. I should like to get to him right away." The Colonel nodded and I sincerely thanked him for the information.

Before I called the company, I requested Abiatha's presence at my tent. Abiatha was ten years younger me, in his early twenties. I asked him to sit and immediately informed him of his brother. At Abiatha's blank look, I placed a mug of rum in front of him. He spoke for the first time saying, "Thank you, Captain." I understood the man's emotion having gone through it with Daniel. I began, "Abiatha, I can only comfort you with the fact he must be still alive or they would have killed him with the others. Have some hope with that." He didn't acknowledge my comment but asked, "What about my other brother, John?" He was visibly relieved when I responded, "He is alive and well."

He finally picked up the mug and drank it down. I spoke again when he finished, "I promise to keep you informed of anything I hear." He wiped his mouth with the back of his hand saying, "I appreciate hearing this from you away from the men." I nodded and offered him an option, "I am calling the company up to inform them of what I know. You may join us or have a minute here with your thoughts." He took a second and stood saying, "I would like to stand with the company, Sir. There are others here with family in Daniel's company." He offered to round up the company and this I allowed even though it was Moses' duty to do. I followed him out and gave a sign to Moses who was waiting outside.

When Abiatha was out of ear shot, I filled Moses in. He watched the man walking away and murmured sadly, "Very well, Sir." The company received the news well. While they were pleased to hear their loved ones were okay, there was some concern and respect shown to Abiatha for his brother.

Camp continued on with the same monotonous routine. We were to remain here for the winter. I wasn't entirely glad about the situation. We had spent the last few years, marching and fighting. It seemed the war was dwindling down in this area. The British had pretty much been driven out of the North, at least for the moment, I hoped. We hunkered down for the winter, waiting to see what spring would bring.

8

1779

January 15, 1779, Moses came to me. He didn't waste any time in getting to the point. "I have just heard news about your brother, Daniel has been arrested for affronting another officer. He is being brought to Fort Plank for court martial." "When will he arrive?" I asked the him. "He should arrive at Fort Plank in the next day or so, Captain."

Two days later, after receiving permission, I went to where he was being held. It was a day of hard riding. Once I found where he was being held, I was addressed by the guard to which I replied, "Captain Lane to see Captain Lane." I didn't respond to the confusion written on the man's face but he stepped aside and let me enter. There sat Daniel. When he saw me, he jumped up and after a brief embrace he we sat down.

I spoke first, "It's good to see you." "You as well", he replied. He was fidgeting in his seat, "I heard about the attack on Cherry Valley. The report was that it was quite gruesome." He continued to fidget not uttering a word. "Are your sons, Daniel and Isaac, okay?" With a dip of his chin and the expression of his eyes, I could tell the scenes were probably much worse than what was relayed. I soon got the story from my brother's experience.

"The boys are just fine. Alden completely ignored the warning" he began. "First off, he wouldn't let the settlers into the fort. Those people never stood a chance." Instead he sends scouts in all directions to warn the people of any 'possible' approaching danger. Alden remained inside the Wells' family home he was staying. No action for organizing defense was put into action. All of the officers were billeted into the different homes around the fort. I sent Daniel and Isaac inside the fort as soon as I heard the warning then, got as many of my men and settlers there as soon as possible.

Captain Walter Butler, a loyalist directed the attack. He sent Brant and the Indians in first and waited while the Indians destroyed everything in and around the village. Alden, the arrogant fool still didn't believe we were being attacked". The Seneca came in first. They went straight for the Wells Farm, where Alden was staying, surrounded it and slaughtered the entire family but one son, who was away at school. Alden started running down the road with Chief Brant chasing him, calling for Alden's surrender. Alden stopped to fire on Brant but the gun misfired, Brant struck him in the head with his tomahawk and he was scalped before his body hit the ground. Inside the garrison, the men were screaming over the noise encouraging the villagers to run faster. We fired cover shot for those that were running for safety with us. Only a few made it. Some hid in their homes and were dragged out to be massacred. The smoke from the fires, the war whoops from the Indians and screams from the women as they watched their children butchered in front of them before being killed themselves, still haunt my brain. Of my company, five were taken prisoner."

I was horrified at his story. I said, "Dear God!" Daniel was quick to respond saying, "Sixteen soldiers were killed. Thirty-two settlers, mostly women and children, were murdered that day. They didn't just murder the women and children; they scalped them, dismembered them and then let their dogs feed on them." With that, Daniel's head was in his hands. "Children! My God, Jabez. Why display such evil on a child. I will never understand or forgive the butchery they performed on those people!"

I said to Daniel, "You know, when I lay down at night, I can still see the aftermath of battle and the horrific images that come to my mind. I don't know how I could live with the images of those children." Daniel raised his head up and looked at me. His expression was bleak. He said, "It's an image that comes to me during the day, not just at night. We all played with those children. Their mothers cooked food for us. These hardened soldiers that thought they had seen everything. They, we, were ill for days afterward. We had to gather the people up for burial, but all of us saw it through and not one man said a word." His anguish was an emotion I had never seen on my brother.

After a minute or two of silence, I bellowed in disgust, "Brant is the worst of savages." Daniel's face took on a look of bewilderment as he went on with his story. "After the Mohawk, Chief Brant killed Alden, he went on to SAVE the lives of the settlers." My jaw dropped and Daniel nodded and went on, "At the fort, a young girl on her horse came riding toward us. Brant came up behind her, but too far out for our shot. When he caught up to her, he slapped the horse's hindquarters and the horse doubled its speed toward us. Once the girl made it safely to us, he turned his horse and went back to the chaos. When the attack was over and the Indians made off with prisoners, we learned that Brant, knew the girl having actually grown up with these people. That evening, the stories from the survivors were told. Brant got to one house and a woman stood inside hiding her children behind her skirts. He told to get in her bed with the children and pretend to be sick, she did so. The Seneca's arrived at the door of the house and he told them there is only a sick woman and her sick children here. With that, he had the house painted and they were left alone. I learned he is a Mason and when Lt. Col Stacy gave the Masonic sign, he too, was spared.

According to Stacy when he was spared that Brant's words were, "I don't make war on women and children. Stacy believed that Brant was angered by what was happening."

I sat there in silence and let him finish his story. He went on, "There was an elderly gentleman who came back by the name of Vrooman. Brant apparently knew him well and while on the trail, sent him back to find sticks to light a fire. Vrooman said he didn't realize it at the time but, Brant was letting him go. He said Brant's expression of disbelief told him as much when he came back up the road with an armful of wood. Days later all the settlers that were taken prisoner were returned except for Mrs. Campbell and her child and Mrs. Moore and her children. Butler kept them to punish their husbands for their activities against the King during the border wars. A few of the soldiers that were taken have not yet returned. For us, the following weeks were spent trying to find the savages and scavenge what could be salvaged from the burned homes. The village is spending the winter, over one hundred settlers and fifty officers huddled in a barn for warmth. Supplies that come in are scarce. People are sick and close confinement was the cause of short tempers and quarrels. Going out to scout is a relief from the overcrowding."

I realized he was finished with talking and said, "The word we received was that Brant was in total blame for the massacre." Daniel replied, "He only went for Colonel Alden and any soldiers that tried to protect him." I could only respond with, "That is an amazing story. So, if Brant had not done what he had done, many more settlers would have been killed." Daniel just nodded his head.

I decided to get his thoughts away from such horror and asked him, "So tell me how you are here in this predicament." Daniel now looked disgusted and began this story. "Captain Ballard was sent out to hunt and/or confiscate Tory livestock. What he did was raid everyone, friend or foe and even burned a few houses. I could not abide that and called him on it. Well after a few shoves back and forth, I got arrested and here I am facing a bogus court martial." I could understand Daniel's anger. The idea of women and children without homes or food would be something even I could not abide, friend or foe.

That is all he would say on the matter and I was happy to talk about other things. I asked him about his sons. "They are still with the company. When this charade is over, I will re-join them. I don't want them here. If I am to be lashed or worse, they should be somewhere else." I nodded in agreement and understood his fatherly protection of them. I also believed in his pride. A father would not want his sons to see him humiliated in such a way. I assured him with a slap on his shoulder, "I will make sure of it, Daniel, in any way I can." He brought his hand to my shoulder and gave it a firm squeeze saying in a choked voice, "Thanks, little brother."

He now wanted to know about my company and I. "Since Saratoga, we have been mostly scouting the area, there have been skirmishes here and there. With Burgoyne's surrender, the area has been mostly quiet. The officers from the South are grating on my nerves. They honestly believe that they are our betters here in the North. I hope they are sent back soon." His expression of surprise was quite clear when he said, "I don't think I've ever heard you speak badly of a person. I hope the situation gets better." I shrugged and explained, "They keep to themselves pretty much. For myself, I only see them at officer's meetings. Other than that, I have no reason to be in the same proximity."

I went on with my thoughts, "Sarah and the boys are constantly on my mind. The war seems more directed to the South and I think I'm needed more at home than here at this point. Most of the company are beginning to feel the same way and I no longer have the energy or inclination to persuade them otherwise."

Daniel's words were kind toward me. "Jabez, you have been away from your family for four years. You deserve to get back to the comfort of your home and Sarah. You have young sons at home that need their father to raise them and they should know their father. Go home. For myself, one of my reasons for staying is that my sons are here, I have no intention of leaving them at this moment. If and when you go home, I will do what I can for John and Joanna's sons." I said to him, "I appreciate your thoughts. I promise to think some more on it." Daniel's tone became his old boastful self and he said, "I have heard great things about you and your men and I am very proud to say 'that is my brother.'" I was so grateful to hear his words. "I'm proud to say you're my brother, too. I feel terrible burdening you with this now with your court martial.", I told him. We talked more about trivial things and then his supper arrived. After one more brotherly embrace, I went off to find something to eat myself.

The next day, both of my nephews Isaac Lane and William Hancock, Joanna's other son appeared. Storming over to them I demanded, "Whose idea was this? Do you have permission to be here?" Isaac, now a Private, stepped in front of me speaking in a confident tone, "Yes, we do." William Hancock came to stand beside him adding, "We want to be near whether the outcome is good or bad." Isaac finished with, "It's nothing less than what you or my father would do if it were one of us", cocking his head in William's direction.

What stood before me were not boys, but men. War had taken care of that at their young ages. After all they had done and seen, I did not have the right to send them away. Carefully thinking how best to handle this new twist I offered them some advice, "The best thing we could do for him is to not let him know you're here until after the trial. He will get upset and we need him calm for his trial." Both young men nodded in understanding.

In a sterner tone to honor Daniel's wish, "However, you must understand, as a father, he does not want to be humiliated in front of his son. Promise me if comes to a whipping, you will not be in attendance. Some day you will become a father and you will understand this." Isaac wiser than his years nodded, "Agreed, Uncle. I understand but you must understand, as his son, my place is near him." I realized at that moment whether he had permission or not, he would be here. My admiration for the young man before me grew immeasurably. Sending them off to the space I had set camp, I went in and sat with Daniel a while.

Walking back to my temporary camp, Isaac met me halfway. I told him how his father was doing as we walked back. Isaac was pleased to hear about his father. As we approached, there were men milling about. Isaac announced, "I found these men while you were with my father."

Some of my company had gotten permission to come and to my astonishment managed to follow me here. I was anxious to have the court martial over and learn the results. The company and all four of my nephews stayed close to the house where the trial was taking place. An officer came out seeing me, saluted and informed me that the trial was over. I glanced over at Isaac and William who quickly moved to the back of the company so as not to be seen.

In a fashion that only Daniel could pull off, the door exploded open and there was Daniel filling the doorway with his hands on his hips. There was that devilish grin and the glint in his eyes. That posture alone told us all we needed to know. He was cleared of the charge. The men were cheering and I felt relief wash over me, so much so that I had to sit down. Daniel came right over to me and said, "Time for a pint or did you drink it already?" I couldn't hold the laughter. He had to help me to my feet and once I stood, I said, "come on let's go find us some".

Before we took a few steps, Isaac appeared in front of his father. I held my breath waiting for Daniel's reaction. For a moment, I thought he was upset at his son. Isaac stood waiting for his father to speak first. Instead, Daniel wrapped his son in a huge bear hug which brought Isaac's feet off the ground. Neither one of them spoke, they just smiled at each other. Daniel was overcome with pride and emotion toward his son. He could not speak but placed his arm around his son's shoulders as they walked together. Daniel looked back at me and I believe his eyes were moist with tears when he said, "Come on, Jabez, we will share some ale with my son today."

To our surprise, our nephews; John Jr, John Hancock and William Hancock approached us waving mugs and said, "If you want them filled, the pints are in our tent." Daniel not missing a beat said to the poor kids, "What? You would have me court martialed again for socializing with a private?". Rules were strict about that and the poor nephews looked crushed. I leaned over and whispered, "Go and get the pints." In a louder voice I said, "Privates, you will please report to my tent." Their expressions were pure delight as they scampered off.

Daniel and I headed toward the tent with the men accompanying us. He answered all of their questions and they answered all of his, not once removing his arm from Isaac. I was glad for the comradery with the men and Daniel. His old bluster was back and he had a good time with the teasing back and forth. There were smiles all around. Daniel directed his gaze at Elijah Bradbury and said, "I hope you're keeping a good eye on my nephews. I would not be happy to hear anything had happened to the boys." Elijah who still had affection and hope to court our nephew, John Jr's sister when he got home, looked terrified at the thought. "I'll make sure they stand behind me at all times, Sir." Daniel tried to look serious but wasn't successful and shot back, "See that you do!".

With that, he went into a fit of laughter having scared the poor man to death. Elijah was receiving slaps on his back and promises to help him out. Phineas Towle said, "If I see a bullet coming, I'll just throw you in front of the lads." This was followed by another round of laughter. I asked, "How did they come by the pints?" James Woodman answered me, "Just plain found it, Captain." Samuel Brooks chimed in "Yes, Cap. That's true. The boys wanted to do something in case things went well."

He looked at Daniel and said, "When we all left, the boys were youngsters. John's son has spoken much of when you went home sick. He said he would come with his father to visit you. He admires you very much, Captain Daniel." He finished with a look toward me and said, "He came to your company because he wanted to know his other Uncle, too. For the boys' sake, share a pint with them. They all work very hard to help out with the work." The men were nodding their heads in agreement at Samuel's words. Over Samuel's shoulder, I could see the cousins running toward us, faces flushed from running and a wave of affection slammed into me. I thought about it and in fact, they are good lads, always eager to please and never complained. I had never acknowledged it.

Phineas Towle came forward, "With your permission Captain, may we light a fire outside your tent?" It was still a regulation in camp that the officers not fraternize with the privates but today I didn't give a damn. I gave him my permission while Daniel zeroed in on the boys trying to act fierce and bellowed, "I believe your Captain said 'in the tent!'". The boys ran on by him and into the tent. Daniel gave the company a grin and a wink and followed the boys. I addressed the men standing before me saying, "Thanks men. We will join you all shortly." Off they went and I entered the tent.

Daniel was already in conversation with the boys. Daniel's demeanor towards the boys was much like I had seen with his own sons. They seemed to be nervous yet overjoyed to be included. I longed for my own sons and the guilt of not being home at that minute, felt unbearable. John Hancock looked at me with wide eyes and raised a mug to me saying, "Captain?". I took the mug he offered and said, "Boys, when we are alone and only in this tent, I am Uncle." His face flushed and he said, "Yes Sir, Captain Uncle!". I was undone. The laughter between the four of us lasted for the next few hours. We talked and talked until we could hear the bonfire outside cracking.

The boys, so pleased with themselves, were now so inebriated, that Daniel and I were roaring at the sight of them stumbling out of the tent to join the men. Daniel and I sat for a few seconds more. We heard the men greeting the four young men as they approached with roars of laughter. I could only grin like an idiot at Daniel as I was feeling the effects of the liquor as well. Daniel with a sly grin said, "That was fun." "Aye", I answered. Taking another swig, I asked Daniel, "Where in hell had they found rum?We were issued ale for rations!" Daniel chuckled and raised his mug saying, "There are some things we don't need to know. Let's go out and join the fun."

We stood up and headed outside. We all sat around the fire, talking well into the night. Somehow, they managed to find more liquor and the hilarity was at an all-time high. If any officers passing by saw two Captains sitting around a fire drinking with the Privates, they blessedly never said a word.

The next morning when I woke up, there was Daniel sprawled on the floor of the tent. In his inebriated state last night, he totally missed the bed and just slept where he landed. I quietly got up and left him sleeping. The fire from last night was down to coals so I stoked it and made us some breakfast. By the time it was finished, Daniel joined me. "Hell of a night, last night", he murmured. I nodded in agreement, the two of us grinning.

As we sat and ate, I asked him, "What are you going to do now that your cleared of your charges?" He answered, "I have to report to the Colonel this morning and get my papers. I'm going back to the company at Cherry Valley. I'm not sure of where we will be going from there." Thoughtfully I said, "I'm glad we fortunate enough to be here and have some time." Daniel sat quiet for a few minutes and said, "Me too, little brother. I hope you think hard about getting home. As I said, I'm not leaving my son behind. The nephews will be watched over. I'll do what I can to get them into my company."

In a mock, derisive tone he added as he stood, "Now I have to find Isaac and William and listen to their chatter all the way back." With that, I stood chuckling. He looked around saying, "It's time for me to report to the Colonel." With a wink he said, "Can't be listed as 'deserted' now can I?". I stood and wished him well. A brief brotherly hug and I watched him stride away. I sat a while mulling over his thoughts.

The next few months were spent in the Highlands in anticipation of another British attack from Canada which did not happen. The Onondagas were leading raids on the villagers around New York. The Generals were discussing an expedition to put a halt to this. We spent our time, scouting and once in a while there would be a skirmish with Indians. We often brought prisoners in so we could obtain intelligence. It was relatively quiet in this area.

It wasn't long before I received word from Daniel that his company was joining General Sullivan on his expedition mounted to put down the Indian uprisings.

One evening in late March, the officers held a dinner. The food was good and the liquor was plenty. All of us were in a good humor and quite drunk. I was enjoying the evening.

As the night went on, the drunker we got, the more obnoxious one particular Virginian officer became. His words became more and more offensive. The others were trying to quiet the man but he somehow was now standing before me. I looked him straight in the eye and would not step back from him. In a loud, obnoxious voice he said, "I cannot wait to get home. You Northerners are a bunch of 'noggs.'" It was term that meant we were clumsy fools. My hand shot out and slapped the man in the face. My anger was now at its peak. The other officers were quick to separate us. He shot out at me, "Tomorrow morning we settle this." I should have thought a minute before I spoke but my answer was, "Why wait?". I shook off the arms holding me and cocked my head toward the door. The Virginian hesitated for a moment but started out with me directly behind him. The house emptied as the officers filed out behind us. Someone said, "Jabez, you're drunk!" I growled back, "I'm not any longer!"

As the rules were declared, others tried to talk us out of it. I remained silent as I stared my antagonist down. Pistols were produced and we counted off the required steps. The loud crack of his shot rang in my ears and I felt a sudden pain in my side. I managed to remain standing and aimed my pistol. I carefully aimed my shot, once again the loud crack of my pistol rang in my ears and the Virginian went to the ground. "Jabez, what have you done!", cried someone. Despite the burning pain starting to spread, I growled, "Relax, he's not dead. I aimed for his leg." I stumbled back to my quarters and laid down on my cot. Men came running in to see how bad my wound was. Phineas announced to the men crowded around me, "No fear, it's only a flesh wound. Now get out and speak no more of this!" Once everyone left, I could see the relief in his face. "Captain, you could get court martialed for this."

My mind was now completely resolved. "Let them do as they wish. I've had enough. When we start shooting at each other, it's time to go home." Phineas with a nod said, "Aye Cap". Once he had me cleaned up. He left me and I fell into a deep, sound sleep.

The next day, I stiffly got out of bed and had the men called to parade. Ephraim came to me and said, "The Virginian had only a flesh wound to his leg. He'll be okay." I didn't bother to respond to the comment.

I don't know how I got through the morning exercises, but I did. The only thing I could not manage was lifting my rifle. Instead, I used it as a prop to help me stand straight. I had hoped that I could fool everyone that nothing was wrong with me. In a short time, I realized my wound had opened up as I could feel the moisture of my own blood beginning to creep down my side. I had to get back and check my wound. I finished the parade and I ordered the men to see to cleaning the camp area as an excuse to return to my lodging.

Once again, Phineas was there along with Moses Atkinson. I was irritated and said, "I'm not in the mood for your mothering." Ignoring my complaint and reaching out Moses snapped, "Captain, Sir. The quicker you cooperate, the quicker we will leave you to your grouchy self." I protested, "I'm not grouchy!" Phineas looked nervous when he said, "Begging your pardon, Sir, but I would rather swing at a bee's nest than be here right now." Moses having no fear at all, uncharacteristically snapped at me again, abandoning all formality saying, "Jabez, you want to get drunk and get yourself shot at, go ahead. I'm going to finish this dressing. You are going to sit still, let us do what we need to and then we will leave you to your miserable self."

I gave up and let them do what they wished. The shirt came off and in fact, it had a spot of blood on it. My side was washed and they ripped my shirt into strips and wrapped it around me to keep the wound from opening up again. I had another shirt put on and they seemed satisfied with their work. The tight binding did feel better and I grudgingly told them so.

"Thank you, I do feel better. I'm sorry if you think my attitude is so poor." "Well it is.", Moses cut me off, holding the bloody remnant he had torn away. I asked him, "What are you going to do with that?". "Tie it to a stick and march around so the rest of the camp can see what the two drunken fools did last night.", he smacked back at me. Obviously, he was still angry with me. Phineas stood rigid and fighting back a giggle he tried so hard to suppress. He was undone when Moses gave him a wink, he started to choke but the laughter doubled him over. The three of us found the hilarity in Moses' comment and within seconds we were laughing but I found that to be a little painful. Moses saw my grimace and said, "Serves you right."

Phineas left and Moses stayed a bit longer. I looked at my friend and said, "I'm really sorry to have angered you." Moses' tone softened a bit and said, "I was really worried as I know these wounds can turn infectious. I came in here to help you and your attitude just made my temper flare. I'm sorry to have yelled at you." I felt terrible that I had caused him so much trouble and said, "You have nothing to apologize for. The blame is mine you were right in what you said. Thank you for everything." With that he raised the bloody rag and said, "With your permission, I'm going to find a fire to throw this in." Gratefully, I nodded at him, "Thank you, Moses. I would appreciate that."

Later that afternoon, Colonel Nixon allowed me to enter his quarters. The expression on his face told me he had heard about the event from the previous night but he didn't say a word about it. After reading my resignation, his shoulders sagged a bit. He started with, "Jabez, this will be a huge loss in my regiment. Is there anything I can do to change your mind?". "I'm afraid not Sir.", I answered.

Taking a breath, I continued, "My enlistment is up in a few weeks and I need to get home to my wife. After four years, I'm sure my home needs a lot of work. I have two small sons who don't even know me." He nodded in agreement. After a second or two of silence he said, "I imagine some of your company will be resigning as well." I stood stiffly and said, "I can't speak for them, Sir." He looked down and said, "Here's the thing. General Washington is denying all resignations at this time. However, I will report you as deranged which could mean, 'you've lost your mind, sick or seriously wounded'." As he took a pointed glance at my side I answered, "That will be fine, Sir." He nodded and stood. He came before me and offered his hand. I shook it. "Jabez, it's been a privilege to serve alongside you. I shall miss your presence. I wish you well on your return home to your family." "Thank you, Sir.", I replied. He smiled and said, "Once I sign that paper, you will call me Thomas and hopefully your friend." I smiled back and said, "Whether I call you Sir or Thomas, we will part friends. Thank you for all your kindnesses. I have always appreciated your fairness toward me and the men. I will stay until the company is in proper order and everyone is placed properly." We shook hands once more and I left him.

It took a couple of weeks and in that time, about half the company had resigned. Most of the resignations were approved and I spent most of my time looking for and suggesting placement of the remaining men. Once I was satisfied that they would be in good hands, I got word to Daniel of my departure and who would be leaving with me. John Hancock was to finish his enlistment. John Jr would be coming home with me. I said my good byes to each man during the last week. I would miss them all but I was excited to get home

The first few steps seated on my horse my heart was heavy for those I were leaving behind. I could only pray that they would get home safely to their own families.

I was taken by surprise when I began to ride out of the camp. Everyone in my company, a few of the Captains and their men along with Colonel Nixon, who was mounted on his own horse, stood making a path for us with their rifles on their shoulders. They stood straight and tall and had cleaned up and carefully dressed. Stunned with the impact of this high honor I looked toward the Colonel first, who saw the tears I was holding back. I could not speak and he knew it. He nodded and smiled.

Captain Buckmaster broke the line to approach and shake my hand. "Get home safe my friend". I could only nudge my horse forward. I saluted them back by removing my own hat, holding it to my chest and held it there as I passed them all for the final time.

I quietly left camp that day with Ephraim Sands, Moses Atkinson,

Elijah Bradbury, Ebenezer Redlon and John Lane, Jr.

9

LIFE IN BUXTON

Riding into town from the war, everyone came out to greet us. I saw John first. He stood in the middle of the road. I gestured behind me and saw the relief spread across his face. He came toward us with his long-legged stride, he briefly stopped and looked up at me. We both nodded at each other. John Jr. jumped off his horse and yelped, "Father!", as he ran toward him. Father and son embraced as if they would never let go.

The rest of us dismounted. John was holding his son at arm's length. Still looking at his son, he said, "By God, I'm glad your home". John, Jr. responded, "It's good to be here. Uncle Jabez took good care of me like you said he would." John turned to me and his arms had me in a bear hug. In my ear he whispered, "Thank you for bringing him back to us." Once he released me and I could breathe again I said, "You can be proud of your son. He did well and at times, he actually took care of me.", I said with a chuckle. John stood taller, as proud as a father could be. He turned and shook the other men's hands and welcomed them home. Meanwhile, the women surrounded me to ask what I might know about their loved ones. In the crowd I lost sight of Ephraim, Moses, Elijah and Ebenezer as their families mobbed around them. I still hadn't found the one face I came home for.

Finally, there she stood, with our small boys on either side of her, holding her hand. Sarah was much thinner but the boys looked healthy and so grown! She had lost so much weight, her dress looked to be too large for her. I concealed my shock and strode toward her, gathering her up to breath in the scent of her. The boys seeing their mother's happiness joined in by wrapping their arms around my legs. Looking down at them I teased, "Who might these little men might be?" Samuel fired back, "Your sons!". I shook my head saying, "No, no. There were two small babies when I left here last." Jabez answered that remark with, "Mother said we should eat all our food so we will be as strong and brave as you. Then we could come to help you."

I looked at Sarah. She had kept me close with the boys and I was grateful for that. I patted them on their heads and said, "I'll not be needing any help with the war but, I could surely use some help around the farm. Why don't we head there now?". I lifted each one up on my horse, much to their delight and had my arm around Sarah. Leading the horse with one hand and Sarah's hand in the other, we walked down the road toward the farm. Sarah was my home and I felt overwhelming happiness.

That first day home, the boys had to show me everything they knew. Samuel informed me he had chores to do. Scooping up Jabez, I followed Samuel and Sarah went inside the house to get some food prepared. It was an excuse for her, she gave me time to reacquaint myself with my sons. We entered the barn and Samuel handed Jabez a bucket of grain. Jabez wandered off to toss it to the chickens. Samuel had to feed the cows and horses. First, he took my filthy saddle and put it over the fence post. Then he went over to brush the horse down. I filled the buckets with water and food for the animals. By now Jabez was done with the chickens and beating the stuffing out of my saddle trying to clean it. We had the chores done in no time and we headed back to the house. My heart swelled with fatherly pride in my boys. Samuel was now only six years of age and Jabez only four yet, they handled the manly chores quite well.

I was at a loss on how to speak with my sons so I asked, "There seems to be some things that need to be tended to around here. What do you think we should do first?" Samuel thought for a second and said, "Well, there is a problem with the roof on the barn. I tried to fix it but rain still gets in and ruins the hay. I had to move the hay somewhere else but it still gets damp when the rain gets in the barn." I stopped in my tracks, "You were up on the roof?". Quite seriously he responded, "That is how one would fix it, is it not?". Jabez in his innocence piped in, "Momma was very mad when she found us up there". I could not fault the boy for doing what he did.

I knelt down in front of them and said, "You have done a wonderful job taking care of everything. I'm very proud of you both for it. Tomorrow, we will go up there and see if we can fix it securely." Samuel's smile was absolutely brilliant in reply. Jabez said in a frightened voice, "Momma said if she catches us up there again, she will beat our bottoms so hard there will be no fabric left to cover them. I hope you have another pair of pants." The seriousness of his tone stopped me from laughing. I understood the fright they must have given their mother. To ease the little man's worry I said, "I will speak with your mother tonight. I'm sure she will be fine with us doing it together."

Dinner that evening became a small battle as to who could sit closer to me at the supper table that evening. I ate listening to their chatter and from the mouths of babes I learned the truth of what was happening under this roof. Once all the food was on the table. Jabez innocently said, "Are you eating tonight, Mother?" Sarah sat in front of me and I could see her body stiffen up. "Of course.", she said. "Why wouldn't she?", I asked him. He looked at me, unconcerned at the tension he had caused saying, "Lots of times there was only food for Samuel and I. Sometimes Uncle John and Aunt Joanna would send food over to us." Sarah said, "That will be enough, now eat your food." I kept my silence. I had my answer as to why she was so thin. Her struggle here was much harder than I realized. It felt like someone had struck me hard in my stomach. I had no right to challenge her on anything that happened here. Actually, I admired her for her strength. She had put her children's health before her own. When she finally looked at me, her eyes swept over my own thin body pointedly. As I watched her eat, I vowed to myself that this woman would not feel hunger again.

I was so enamored with my sons, that when Sarah put them to bed, I stood over them for the longest time soaking in every detail of them. Sarah, with the pride of a protective mother stood beside me holding on as if I would disappear said, "They are good boys, Jabez. Samuel is more serious than Jabez. He works so hard at anything that needs to be done. Too much actually for a little boy. He is much like you in personality. Jabez however, has no fear. He is eager to for anything new. Samuel spends much of his time keeping his little brother out of mischief." I smiled at the thought and whispered, "Much like John was with Daniel and I growing up."

Sarah and I took a moment just gazing at each other and finally left the boys' room. Sarah had drawn up a nice warm bath for me and I could not wait to wash the war off of me. For the first time in years, I had the luxury of relaxing for more than a minute. Sarah came up behind the tub and gently washed my hair with soap and then playfully pushed my head under the water. When I rose from the tub, she wrapped a blanket around me and led me to our bedroom, eager to begin our lives again in our marriage. Quite happily, I obliged.

The next morning, when I awoke, it was not Sarah beside me but two little boys anxious to get me out of bed. Jabez even managed a kiss on my cheek. I swooped him up over my shoulder and marched out to the kitchen with Samuel close behind. "Wife!", I bellowed. "I found two bugs in our bed!". This brought on the heartwarming sound of children's laughter. How long had it been since I heard a child laugh? Sarah put the food on the table with a stern, "Have you washed your hands? No breakfast until you do!". Samuel took my hand and said, "Come on, Father. She is *very strict* on that rule." I let the boys pull me towards the basin of water with a glance over my shoulder at my wife smirking. Cleaned and anxious to eat, I waited until Sarah sat down with us.

Jabez, the little darling got right down to business. "Are we fixing the barn roof first Father?" I froze. Dear Lord, I forgot to mention it to Sarah last night. Sarah was sitting very calmly across from me. Testing the mood, I answered, "Yes, but I have rules. You will do exactly as I say or it is back to the ground you go, understood?" Still looking into Sarah's eyes, her expression relaxed and I knew it would be okay. Jabez between bites agreed, "Understood, Sir."

A month or so after I arrived home, John asked me to meet him at Garland's Tavern. I got there early in order to spend a few minutes with Joanna and her husband, Peter. They had a good marriage and did quite well with the tavern. They stopped what they were doing and sat with me for a while until John arrived. Joanna, still beautiful as ever, immediately placed breads and dishes of food on the table. "Whoa!", I said with a chuckle, "Sarah will be upset if I don't eat the supper she is cooking." Joanna insisted and I took a pretty piece of pastry that was too tempting to resist.

"How are you and the family these days." Cheerfully she answered "Quite well. I would feel much better if Daniel was home too." "Where is my nephew?", I inquired. She plopped down beside me and said, "I have to get used to the idea that he is not a little boy anymore. In my excitement to have him home, I believe I'm mothering him too much." I felt bad for her, "Joanna, I don't believe it is you so much. These past few years, he has endured crowded conditions. It was not easy for any of us. Home must feel strange to him." Joanna was listening intently, wanting to understand her son's behavior. Solemnly I went on, "Joanna, give him time. He has seen such terrible things and fought bravely. He's turned into a good man. Have patience." She leaned in and hugged me so hard I could not breath for a minute.

Just then, our brother, John came in. He saw Joanna's teary eyes and gave me a nasty look. Joanna was quick to calm our brother saying, "Everything is fine, John. I'm a foolish mother whose son has grown up." He smiled at her and patted her hand gently saying, "It will all turn out well." She rushed off to her cooking and John sat down across from me. We watched her hurry away. John said in a thoughtful way, "I believe a lot of families will have to deal with similar issues when their loved ones come home." "Aye", I agreed.

I could see something weighed heavily on John. "Out with it", I finally said. He spoke with purpose, "I am leaving. I wish to see if I can aid the Penobscot." I exploded, "You can't! You will be arrested!" "No, I won't. I plan to enlist as a private." I realized my mouth was agape and could only say, "Why"? "I owe something to the Penobscot. It was me who talked them into joining our side. If there is danger to them, I want to be there to help them." I remained silent. John had always thought well of the tribe, especially Orono and Sabattus. It was obvious the situation was heavy on his heart and he wanted to see his friends once more. I could understand leaving his wife and children weighed just as heavily on him. I tried to ease his mind saying, "I will keep a close eye on your family while you're gone." He smiled finally and responded, "I would be grateful."

To put a lighter air on the subject and with a stern voice I added, "You better get yourself back here. I can't imagine how you feed all those mouths. How many children do you have now?" "By God, Jabez, I've lost count." With the matter settled, we shared another ale before we returned to our homes.

He came back six months later. I met him at Garland's Tavern. "You look good, John.", when I sat beside him. "Thanks. So, do you", he said. "I'm sorry to hear that the expedition was a disaster." "Aye, it was." The British gained control of the Fort and when we arrived by land, we laid siege on it. The American ships arrived from Boston, hundreds of them. We on the land, were under constant firing from the British. Our ships weren't firing on them and this gave the British fleet time to sail up from New York. When they arrived, our ships were boxed in. There was a lot of cannon fire between the ships and then the Americans tried to sail up the Penobscot River to escape. Some were captured and others were sunk. The men fled to land to escape." "Good Lord.", I said. "I'm glad to see you home, brother." He said, "Aye, me too."

He followed that with, "I appreciate your helping to keep my family fed as well as helping out with my farm while I was gone." Surprised I said, "Did you not do that for my family? I couldn't have done anything less." He nodded and said, "I did what I could. Sarah is quite remarkable and quite prideful. She insisted on helping with my children before she would take food from me. I saw her yesterday and was very happy to see she has gained some of her weight back. I was terrified for her health." I said to him, "I see that most of the women here are quite thin." "Aye", he said. "They pretty much survived on berries in the fall and what food they could grow during the summer. An awful lot for any woman with small children."

It was almost a year after I returned before Sarah questioned the scar on my side. I thought carefully and decided to tell her the truth. "Sarah, my love, it is something I am not proud of. There is no bravery attached to this. I received it in a duel." Her eyes widened in shock but I had to tell her the whole of it. "We were at an officer's banquet and all of us had too much to drink. A southern officer insulted the

Northerner's and I slapped him in the face. That I am not sorry for. However, when challenged, I did not back down. We had fought battles together against the British and now we were fighting each other. I felt then and I feel now, we had lost our dignity and our honor." She understood the torment of my thoughts and only said, "I will say this and we will never speak again of it. You carry honor and dignity in all you do. It was but a moment in your life, a human response. That does not define you."

She made it sound so simple. I finally said, "If one of the boys lashes out in anger as I did that day, I would be a hypocrite to correct him." Sarah sighed, "First of all, let's hope our sons never have to live like you did these past four years. I cannot imagine the conditions you and the men must have suffered. You will explain it to our children as you just did with me. It's that simple, my love."

Over the next few years, the war raged on, mostly in the South. John and I remained at home. Our little family had grown by two more children, Polly, who was the apple of my eye and then Joshua. In that time, food on the table was plentiful, my clothing was intact and warm. I now had a roof over my head, a bed to sleep in each night and enjoyed blissful sleep with the woman I love. During the day, Samuel and Jabez were constantly at my side helping me to get the farm in order. Their antics kept a constant smile on my face.

Daniel came home a year later. He had gone on the Sullivan Expedition that clamped down on the Indians in New York that were raiding the settlers' towns burning, killing and taking prisoners. On one of the many occasions that I visited him, we managed to have a quiet conversation. He told me that a few months after I had left, he had been court-martialed yet again. I had asked him, "What were the charges?" He simply produced a paper and I read it:

Camp, Oswego Lake,

July 27' 1779.*

At a Gen 1 Court Martial, held in Camp, July 24th, whereof Col, Duboys was President, was tried Captain Daniel Lane of the 6 Massachusetts Regiment, charged with ungentlemanly-like Behavior towards Captain Day and other Officers of said Reg., before Officers of their Reg", in saying many Things prejudicial to their Characters, likewise in saying he was broke by a scandalous Authority, of which Court the Complainant was a Member. The Court having duly considered the Evidences for and against Captain Lane, do honorably acquit him of the Charges exhibited against him, and are further of Opinion that the Complaint was vexatious and malicious.

The General highly approves the Determination of the Court, and discharges Cap. Lane from his Arrest.

"I'm glad you were cleared.", I said when I finished reading. "How in God's name did you manage to be cleared of the charge?". Daniel smiled wickedly and said, "It was a difference of opinion between us. Captain Day chose to exaggerate the argument. Colonel Duboys saw through it. There were also witnesses that confirmed the actual argument.".

In 1781 the news arrived of Cornwallis' defeat at Yorktown, VA, marking the end of the war. Delegates met in Paris France to exact the peace treaty. It took almost two years to come to terms. During that time there were skirmishes, mostly in the Carolinas. The men trickled home and the reunion of families began to make the town whole again. Here in our town, the last of the men returned from the war. Like me, their return found their fields overgrown and homes requiring much needed repair. The bond we forged in our struggles during the War were unbreakable on our return home. Everyone did what they could to help each other out. The women had done the best they could. Everyone suffered during this war.

The first thing Elijah Bradbury accomplished on his return home from the war was to marry his love Sarah. John, in spite of himself, was happy to see the young man come home and seeing his daughter's love for Elijah, approved of the marriage. Phineas Towle married Sarah Leavitt in 1778.

Finally! In 1783 the war was over. That same year, John Elden, Samuel Merrill and Thomas Bradbury who were appointed under the authority of the King of England resigned their commissions under the King.

To celebrate, an iron three-pounder was hauled up from Saco and fired near the Garland tavern. A young fellow by the name of Andrews, swung the match. Never having been near a "big gun", he became so alarmed at the spring of the gun and the heavy discharge, he fainted from fear. The women made a fuss, wrapped him in flannel to recruit him.

While the women were fussing over him, the rest of us men were doubled over in laughter. Ephraim simply said, "Knew that as going to happen!" This sent another wave of uproarious laughter through our bodies. The women however, were not the least bit amused which only made the situation that more humorous to us.

All the women had brought food and the men of course brought rum and ale. The men made toasts to those that made it home and then another round of toasts for those who had not. It was a healing day for us all.

I sat with Captain John Elden for a time and we had a pleasant conversation. "It's good to be home, Jabez", he said. "Aye", I responded. "I still see the faces of the men we lost along the way but to see the men here today not suffering any longer from the depredations of war, warms my heart." He nodded, leaned toward me and quietly confided, "Aye. The horrible scenes sometimes invade my sleep, Jabez." "Mine too", I responded.

Elden in a solemn tone said, "I'm sorry to hear about Samuel Woodman but I was glad to see his brother Joshua make his way home.

He was a lucky man." I agreed, "Yes, Joshua transferred to the Navy half way through the war and his ship was captured. They were sent to Mill Prison in England. Somehow, he and this other fellow Roger Plaisted dug under the wall and escaped to France. Captain Samuel Harding found himself in England and heard about Roger and Samuel. He found them in France and got them home."

"Amazing that another man from Buxton happened to find him.", whispered Captain Elden as he glanced over at Joshua deep in conversation with Captain Harding. Looking to where Elden's eyes were focused, "Aye. They have become friends since they both came home." Elden told me what he had heard about Samuel Woodman's death. I nodded sadly and answered, "Yes it's true. He was in fact one of Washington's Life Guards and he did so honorably. He was discharged and died on the way home of small pox. Sarah took his death very hard. She was always very close to her brothers."

To get away from the morose thoughts I raised my mug, "To never eat another fire cake!". He quickly raised his mug to the toast, responding, "They were horrid, weren't they?" Musicians began to play and I went to find Sarah to join in the dancing. The rest of the evening, I spent dancing (or tripping over my own feet) with Sarah. We finally found our sleepy children, bundled them up and headed home.

The following years were peaceful and happy for me. John and I returned to being involved in the affairs in town. John being voted Moderator many times. Most of the men didn't find the everyday struggles to be a burden. Educating our children became very important as well as learning that hard work would help our children to prosper. Slowly, the town began to restore itself through the hard work of all the townspeople working together to rebuild their homes, farms and their relationships with their families.

It would be many years before towns recovered from the war. A government had to be established. It would not be until 1787 that the

U.S. Constitution would be signed. Each state would define their own government within the Constitution and each town would define their government within that.

It was a difficult process but, in the end, we had our own government set up by the people. The idea of electing our governing bodies was appealing to all. We enjoyed the idea that if a Representative or Senator did not speak for us as we wished, he would be replaced at the next election. We now had many rights that we previously did not. By God, I pray those rights are never abused or taken away. All across the country men spoke proudly of this new government. It was, in fact, what so many men died and were wounded for. Those of us that survived made sure their children understood what took place and that our country would be tested in the future from within and from foreign influence. It is up to the future generations to keep our country intact.

The years after Daniel's return from the war, Daniel had his struggles with the ale and was a frequent visitor at Garland's Tavern. He never talked about it but, I think his images of the Cherry Valley Massacre haunted him. He was well liked in town and it seemed everyone understood, however, a few times when he had imbibed in one too many, he would return home and toss his wife and children out of the house, followed by the furniture, into the night. The next day he would be horrified at what he had done and would beg for forgiveness from his family. Joanna was approached once about not serving him anymore ale to which she answered with, "I cannot deny my brother."

On Sundays, everyone went to church. Well, almost everyone. Ebenezer Redlon developed the eccentricities that were quite common in his family. He was often seen enjoying his grog at the tavern. On one particular Sunday, Parson Coffin came questioning why the men were not at church instead of drinking. One excuse such as, "bad cold", another "pain in his back" while another said "rheumatism". Rough

Old Ebenezer understood their hypocrisy walked up to the counter and looked the Parson in the eye saying "Nothing ails me, but I want a glass of grog because I love it!". He was an honest and amiable man however, he would never back down from anyone or anything. He and the rest of his brothers who fought in the war, were noted for their bravery.

Abiatha Woodsum became the tax collector of Buxton for a number of years after which he moved to Limington. Not long after peace had been declared, his brother Samuel walked into town. Samuel Woodsum had been held in Niagara by the Indians until the end of the war. While there he had learned to speak their language and was used as an interpreter. To gain his freedom, he had to run the gauntlet, which meant he walked through a path of fire on the ground. Coming home he settled on some land here and built a prosperous farm.

Ephraim Sands returned home and continued as a millwright. Shortly after the war, his son John, who had survived the war, was found drowned in a river. Some believed he was murdered. Ephraim lived with his son, James at the end of his life.

My nephew, Isaac, returned having obtained the rank of Corporal. He married Ruth Merrill in 1794. Their daughter, Hannah was born in 1795. Ruth died when Hannah was only five years of age. Isaac saw that she was well educated. He would take her everywhere with him and everyone loved the happy, rosy cheeked child. She could always be seen singing. She grew to be a remarkable woman; more graceful, gracious, dignified and impressive than other women of her day. Isaac not only became a successful business man, he also held many positions.

Sarah and I faced our own personal tragedy when our son Jabez, went to sea in 1800. The ship was never heard from again. We never knew what happened. A year later, I found Sarah one night, outside, gazing off into the distance. I brought her shawl out to her, "My love, it's cold out here." I put my arm around her and she leaned heavily against me, "Jabez, my heart is broken."

With that statement, she broke down. I held her tightly while she finally grieved. When she was through, for the first time we could talk about him. I cheered her with my memories of him, "My first sight of him, this little boy who stood tall and brave in front of me, a man he didn't know. The next day, he stood in the same manner on that barn roof we had to fix. That is how he was his whole life. Tall and brave." I choked on my own sorrow and could barely get the words out. "There was no fear in anything he did." She interrupted, "He got that from his father." I squeezed her around the shoulder responding, "His lovable nature came from his mother". She spoke wistfully, "He had that damned devilish grin when he got the better of Samuel or, when he accomplished what he set out to do." We stood that way for a long time trying to come to terms with the loss of our son.

My brother, Daniel passed away at his son's house in 1811. Daniel and his wife Molly had eleven children. In his later years, his nature became more moderate. He seemed to be more relaxed and less easily angered.

It was at this time, after many years of peace in our newly formed country, we would be tested yet again.

10

WAR OF 1812

Overseas, Britain and France had been at war since the 1790s. The United States took a neutral position. Britain not being satisfied, passed a Parliamentary Act on neutral countries, forbidding them to trade with France. They followed with another Parliamentary Act forbidding any trade with any neutral country. By 1807, the Britain as well as France began confiscating American trading ships but, it was Britain who began the practice of impressing American sailors into the British service against their will. Soon Indians were attacking settlements again in the Great Lakes region. The rumors were that the British in Canada was instigating this. James Madison was sworn in as the 4th President of the United States of America. He declared war in 1812. He sent a force to Canada but that ended in disaster as his troops were defeated.

Isaac received a commission as Colonel. He immediately raised a regiment. Among those that signed with him were his brother Daniel (who became a Lieutenant Colonel), my son Stephen became a Captain. My other sons Joshua, Rufus and Silas as well as sons of John and Joanna signed for the cause. A few of them left for Boston in the first half of 1813. We received word that their regiment left Boston headed for the Great Lakes area in New York. At seventy years of age, I could not leave with them. It was difficult to see my boys off. I feared what was ahead of them. Could they stand up to the deprivations of war?Worse yet, would I have to console their mother if they did not return?

My mind was in a turmoil and yet Sarah was my comfort. I was out working in the barn and she came in with a bundle. "I thought we could enjoy our lunch outside, just the two of us." I put the saddle I was mending to the side and said, "I like the sound of that". We went outside where she had spread a blanket and we sat. She opened her bundle and presented me with a dish of chicken and some vegetables she had cooked. "What else is in your bundle?" She smiled and produced a bottle of rum from the bag. Suspicious, I asked, "What are you up to, my dear?" Trying to sound nonchalant she answered, "The rum is to relax us so we can enjoy this fine meal I prepared." I protested, "I always enjoy my meals with you". Sarah straightened her back, "I know you are worried about the boys, so am I. I am worried about you as well. We might as well talk about it."

She poured the rum into two mugs and we sipped in silence for a few moments. I started first. I could not help but answer in an irritated tone, "Yes, I am worried for them. I feel I should be with them. I don't think they have a clue of what they are in for." Somehow, I had angered her and now it was Sarah's turn to speak and speak she did, "Did you have any idea of what you were in for when you left? No. You had your father and brothers the first time you went. You were just a babe. Yet you entered again during the last war to end England's rule over us. Because of your participation, our family has lived in peace and freedom all these years. Your sons have gone off to defend the prize you and many others fought and died for, for their families. I should think you would be proud of that, you pouting pup."

Her uncharacteristic scolding caught me by surprise. "Of course, I'm proud of my whole family. I'm just worried for them and the worry they have brought on you." Sarah smiled and said, "My sweet husband, I have worried about each of my children since the day they were born. I will do so until the day I die. I have faith they will come home, just like you did. We will mourn when it is appropriate." Sarah at fifty-nine years of age still looked as beautiful as the day I married her and she still surprises me with her strength of spirit.

After Isaac took his regiment off left to fight, Moses left his home at Bar Mills, unknown to his family. He just left. He kept going until he found Daniel and Isaac somewhere near Plattsburgh NY. He was 75 years of age. They tried to send him home, but he would have none of it. They informed their commander who said, "Indulge him". They kept him as close to them as possible and in November of 1813 when the army made for winter quarters at Plattsburg, they had a large tent and had a large fire at their feet. Daniel told us he had lain down on one side of Moses and Isaac on the other side. They had him covered with all the spare blankets. Sometime during the night Daniel woke to stoke the fire. He looked over at Moses and noticed he laid just as he did when they first laid down. He spoke but got no answer. He then shook him and found him cold and stiff. He had died peacefully in his sleep. Moses' body lies in Plattsburgh.

In 1814, the British came down from Canada and began to attack our coastal towns. They came as far south as Bangor and burned the town down. When they reached Limington, just one town away from us, our militia prepared. A group of men had talked about it at the Tavern. John was there. I went over to sit with him. Age had slowed him as it had with the rest of us. John was talking to Phineas Towle who was complaining, "Repeated requests to Boston for assistance have gone ignored." John pointed out, "Boston is busy trying to secure the harbor, but other towns could have come to assist." I added, "Massachusetts has voted against the war, so militias are not being raised." Phineas complained, "When Boston called for our assistance, we didn't hesitate when British ships were in their harbor." "I understand", sighed John. Phineas still upset added, "Now we have the British practically in our backyards. Britain now occupies north of us, all the way to the Canadian border and we receive no assistance!"

At that moment, James Woodman entered the tavern. He listened quietly to the conversation before adding, "There is so much anger and talk about Massachusetts. When this is over, will we become part of Canada, Britain or should we form our own state?" John in a disgusted tone yelped, "Too many died freeing ourselves from British rule. It would be an insult to their memories and our efforts." Ephraim choked out, "If the British got control of us again, things would be worse. Retaliation would be their priority."

There was a hush over the tavern. We had not thought that others would be listening. One voice yelled, "Never British rule! Send them home!". John trying to stay a riot, brought his hands up. His voice still commanded attention, "Delegates are headed to Paris to draw up a treaty. Rest assured, Britain will not be ruling our lands." There were some mumbles but otherwise the heated conversation ceased.

We like the rest of the towns, waited for word to arrive. The air was tense until the Treaty of Ghent was signed. However, the anger toward Massachusetts never subsided. We felt betrayed.

When our sons and nephews returned from the War of 1812, it was a most joyous sight to see. The whole town heard of their coming and all were there to see them march in. Standing beside Sarah, I could not hold her back.

We heard the drums from a distance. Gradually they grew louder. The first we saw was Isaac, as Colonel riding in front of his brigade. On the second horse in line, sat his brother, Daniel wearing the rank of Lieutenant Colonel. Behind them, came the rest of the men on horseback. The men marched into town, tall, straight and proud.

Their footsteps, crisply matching the beat of the drums. John suddenly appeared beside me. He leaned over, his thoughts matching my own. "Our sons do us proud today." Not taking our eyes off of the soldiers coming our way, I answered, "Aye. I wish Daniel were here to see his sons." Ephraim surprised us from behind saying, "Good Lord, he would have been telling Isaac how to do things. Isaac would have had to shoot him." The three of us, burst out laughing. I felt the tears running down my cheeks and saw that John and Ephraim did as well. Colonel Isaac Lane dismissed the men and it was mayhem with loved ones trying to find each other.

Sarah spied her sons and ran with remarkable speed to them. By the time I caught up, she had her arms wrapped around them weeping with joy.

When she finally let go of them, I got a good look at them. Their uniforms were too large disguising their thin bodies. Samuel was preoccupied. I knew he was looking for his wife. There she came up the road. I saw myself thirty years ago in him. He could not take his eyes off of her. When his oldest son, Nathaniel ran to him, Samuel looked shocked. Instead of the boy he left behind a few short years ago, stood a teenager of fifteen years of age. He embraced his son and wife. His two little girls had wrapped their arms around each of his legs. He picked each one up and sat them on his horse. Nathaniel took the reins from Samuel and led horse while Samuel, holding Martha's hand, walked with his family down the road to home. Sarah whispered, "They look just like we did when you returned. Did we look that happy?" I smiled down at her with a quick kiss saying, "Happier".

Stephen, Rufus, Joshua and Silas came back to the house with Sarah and I. They looked very tired. I saw it in their eyes, men that had seen war at its worst and at its best. I'm sure they had their stories to tell, but they would not be told today. Sarah in her excitement cooked enough food to last us the week.

The months passed and gradually the men returned to their normal lives as best they could. I often saw the young men come into the tavern after work. Conversation was easy for them when talking to us old Revolutionary War men. We understood each other. I found that they developed the same strong bonds as we did so many years ago.

11

REFLECTIONS

My son, Silas, became a lumberman. He did not want to stay here in Buxton and heard of profit to be made at St. Stephens in Canada. Stephen lived on the farm with me and which was quite convenient as I have become too old to maintain the farm by myself. Joshua bought his own farm nearby and raised his family. Rufus stayed around a while before moving to Readfield to become a Justice of the Peace.

Isaac showed up at Garland Tavern one day with his brother Daniel. He and Daniel were amiable men but, Isaac came in with an unusually, mischievous purpose in his eye.

After greeting everyone and having his mug filled, he began. "I had been in the city of Washington and met a gentleman there. He stated that while the army was stationed in the South, the officers gave a dinner at which his father and a Captain Lane were present. They became rather hilarious and boisterous over their wine and somewhat excited. The gentleman's father said something derogatory to the character of Yankees, at which Captain Lane slapped him in the face. A challenge and duel followed. The gentleman's father was wounded in the leg and Captain Lane was wounded in the side." At the gasp in the crowd he added, "Flesh wounds only."

Now Isaac was looking directly at me and went on saying, "After thinking the matter through, it could not have been my father or John for they would surely have spoken of it but my Uncle here would have definitely kept it quiet. What say you, Uncle?" The room was silent, all eyes were on me and Isaac had that idiotic grin on his face.

In response, I unbuttoned my breeches and showed the crowd the scar. There was a roar of cheering, the mugs were all filled with ale and my secret was out. Isaac, the little rascal bought me an ale and gave a toast. "Uncle, tell us more about it.", he said. "You just told it", I answered. His face became serious, "I hope you are not angry". I told him, "No son. It was many years ago now. I never told anyone because I was never proud of my lapse in temper, especially toward a man fighting for the same cause as me."

Isaac went on to be a man of great accomplishments. He participated in a large part in the groundwork laid down in the forming of the State of Maine. He held many important positions, a few of them being Justice of the Peace, Sheriff of York County, Deputy Postmaster for Hollis, Member of the council of the Governor Maine and a Presidential Elector. His brother Daniel was appointed by James Monroe as the Collector Customs for the District of Belfast. Huge feats for the young boys that served in the Revolution.

In 1817, President Monroe came to Maine for a visit. Isaac's daughter, Hannah, at twenty-two years of age was invited with a few other young ladies to breakfast with him at the home of Judge Sewall. She conducted herself with grace and dignity. Isaac was so very proud of her. He was always close to his beautiful daughter and her happiness was what mattered most to him.

When Ellis B. Usher came to Hollis as a young boy to Buxton to stay with his uncle, his clothes were ragged and his circumstances were poor. He worked at his uncle's tavern and then for Isaac at his mill. He worked harder than most. One Sunday morning, Isaac's men teased him about the clothes he wore to church. He answered them saying, "One day I will be able to buy clothes for all of you."

Isaac always commented on Ellis' integrity. He did admire the young man's ability to overcome his circumstances. Ellis worked very hard and prospered well. He first married Rebecca Randall, who tragically died young. After Rebecca's passing, Isaac watched as love blossomed between Ellis and his daughter Hannah. Isaac worried for her as any loving parent would. It would not do, if her heart was broken. She quite obviously adored Ellis. When Ellis asked Isaac for her hand, Isaac approved. He knew Ellis would take great care with his daughter.

Ephraim passed away in 1820 at the age of ninety-eight at his son's home. After the war, I enjoyed his friendship and humor for many years at the tavern. We liked to reminisce in our old age. Joanna had visitors at the tavern and one particular evening, visitors staying the night got caught up listening to our chatter. Ephraim realized he was being heard and went right into what had happened after the War of 1812.

Ephraim said in a giggle, "Anyone remember when we built the blockhouse?". There was a rumble of laughter and now Ephraim was warmed up to the subject saying, "After the last war, we menfolk decided to build our own powerhouse for defense. The men would be away at night which left the women and children alone here. Someone had informed the women that there were Indians lurking around. Captain Elden's wife, Ruth, rallied all the women. She had them don their husband's clothing and arm themselves with anything they could get their hands on.

We came back in the morning to find Ruth with her husband's old rusty sword in one hand, bellowing in a deep loud voice at all the women parading around." He directed his attention to his attentive audience, who had sat down to listen. He threw out his arms and put an astonished expression on his face and said, "What else could we think when we first saw them? We thought they had been indulging in the rum!". Everyone was in hysterics with the story. That was the last time I shared a pint of ale with my friend. He passed away a week later sitting on a block at the door of James' home. He was in his 98th year.

John passed away in 1822. John married three times and produced twenty-two children. His obituary in the Columbian Centinel on August 7, 1822 read:

"Died in Buxton. July 14, 1822, Captain John Lane, aged 88 years. Captain Lane was a patriot and hero of the Revolution. He was appointed at the age of 20 a Lieutenant under his father, and had, himself, the command of Fort Halifax, on the Kennebec river, in the old French war. In 1756, the command developed on him in consequence of the death of his father. He took an active part in the war that severed America from England; as early as the Spring of 1775 he was appointed commander of a company which he and his under officers raised, consisting of one hundred and twenty men. He was also appointed Commissioner to treat with the Penobscot Indians, then on the point of joining their forces to the British army; he succeeded, and agreed upon the preliminaries of a treaty, after encountering every obstacle that the British agents could devise to prevent it, and prevailed on Orono, their Chief, and some others of the tribe to accompany him to Cambridge, where the treaty was ratified, and has always been strictly adhered to. (The Oldtown Indians.)"

"Immediately after his return from Cambridge, he was joined by his recruits and ordered to repair to and take command of Cape Ann Harbor an important port. He was at the place when the famous prize was taken from the enemy by Captain Manly, consisting of ordinance and military stores arrived, and defended and repulsed the British, who made an attempt to retake the prize

(which was then considered a very important acquisition.) The stores were immediately landed and sent to Cambridge. He was a man of strong mind, invincible and sanguine in whatever he undertook, and always exhibited striking specimens of bravery and foresight; his genius soared above all vulgar enterprises; he gloried in defending his country against outrage and oppression."

The worst day of my life was March 11, 1825. My beautiful Sarah was taken from this world. Now I sit outside of our home at night without the loving companionship of my devoted wife, Sarah. The years after the War, she was my constant companion and my pride for her was immeasurable. Sarah was constantly busy ensuring my comforts. Each night entering our home, I was met with the pleasant aroma of dinner she had prepared. She was always willing to help others within the town when needed and the townspeople spoke highly of her. She was never idle. Our children dote on me constantly but my mind is most at ease sitting outside at night where she and I used to sit. I have never been in so much pain, body and soul.

Within a month after Sarah's death, Isaac stopped by to see me as he did quite often. "Uncle, Marquis de Lafayette will be coming to York in a week. There will be a banquet at Cleaves Hotel. I would like you to accompany me." I thought about it for a long minute but, my answer was, "No, thank you. I get tired too easily now and it would be a burden for you. You should have some fun. Go and see your old friend." "Uncle", he started to say. I patted him on the arm and said, "Please give the Marquis my best. It would have been nice to see him." He was disappointed, "Are you sure Uncle? I am sure he would like to see you." I chuckled a bit, "I'm quite sure. Come and tell me about it when you return." He stood saying, "Right then" and left.

As promised, he was back a few days after the ball. "It was a grand affair, Uncle." "Did you get a chance to speak with him?", I asked. "Yes, we managed a conversation." He chuckled a bit and said, "He's old." I teased him saying, "I believe we all got old". He laughed and went on in amazement, "He left his family to journey here to help us fight for our freedom in this country. He went home and when the French Revolution occurred, he and his family were thrown in prison. A few of his family members were even put to death by the guillotine." I was shocked by Isaac's words, "What about his children?" "Ah, he has a son who is here with him, 'George Washington Lafayette'. When trouble arose, he sent his son to George Washington here in the states. George Washington saw to Lafayette's son's education and welfare. He is here with his father as well. Imprisonment weakened his wife and after she was released, she never fully recovered. She died in 1807. He is still devastated by it." I was having a hard time comprehending why this man who believed in freedom for all, could have been imprisoned along with his family. "That's shocking", was all I could muster. I asked Isaac, "Does he look well?". "Yes, he does. I liked his son. I believe he will do well with his life." I nodded at Isaac's words.

"So, tell me more about the ball!". Isaac said, "First, I did send your regards and the Marquis was quite happy to receive it. He went on about a scouting party you had taken him on". "He remembers that, does he?", I chuckled. He continued, "Yes. The best part of it all was Hannah's reaction when the Marquis came over and welcomed me as compatriot. I have never seen her let her jaw drop." My response was, "I bet that was pretty." Isaac and I both laughed at the thought. "Well, it was very good to see the man. The town did a very nice job in preparing the banquet for him. The speeches were eloquent and the Marquis mingled with everyone there."

I sighed, "I remember meeting a very young man with the title of General. I liked him." In a teasing tone and a side way glance, I added, "You followed him around like a puppy." Isaac protested, "I did not." Smiling I insisted, "Yes, you did. Why did you bring him to my tent that day?" Isaac hesitated, "He had been impressed with the scouting party you had brought him on. When I informed him you were my uncle, he wanted to know more about you." "And, what did you tell him?" Isaac sat up straight, "I told him of you as a drummer boy, losing your own father in the French and Indian War, your mother dying a month after your return. How brave you had always been. How the men respect you. Should I go on?" "No", I answered.

Isaac continued, "The Marquis said once, 'a brave man with honor, respect and dignity is a rare man to find. Hold on to that friendship as if your life depends on it.'" I said, "That was very good advice." Isaac leaned in close and put a hand on each of my shoulders, "I thought of you when he spoke those words. I never forgot that. It was you who helped me start the sawmill and put me on the road to wealth. I have never thanked you for all your kindnesses toward me." Isaac had never spoken his feelings to me before.

Uncomfortable with the praise, I murmured, "Isaac, even as a young fifer, you had an open friendliness about you. I had always thought you would do well. Being a small part of that was my honor. I have been very proud to watch you succeed. That you did with your own hard work." At that moment, my son Stephen appeared. The younger men shook hands and Stephen invited Isaac to stay for supper and Isaac happily accepted. Stephen's wife Alcestis, who was my brother John's daughter, put out a delicious dinner while the three cousins chatted away.

While the two men talked, memories of the conversation I had with Ephraim so many years ago at Morristown came back to me. That vision of freedom and a new country was no longer a dream, I lived to see the results of our sufferings with complete satisfaction. Our children, a new generation all over this country had grown. Each of them chased their own destiny and with the freedom earned and had molded their own government. They stood up and succeeded in defending it in 1812 when a foreign country invaded our borders. I sat there in my living room, watching a farmer and a Colonel turned politician exchanging ideas as equals. Both quite happy with their own lives with no envy toward the other.

Our sister, Joanna left this world in 1827. She was well known far and wide for her hospitality, intelligence and her beauty. People came from far away to dine on her food.

When she died, Rev Paul Coffin spoke of Joanna:

> "Madam Garland was known as one of the best cooks of the times; and her eight daughters were no less accomplished in that very useful, but much neglected art. It was not alone the famous bowls of punch, the mugs of Flip and Samson (cider and rum) and the choicest viands the forest, as well as Portland market afforded, that so often attracted to that tavern its distinguished guests. This hostelry became noted for its hospitality and its mistress's appetizing cooking. I loved to gather there in the evening with neighbors and guests of the tavern. I remember that the long high-backed settle, drawn up before the blazing fire was a famous place for talk and laughter. Often the tavern room might be cleared and a fiddle produced by some local genius and the high rafters overhead would resound to the lively strains while the young folk gaily joined in a good old-fashioned dance."

It was a wonderful tribute to a wonderful woman.

Most of the Woodman's I had fought with are now gone as are most of the Redlons and men that had traveled with me so many years ago.

It is 1830 and I am now 88 years old. The children we all had produced are adults now with their own families. The number of grandchildren and grand nieces and nephews are too many to count. Between my brothers, Joanna and I, we raised families who sons and daughters, grandsons and granddaughters grew up as the first generations of a new Nation. Free to live their lives as they chose. The hardships we had endured for their futures were worth it to me. I have known more content with my life than most men. Now that my story is told, it's time to rest.

THE CHRISTIAN INTELLIGENCER & EASTERN CHRONICLE

May 14, 1830 & May 21, 1830.

Another Revolution worthy gone. Died in Buxton, on the 30th ult., Captain Jabez Lane aged 88. He entered the Revolutionary Army in the summer of 1775, in the capacity of 2nd Lieutenant. In 1776 he was in the army under the command General George Washington when New York was evacuated by the American troops and bore a part in the action at Harlem and White Plains, and in the capture of the Hessians at Trenton. In the spring of 1777, he received a captain's commission, and at Fort Edward, joined the army, then on its retreat from Ticonderoga, and took command of a company in Colonel Nixon's regiment. The regiment to which he was attached bore an active share in all the action which preceded the capture of Burgoyne. Captain Lane continued in the service until 1780, when his domestic affairs requiring his attention, and believing that the independence of his country was virtually accomplished he requested a discharge.

During this period, he was engaged in much active service and no officer of his grade bore a higher reputation for bravery and military skill. Although he took part in many engagements, Captain Lane had the good fortune to escape from them all without a wound. His company when it left Long Island, numbered 120 men, but the battles at Harlem, White Plains and Trenton, and the suffering of retreat through the Jerseys, reduced it to 20. After he retired from the service, he resumed the business of a farmer, and continued in that peaceful and respectable occupation through the long remainder of his life, sustaining to the end the character of an industrious intelligent and upright citizen. His latter days were cheered, in some measure by the tardy justice of his country, having awarded him a pension-and he went down to the grave full of years and liquor. It may perhaps, not to be amiss to mention that at the commencement of hostilities, two brothers of Captain Lane also entered the service of their county; one of them as Captain and the other as 2nd Lieutenant; of the same company with the subject of this brief and imperfect notice, they having enlisted the whole company by their own efforts.

The generations that followed in the Lane family included; Council to the Governor of Maine, Maine State Legislators, Judges, lawyers, a Consul to Brazil, mill owners, successful business men and some chose to remain farmers. However, that is a story that one of them should tell.

12

REFERENCES

Captain Leonard Bleeker, *"The Order Book of Captain Leonard Bleeker Major of the Brigade in the Early Part of the Expedition Under General James Clinton against the Indian Settlements of Western New York, in the Campaign of 1779"*. New York: Joseph Sabin, 84 Nassau Street, 1865. (Court Martial of Daniel for ungentlemanly conduct to Captain Day)

Rev. Jacob Chapman and Rev. James H. Fitts, *"Lane Genealogies, Volume I"*, Printed by The News-Letter Press, 1891

W. Woodford Clayton, *"History of York County, Maine: With Illustrations and Biographical Sketches of Its Prominent Men and Pioneers"*, Philadelphia, PA, Everts and Peck, 1880.

"Council of War, 13 March 1776," *Founders Online,* National Archives, version of January 18, 2019, https://founders.archives.gov/documents/Washington/03-03-02-0337. [Original source: *The Papers of George Washington*, Revolutionary War Series, vol. 3, *1 January 1776–31 March 1776,* ed. Philander D. Chase. Charlottesville: University Press of Virginia, 1988, pp. 459–461.]

Peter Force, *"American Archives Consisting of Authentick Records, State Papers, Debates and Letters and Other Notices of Publick Affairs"*. Prepared and Published under authority of an Act of Congress. Pages 1090, 1427, 1428, 1431, 1433, 1437 through 1445, 1482, 1501, 1503,1505.

"General Orders, 24 March 1776," *Founders Online*, National Archives, version of January 18, 2019, https://founders.archives.gov/documents/Washington/03-03-02-0389. [Original source: *The Papers of George Washington*, Revolutionary War Series, vol. 3, *1 January 1776–31 March 1776*, ed. Philander D. Chase. Charlottesville: University Press of Virginia, 1988, pp. 520–521.]

"General Orders, 29 March 1776," *Founders Online*, National Archives, version of January 18, 2019, https://founders.archives.gov/documents/Washington/03-03-02-0420. [Original source: *The Papers of George Washington*, Revolutionary War Series, vol. 3, *1 January 1776–31 March 1776*, ed. Philander D. Chase. Charlottesville: University Press of Virginia, 1988, pp. 559–560.]

"General Orders, 29 April 1776," *Founders Online*, National Archives, version of January 18, 2019, https://founders.archives.gov/documents/Washington/03-04-02-0131. [Original source: *The Papers of George Washington*, Revolutionary War Series, vol. 4, *1 April 1776–15 June 1776*, ed. Philander D. Chase. Charlottesville: University Press of Virginia, 1991, pp. 162–164.]

"General Orders, 7 May 1776," *Founders Online*, National Archives, version of January 18, 2019, https://founders.archives.gov/documents/Washington/03-04-02-0185. [Original source: *The Papers of George Washington*, Revolutionary War Series, vol. 4, *1 April 1776–15 June 1776*, ed. Philander D. Chase. Charlottesville: University Press of

Virginia, 1991, pp. 224–225.]

William F. Goodwin, Captain U.S. Army. *"Records of the Proprietors of Narraganset Township, No. 1, now the Town of Buxton, York County Maine from August 1ˢᵗ, 1733 to January 4ᵗʰ, 1811.",* Privately printed. 1871

A. Maria Higgins, *"Genealogy of the Lane Family from 1693 to 1894",* Washington, D.C.

Charles A. Lane, Esq., volunteer. *"Lane, Isaac, 1765-1833 Collection".* 1777-2000". Maine Historical Society.

J.M. Marshall. *"A Report of the Proceedings at the Celebration of the First Centennial of the Town of Buxton, Maine, Held at Buxton, August 14, 1872".* Portland: Dresser, McLellan & Co. 1874

William McKendey, *"Journal of William McKendey",* Cambridge: John Wilson and Son. Press, 1886 Massachusetts Historical Society. Massachusetts Historical Society. (Court martial of Daniel for affronting Captain Ballard)

Philip Hildreth Reade. *"Dedication exercises at the Massachusetts military monument, Valley Forge"* Wright & Potter Printing Company, 1912

Gideon T. Ridlon, *"Saco Valley Settlements and Families"* A reprinting of the 1895 Edition, New England History Press, Somersworth, 1984.

John Francis Sprague, *"Sprague's Journal of Maine History",* Volume 6 Page 106-108. April 1918 – April 1919

Ellis Baker Usher, "A biographical sketch of Hannah Lane Usher of

Buxton and Hollis, Maine : with historical and genealogical facts relating to the Lane family of Buxton" Boston Public Library, Privately printed 1903

"To George Washington from the Gloucester Committee of Safety, 7 September 1775," *Founders Online*, National Archives, version of January 18, 2019, https://founders.archives.gov/documents/Washington/03-01-02-0321. [Original source: The *"Papers of George Washington*, Revolutionary War Series, vol. 1, *16 June 1775–15 September 1775"*, ed. Philander D. Chase. Charlottesville: University Press of Virginia, 1985, pp. 429–430.]

"To George Washington from the Gloucester Committee of Safety, 28 September 1775," *Founders Online*, National Archives, version of January 18, 2019, https://founders.archives.gov/documents/Washington/03-02-02-0054. [Original source: The *Papers of George Washington*, Revolutionary War Series, vol. 2, *16 September 1775–31 December 1775*, ed. Philander D. Chase. Charlottesville: University Press of Virginia, 1987, pp. 59–60.]

"To George Washington from the Gloucester Committee of Safety, 28 September 1775," *Founders Online*, National Archives, version of January 18, 2019, https://founders.archives.gov/documents/Washington/03-02-02-0054. [Original source: The *Papers of George Washington*, Revolutionary War Series, vol. 2, *16 September 1775–31 December 1775*, ed. Philander D. Chase. Charlottesville: University Press of Virginia, 1987, pp. 59–60.]

"From George Washington to John Hancock, 7–9 March 1776," *Founders Online*, National Archives, version of January 18, 2019, https://founders.archives.gov/documents/Washington/03-03-02-

0309. [Original source: *The Papers of George Washington*, Revolutionary War Series, vol. 3, *1 January 1776–31 March 1776*, ed. Philander D. Chase. Charlottesville: University Press of Virginia, 1988, pp. 420–428.]

"To George Washington from Nicholas Cooke, 4 April 1776," *Founders Online*, National Archives, version of January 18, 2019, https://founders.archives.gov/documents/Washington/03-04-02-0026. [Original source: *The Papers of George Washington*, Revolutionary War Series, vol. 4, *1 April 1776–15 June 1776*, ed. Philander D. Chase. Charlottesville: University Press of Virginia, 1991, pp. 29–30.]

"From George Washington to Major General Artemas Ward, 13 May 1776," *Founders Online*, National Archives, version of January 18, 2019, https://founders.archives.gov/documents/Washington/03-04-02-0233. [Original source: *The Papers of George Washington*, Revolutionary War Series, vol. 4, *1 April 1776–15 June 1776*, ed. Philander D. Chase. Charlottesville: University Press of Virginia, 1991, pp. 293–294.]

"To George Washington from Brigadier General Nathanael Greene, 5 July 1776," *Founders Online*, National Archives, version of January 18, 2019, https://founders.archives.gov/documents/Washington/03-05-02-0148. [Original source: *The Papers of George Washington*, Revolutionary War Series, vol. 5, *16 June 1776–12 August 1776*, ed. Philander D. Chase. Charlottesville: University Press of Virginia, 1993, pp. 211 "From George Washington to Major General Artemas Ward, 13 May 1776," *Founders Online*, National Archives, version of January 18, 2019, https://founders.archives.gov/documents/Washington/03-04-02-0233. [Original source: *The Papers of George Washington*, Revolutionary War Series, vol. 4, *1 April 1776–15 June 1776*, ed. Philander

D. Chase. Charlottesville: University Press of Virginia, 1991, pp. 293–294.]

"From George Washington to Major General Artemas Ward, 16 June 1776," *Founders Online*, National Archives, version of January 18, 2019, https://founders.archives.gov/documents/Washington/03-05-02-0007. [Original source: *The Papers of George Washington*, Revolutionary War Series, vol. 5, *16 June 1776–12 August 1776*, ed. Philander D. Chase. Charlottesville: University Press of Virginia, 1993, pp. 13–15.]

"From George Washington to Major General William Heath, 9 February 1777," *Founders Online*, National Archives, version of January 18, 2019, https://founders.archives.gov/documents/Washington/03-08-02-0305. [Original source: *The Papers of George Washington*, Revolutionary War Series, vol. 8, *6 January 1777–27 March 1777*, ed. Frank E. Grizzard, Jr. Charlottesville: University Press of Virginia, 1998, pp. 287–288.]

"To George Washington from Major General William Heath, 28 March 1777," *Founders Online*, National Archives, version of January 18, 2019, https://founders.archives.gov/documents/Washington/03-09-02-0003. [Original source: *The Papers of George Washington*, Revolutionary War Series, vol. 9, *28 March 1777–10 June 1777*, ed. Philander D. Chase. Charlottesville: University Press of Virginia, 1999, pp. 2–4.]

"To George Washington from Major General William Heath, 1 April 1777," *Founders Online*, National Archives, version of January 18, 2019, https://founders.archives.gov/documents/Washington/03-09-02-0038. [Original source: *The Papers of George Washington*, Revolutionary War Series, vol. 9, *28 March 1777–10 June 1777*, ed. Philander D. Chase. Charlottesville: University Press of Virginia, 1999, pp. 37–39.]

"To George Washington from Major General William Heath, 9 April 1777," *Founders Online,* National Archives, version of January 18, 2019, https://founders.archives.gov/documents/Washington/03-09-02-0102. [Original source: *The Papers of George Washington,* Revolutionary War Series, vol. 9, *28 March 1777–10 June 1777,* ed. Philander D. Chase. Charlottesville: University Press of Virginia, 1999, pp. 99–101.]

"From George Washington to Major General Israel Putnam, 20 June 1777," *Founders Online,* National Archives, version of January 18, 2019, https://founders.archives.gov/documents/Washington/03-10-02-0088. [Original source: *The Papers of George Washington,* Revolutionary War Series, vol. 10, *11 June 1777–18 August 1777,* ed. Frank E. Grizzard, Jr. Charlottesville: University Press of Virginia, 2000, pp. 88–89.]

"To George Washington from Major General Israel Putnam, 23 June 1777," *Founders Online,* National Archives, version of January 18, 2019, https://founders.archives.gov/documents/Washington/03-10-02-0113. [Original source: *The Papers of George Washington,* Revolutionary War Series, vol. 10, *11 June 1777–18 August 1777,* ed. Frank E. Grizzard, Jr. Charlottesville: University Press of Virginia, 2000, p. 113.]

"To George Washington from Major General Israel Putnam, 30 June 1777," *Founders Online,* National Archives, version of January 18, 2019, https://founders.archives.gov/documents/Washington/03-10-02-0156. [Original source: *The Papers of George Washington,* Revolutionary War Series, vol. 10, *11 June 1777–18 August 1777,* ed. Frank E. Grizzard, Jr. Charlottesville: University Press of Virginia, 2000, pp. 158–159.]

"To George Washington from Major General Israel Putnam, 4 July 1777," *Founders Online,* National Archives, version of January 18, 2019, https://founders.archives.gov/documents/Washington/03-10-02-0187. [Original source: *The Papers of George Washington,* Revolutionary War Series, vol. 10, *11 June 1777–18 August 1777,* ed. Frank E. Grizzard, Jr. Charlottesville: University Press of Virginia, 2000, pp. 192–193.]

"To George Washington from Major General Philip Schuyler, 22 July 1777," *Founders Online,* National Archives, version of January 18, 2019, https://founders.archives.gov/documents/Washington/03-10-02-0357. [Original source: *The Papers of George Washington,* Revolutionary War Series, vol. 10, *11 June 1777–18 August 1777,* ed. Frank E. Grizzard, Jr. Charlottesville: University Press of Virginia, 2000, pp. 365–366.]

"From George Washington to Major General Alexander McDougall, 23 October 1778," *Founders Online,* National Archives, version of January 18, 2019, https://founders.archives.gov/documents/Washington/03-17-02-0556. [Original source: *The Papers of George Washington,* Revolutionary War Series, vol. 17, *15 September–31 October 1778,* ed. Philander D. Chase. Charlottesville: University of Virginia Press, 2008, pp. 547–548.]

"From George Washington to Henry Laurens, 29 October 1778," *Founders Online,* National Archives, version of January 18, 2019, https://founders.archives.gov/documents/Washington/03-17-02-0650. [Original source: *The Papers of George Washington,* Revolutionary War Series, vol. 17, *15 September–31 October 1778,* ed. Philander D. Chase. Charlottesville: University of Virginia Press, 2008, pp. 630–632.]

"From George Washington to Major General Alexander McDougall, 19 November 1778," *Founders Online,* National Archives, version of January 18, 2019, https://founders.archives.gov/documents/Washington/03-18-02-0220. [Original source: *The Papers of George Washington*, Revolutionary War Series, vol. 18, *1 November 1778–14 January 1779,* ed. Edward G. Lengel. Charlottesville: University of Virginia Press, 2008, pp. 210–211.]

"To George Washington from Philip Schuyler, 27 April 1779," *Founders Online,* National Archives, version of January 18, 2019, https://founders.archives.gov/documents/Washington/03-20-02-0213. [Original source: *The Papers of George Washington*, Revolutionary War Series, vol. 20, *8 April–31 May 1779,* ed. Edward G. Lengel. Charlottesville: University of Virginia Press, 2010, pp. 244–246.]

Williams, Chase & Co. *"History of Penobscot County"* 1882. pages 520, 521 and 880.

Cyrus Woodman. *"The Woodmans of Buxton, Maine",* Printed by David Clapp & Son, 1874.